GW00367215

BREAKFAST IN BED

Laurie Lewis

Carrick Books

First edition 2005

All rights reserved

ISBN 0-9551101-0-6

Cover: "The Punchbowl", St Agnes, Isles of Scilly

Published by

Carrick Books
"Gelvinak", Pill Creek. Feock, Truro, Cornwall TR3 6SD

Printed by

R. Booth Ltd
Antron Hill, Mabe,
Cornwall

For a very dear
pupil, Anne
love from
Laurie Lewis

For:

Cicely, Mark, Clare, and Shirley

Contents

❧ Introduction ❧

Short stories have always had a special place in my life. My parents both loved story telling and would promise to tell me one in bed, "If I was good." I don't know whether I was or not, but I do remember that special comforting sensation of dropping off to sleep lulled by the dear sound of their voices. In turn I told my children stories and now they tell their children stories.

I have to declare at once that my little collection is not intended for children but for adults only. They are intended to be read aloud, ideally in bed and I like to think that you will find the "Right voice" for each story which will be amusing if you are at all histrionically inclined.

Poor Mamillius in " The Winter's Tale" wanted to hear a story and claimed that, "A sad tale's best for winter." Indeed, a sad story would have been right for him, given the season and his tragic early death, but my Bedtime Stories are intended to make the hearer laugh or think or occasionally, cry. I have included some of those that I wrote for the "Stray Dogs" writers' group if they caused a laugh when I read them. Like the fairy stories that were part of our childhood, I feel that a good Bedtime Story must have a definite element of fantasy about it; it can break rules, stretch the imagination but not introduce too much of the "Real" world with all its worrying problems into the peace before sleep.

SWEET DREAMS

❧ Breakfast In Bed ❧

Rupert had certainly never gone short of sex. It was, after all, the reason he had changed his name. He had become" Rupert " at Cambridge when he found that the most desirable of the few young ladies there granted their favours to "Ruperts" without the usual preliminaries of promises and candle-lit dinners. Since his real name was Albert, he had changed his name and so changed his amorous fortunes. Now he was seventy and lived much of his life in retrospect.

'Enough is enough! I'm not quite the man I once was in some ways you understand,' Rupert tactfully hinted to the second chambermaid. She was a delightful girl and he had taken great pleasure in ogling her ever since she had joined his household. Now she was busy slipping her maid's black uniform over her head as a prelude to joining her employer in bed.

There was one thing that always stirred Rupert to the core and that was the sight of plump, but not too plump, white thighs at the top of black thick stockings held in place by a proper regulation suspender belt, also, needless to say, in black. Tildy had knocked on the master's door with his morning tea and had then begun to undress.

'Please replace your dress, Tildy. It was a kind thought, but, but what I most desire, you see...' but here his voice tailed off, lost in a private sensuous fantasy of his own feverish imagining.

Tildy listened. Her resolution; 'To pay her respects to the master and show herself properly grateful for all he had done for her', as Armitage, the butler, had insisted, began to waver, as did her courage. What might this old man, master of Ploom, the best preserved mediaeval castle in the British Isles, be secretly craving ?

Tildy had heard of the whims of old men. Only last Wednesday, Sally, the kitchen help, had been telling them in the servants' dining hall of how a titled gentleman, her mother's employer years ago, had wanted her mother to dress up as a Christmas fairy, with magic wand and all. She was to do cartwheels in front of the master on the lawn, but she wasn't to wear any underwear.

'That's going too far! Out in the open, on the lawn, in winter, without benefit of woolly underwear! She'd likely catch her death of cold ! Just downright inconsiderate, I calls that,' had been cook's opinion.

Now, thought Tildy, was she to be faced with a similar ordeal? Would she have to do cartwheels, perhaps without her uniform? She'd never been much good at "the gymnastics," but she'd certainly do her best. She might, perhaps, damage herself, or worse, break one of the valuable ornaments dotted round the room if she were asked to perform in the master's bedroom.

Another long drawn-out sigh from the master brought her back to herself. His face was turned from her so she had to lean over the bed to hear what he was saying 'What would please me, indeed the only thing for which I have any desire at all at this time is, is....' At this Tildy began to shake. The master continued in a slightly different tone and with a growing tremor in his voice. Tildy bent closer to hear the next words uttered in a throaty whisper, 'Is a dish, a dish of devilled lamb's kidneys. Ah. There, I've said it,' he gasped, then lay back on his pillow.

Tildy stood her ground. She had been prepared, even determined to remove her uniform, item by item, very slowly, waving each piece of clothing three times round her head. 'They particularly likes that, does the gentry,' Millie, the first housemaid had confided. If it could not have been avoided, she would certainly have been prepared to try at least one cartwheel, for her old master's sake, if he'd excuse any breakages during the proceedings. But what was this she had heard him asking for?

'Tildy, are you still there?'

Shame prevented Rupert from turning his head to look the young chambermaid in the face. It had not been an easy thing to do; actually to put into words the nature of his desires, this fantasy which had kept sleep from him at night and had dominated his every waking moment for the last month.

'Yes, sir, I heard, at least I think I heard what you said. You want, you want me to bring you, in bed a....' She just could not say it; shame utterly overcame her.

Rupert pulled himself together and sat up. 'I want a white plate, you know, one of those from the big cupboard we use when we have the Hunt Ball. Well, one of the big white dinner plates, with a piece of toast on it; hot, crisp, but not burnt, easy to cut, with lashings, absolutely lashings of best unsalted butter dripping from it. And on it, piled on it.' His voice dropped to a throaty gurgle. 'On it, on the toast, must be a generous helping of devilled kidneys, fried in best butter, crisp at the edges. Each kidney must be exactly halved and neatly done so that it stays in a precise half circle, then the sauce, with some fresh mustard-I like there to be plenty of fresh mustard in the sauce and'. But he got no further. The tears of Tildy were almost audible and the anguished trembling of her young body shook the whole bed.

'My child, you're weeping. Oh God, what a beast I am to subject you to all this, but you see, I just cannot help myself. You've been such a decent young girl, always dutifully raising your skirt when we passed each other in the long corridor and all the other little things you've done that you thought would please me.'

'Oh sir! I'll do anything else you want me to. I ironed my uniform specially to take off for you, but, but what you just said you wanted..' Here Tildy's voice failed her. The thought of telling cook and Mr Armitage all the ghastly details of what the master wanted her to bring him in bed was just too appalling to contemplate. Much as she had enjoyed working at the castle, she would have to leave it. Mother would surely understand when she heard the reason.

And so Tildy left Ploom and the employment of Rupert that same day. She did, out of courtesy, go so far as outline to cook and Mr Armitage the reason for her sudden wish to leave.

'Kidneys! And devilled you say? Oh God help the poor old master, and us too if that's the way his mind is turning,' was cook's charitable and understanding view.

'We do come and we do go, we servants. We live out our lives at the beck and call of our masters, but there's certain things a young chambermaid should not be expected to do for any normal, church-going employer,' Mr Armitage declared with solemnity as he attempted to comfort Tildy.

Her farewells complete, Tildy walked down the four miles drive of the castle, back to the main road then on to her simple home where she could but try to blot out the fearful memory of those dreadful words of her master and the unthinkable request he had made.

Rupert, short of being shamed by the innocent Tildy's departure, seemed suddenly to grow increasingly feverish and immoderate in his desires. The position of second chambermaid was filled almost immediately, for times were hard for families that lived from the land. If a daughter could bring in a few more pounds a year and her feeding and clothing cease to be the responsibility of her parents, there was fierce competition amongst the village girls to fill any vacant place at the castle.

Rupert devoted a morning to seeing the seven girls from the village who had come to be considered for Tildy's position. He sat with the window behind him in the morning room. The sun, shining brightly behind him rendered him almost invisible to the applicants Each girl would knock gently on the door which was opened ceremoniously by Mr Armitage who announced the girl's name.

'The usual duties, is it?' the girls would ask discreetly and then lift their skirts to demonstrate their eligibility.

'Lift that skirt properly, girl, the master wants to be sure that you have the right qualifications for the post', Armitage would snap, if the skirt lifting was done in a perfunctory, or worse, a lascivious manner.

By lunchtime Tildy's successor had been appointed. Rupert and Mr Armitage were in agreement that the new second chambermaid looked very promising.

'I could send her up to your dressing room, sir, as soon as Mrs Daboline has furnished her with a new uniform from the housekeeper's cupboard. Black suspenders, of course, sir.'

'Of course', snapped Rupert. 'Absolutely no lowering of standards will be tolerated. However, you can give her the afternoon to find her way around, as it were. Her first formal duties begin tomorrow morning'

At eight precisely next morning there was a careful tap on the door of Rupert's bedroom.

'Enter,'cried Rupert, eager to learn whether the new girl would give satisfaction.

'Name?' Rupert asked, as kindly as he could manage.

'Dora, sir, if you please.'

'I rather think it's a question of if YOU please, what?'And Rupert gave a great laugh at his own, time-honoured joke.

Mr Armitage had been rehearsing the girl in the customary duties of a junior chambermaid in a gentleman's household. Dora had her uniform over her head while Rupert was still laughing at his joke. But he stopped and roared," Stop that. I'll tell you precisely what I want you to do for me. Put your dress on again. Go down to the kitchens, find one of the big white dishes-the Hunt Ball ones. Prepare a plate of freshly scrambled eggs, new laid, mind, then before they have become too viscous in consistency, stir in very gently some small pieces of wild smoked salmon, add a sprinkling of small forest ceps, finely chopped and seethed in non-vintage champagne thickened with unsalted butter. All this to be piping, piping hot, but by no means overcooked. Place this on crisp wholemeal toast, edges trimmed and on a silver chafing dish. Now the coffee.'

But before Rupert had come to the end of this shameful inventory, Dora had fallen in a faint on the Chinese carpet of his bedroom.

Armitage demonstrated his customary skills in discretion and service to the family. He carried Dora down to the comfortable little room that served him as a pantry and revived her with a glass of vintage claret left over from the last evening's dinner. When Dora did recover her senses enough to speak, she burst into tears and cried out. 'Oh,Oh, it was horrible, horrible;the things he wanted me to do for him! I couldn't bring myself to even talk about them. Oh. Oh.'

Dora left the same day clutching her white five pound note and sworn to silence, 'If she knew what was good for her and if her father wanted to keep his job on the estate,' Armitage had cautioned.

Rupert's depravity followed the textbook stages and grew increasingly more alarming. Armitage's ingenuity was hard put to cover the activities of his old master's ailment. Several more girls were appointed, furnished with new uniforms and rehearsed by Armitage in their normal duties. Each time the girl would attempt to carry out those straightforward duties only to hear the master begin some ghastly incantation regarding "Devilled kidneys," or "Kedgeree en croute". Each time they would collapse or else run screaming from his bedroom. The estate's van would convey them from the castle clutching their silence money.

The Lady Solange, Rupert's wife, was cabled to return, as a matter of urgency from the family's summer retreat in Menton. She listened to Armitage's account of her husband's grotesque affliction, thanked the old butler for all he had done to shield the family honour and arranged for her husband to be committed to a private asylum for the insane the day following her return.

When he knew that his secret was out and that there was now no hope of keeping his shameful fantasies and tormenting longings in check any longer, Rupert abandoned all restraint and even as Armitage chauffeured the Silver Ghost out through the noble gates of the castle, his awful cries echoed around the quiet glens;

'A large white plate! A gentle interlayering of smoked haddock and finest wild rice, fresh thyme, flat parsley! Unsalted Highland butter, freshly churned. Wild lovage, two, coarsely ground wild boar sausages! Honey cured gammon sliced wafer thin on ducks' eggs, poached, an Arbroath bloater, succulent and tender. The plate to be large and white! Freshly baked cinnamon rolls and...'

It is much to the credit of Rupert's indomitable spirit as well as the professional expertise of the establishment where he saw out his remaining years that only rarely, and then, only after an unwise over indulgence in the house champagne, would he lift up his head to the skies, his eyes glazing over, his voice baying like a ravening wolf's and he would embark upon that blood-curdling anthem,

' A large white plate, several crisp lamb's kidneys, lavishly devilled, a ....' and then the practised attendants would close round him and after a sedative had been administered by the doctor, Rupert would lie back upon his pillows obediently and passively. An onlooker might even imagine that Rupert was actually watching his personal nurse intently as she began feelingly to remove her crisply laundered uniform, attentively tweak her black suspenders prior to joining her patient in his bed and there carry out those delicate rituals of treatment that are the time-honoured custom in all private hospitals, great castles, lordly mansions and indeed all places where the upright gentlemen of England are wont to spend the last days of their ordered and privileged lives.

A Song for Summer

"Something taut yet elemental; tumescent with insights, felicitous in phrasing and metre, but that, of course, goes without saying." Peter blinked; he'd heard but wished he had not . He was lying on his back under a vast cedar. The sunlight dappled the grass and he shielded his eyes. Between his fingers he could make out Alexander towering above him. The weekend Writers' Course had so far not been a success. First, and for Peter, foremost, the food was indifferent. Things, well fruit sausages, quiches-how he hated the runny cheesy anonymity of those insipid dishes-pies and pastries, all cold, had been spread about on a pink tablecloth on the kitchen table. He picked up one of the bottles of wine in the hopes that something might brighten the leaden indigestibility of it all. "Clarion. The robust popular wine from sunny Nappa Valley." No resort or refuge there! He could have wept.

Alexander moved on. As course director and proprietor of "Sheldrake's Literary Escapes" he had adopted a ridiculous manner towards his clients. He wore a purple corduroy suit, with pink bow tie, suede shoes and a blue felt hat when he walked round the garden where his seven disciples were scattered with their note books poised to record his every word of advice on their literary efforts. Peter wanted to laugh out loud. How could Fiona have done this to him?

'I've got you something rather special for your birthday. You'll never guess what it is, so don't bother to even try,' she'd announced ominously. Peter had nevertheless looked up from his paper and ventured, 'Mini cruise on Lake Garda? Day's flying tuition?' She'd merely laughed. 'No, something I really know you'll enjoy and find helpful , even engrossing, probably.' Engrossing! There were two worm thin sisters in their eighties, Ethel and Edna -'We've always known we've got a book in us, you know.' They had said, as one.

'Like having a gall stone,' It was out before Peter could stop it. He'd become invisible to them after that, not that he cared, but he would need to find at least one kindred spirit with whom to share his growing exasperation at the antics of Alexander and the absurdity of the various word games in which they were ordered to participate.

'A Song. For Summer,' Alexander added . That was the appointed theme for the afternoon's writing. Bill, the middle-aged librarian from Wigan, had committed the words at once into his large and virgin notebook. 'Aye, there's enough there to keep us out of mischief for a bit, eh?' The only female under fifty present, Prudence-'Just call me Pru, everyone does'- giggled, then nodded conspiratorially, as though at a crude invitation.

Peter had run his eye over Pru when they had all been gathered in the lounge yesterday for the *informal get together*. Maybe, just possibly there might, if he played his cards carefully and above all, if he entered into the whole lunatic spirit, be a chance of some slight diversion, some extra curricular gallimaufry, as he used to call it as a student. But Pru, it turned out, was all prudence and had become loudly dismissive when he'd suggested , 'Nipping off to the local, away from this menagerie. Get a steak, a decent bottle of reddo and a roll in the hay after, perhaps,' he added not quite in jest.

'I hope that was just a joke. I don't want to miss any of Alexander's useful advice. Don't you think he is so talented; inspirational and so, well insightful?' Peter had slunk, the only word for it, slunk away and managed a bare hour in the pub, just time to get four pints down and a wrestle with a rubbery rump steak before walking back to find the other members of the course drinking cocoa and giggling with Alexander, who could only be described as "Holding Court".

Peter made some excuse about needing to 'Put flesh on some bones of an idea for a story' and went to bed. Breakfast- all health food nonsense, no sign of the bacon, sausage, mushroom and fried egged cholesterol nightmare that Peter revelled in when on holiday- out of the way, the decks, were now clear for the *readings*.

'Bill, let's hear what sort of song you have for us this summer'

Bill, stood tall, opened his notebook and exposed, as it were, his literary privates to their regard.

"It's just a little poem", he pronounced it,"Poom". "Just a few words about how I feel about being with you all, basking, like, er in the sunshine of your company.'

Peter tried to black it out but some words got through-

'As summer brings us flowers, it brings us hope and love as well.

I think I could spend hours here, far away from work and hell'

This was rapturously received . Edna came next, 'This is just a few words I wanted to put down, and I'm sure I speak for us all, just to say how grateful I am, and Ethel as well, she helped me with this, a few words of grateful acknowledgement to dear Alexander. I 'm' sure he won't mind me calling him dear, everyone's a dear to you when you get to our age. A few words then, not really a *poem*. (nervous laugh.) It's just a little expression, about summer, about Alexander, and about being old.

Now that we're over the hill

And the candle of life's burnt short,

We'd just like to say

How grateful we are

For all the fine things we've been taught.'

Alexander led the clapping, smashing his oversize hands against each other.With a face full of teeth he switched on his great smile, 'And now, Prudence, my dear

Prudence, following that delightful and charming encomium, what have you written to swell our joy?'

Peter felt his stomach churning- was it real, a parting tribute to last night's indigestible hunk of overcooked meat lying on top of Alexander's dinner offering of Sorrel and purple sprouting broccoli ragout, or were his overstrained sensibilities turning in revolt upon these drivelling inanities and their perpetrators? He closed his eyes and tried to keep his flexing and swirling intestines under control.

'Peter's quite overcome!' said Ethel. 'Now come on, we're all friends together; if you feel tears coming on after all these lovely words, you let it all go, we'll understand.' 'Aye, let it go,' said Bill, and patted Peter on the back.

It was then that Alexander addressed Peter, "I think you're a bit of a dark horse, eh, probably had a few poems in the local paper, I shouldn't be surprised, but just give us, quite simply, what you fell about what you've heard and all that we've been doing here and about summer and its very special song for us all.'

There was no mistaking it now, Peter's stomach could take no more and in a sudden violent gush, of sorrel green and broccoli purple, of Guinness and crisps and tough steak he spread his deepest feelings out for their regard, on the carpet, on the curtains but specially on Alexander himself.

' Good course, dear? ' Asked Fiona, hearing his key in the lock.

'Deeply moving' was his honest reply 'Fancy a little cruise on Lake Garda this year, by any chance?'

⨈ .. tells a story ⨈

The last thin flakes of late snow hung uncertain on the still air then scattered and vanished on the wide lawn. It was early yet and no one in the big house was stirring except for the boy. He had seen the few flakes falling from his bedroom window and had rushed downstairs and out to explore the magic element. This then was all there was; a second's splendid whiteness that turned at once to water in his hand.

Last winter all had been so different. The bougainvillea had never lost its brilliant blossom and the boy had swum each day of his holiday warm in the tepid water far out from the surf edged beach and the mangroves. Jamaica, just after the war, had so much to delight the eye and body but there snow was never known and it was snow that Peter longed for especially in a land of unremitting sunshine.

Peter looked up at the sky, willing the snow to settle, thicken and cover the grass deeply, to shroud the house and cloak the trees. Above him the clouds jostled; white bulbous and disappointing. The flurry of snow flakes ceased and the sun began to shine. Peter frowned and went inside.

Peter's childhood had been spent entirely in the sun, in the West Indies; Bermuda, St Lucia and lastly Jamaica. His father had wanted him with him in the sun.

This winter his grandfather, a man Peter had never met before, had fallen ill and this winter would be his last. Peter had been sent by his father to meet the dying man and get to know a him a little before he died. So far Peter's few encounters with his father's father had not been a success. The old man was uncomfortable with children; irritated by their sudden movements and strident voices. He had been a artist, well known and successful in his time . He had made enough money from his skills to buy the rambling mansion where he now lived, looked after by two men, also old now, who had cooked and managed the household for him ever since his wife had left him twenty five years ago.

The boy and the old man sat opposite each other at meal times. Neither spoke much. The old man would try, "I expect you find things a bit quiet here, Peter, after the fleshpots of the West Indies, eh? Sorry your father couldn't come, but I know he's a vey busy man; busy and important."

Peter would nod or mutter self-consciously, his eyes firmly on the table in front of him, 'No, I'm fine' or 'Yes, yes he is'.

"I don't imagine that you've ever seen snow , Peter, there was a flurry earlier, perhaps you saw it?' Peter nodded again but did not look up.

'In the great freeze of '47 I painted a picture of the snow on the lawn in front of the house. It was one of my best but snow clearly wasn't a popular subject and it didn't sell, no one bought it, strange that when pretty well everything else I did found a home pretty quickly'.

The meal ended, the old man would go for his rest and Peter to his room or else for a walk by the sea. He had never needed company and was quite content picking things up on the small beach he had found through the trees at the edge of the garden. The sand was grey and very different from the shining white expanse at Montego Bay. The sea here looked so uninviting, too cold even for paddling.

What happened to the snow when it fell on the sea he wondered. Was it instantly absorbed or did it, for a split second, perhaps float like a white moving blanket.

No more snow fell during his stay with his grandfather and now he was going back to the sun. On the last day of his visit Peter was asked to go up to his grandfather's bedroom as he wanted to see him. He had not been well enough to come down for his meals for a few days.

Propped against a pile of pillows the old man looked smaller and less intimidating. He beckoned the boy to him and patted the bed for him to sit down.

"Well, old chap, you must be my envoy to your father, I shan't be here when you or he come again. There's such a chasm between generations. We fathers and sons, and even more so, grandsons, are like travellers on the same road, facing the same pitfalls, the same challenges, temptations and disappointments. Our destinations are just the same- self-knowledge; the rest is just a procession of events leading to death". The old man's body was then shaken by a great coughing fit and afterwards he lay back, breathing slowly and with obvious difficulty. Peter's eyes followed the pattern on the counterpane, it was quite elaborate, perhaps his grandfather had designed it himself, if artists could be bothered with such domestic matters. His grandfather then seemed to rally and continued, ' Yes, self- knowledge and then- oblivion. There's nothing else, you know. I should have liked you to see the snow, it's a symbol of life for me. Suddenly, it arrives, like unexpected joy or beauty and love…. Then everything is instantly changed; the dirt is hidden, the ugliness obliterated; a wondrous beauty and peace is revealed. But then it melts and the old disorder returns and we lose our sense of hope. Hang on to your moments of beauty, boy; you need to know that there is beauty in the world even if it fades.'

Peter wanted so much to speak; to say that he understood the message his grandfather was trying to pass on before he became forever silent. The old man coughed again and then gathered his energy to talk again. 'You see I failed with your father; we just did not speak about the important things. His wife- your mother- died and my wife walked out of my life. These losses we had in common but they did not bring us together.' Peter looked up from the counterpane and met his grandfather's eyes. The old man resumed, 'I want you to see for yourself what the snow can do, and when you do, you will remember what I have said.'

Peter's grandfather was asleep when the taxi came to take him to the station. His bag was packed and waiting in the hall. He wanted just to go in to his grandfather's room; just to look in and say goodbye. Giles, the cook/companion led him to the great bedroom again at the top of the house. Peter loved the room, he had never before seen such an amazing place just for sleep. There were French windows along one side which opened out onto a wide balcony with a view across the great lawn and on to the pine trees and the distant sea shimmering in the afternoon sunshine.' Your grandfather designed this room,' said Giles as he showed Peter in. He used to like to do his painting here but sadly his eyesight is now so poor that seeing the brushes and mixing the paint is beyond him.' He looked at the bed where the old man was asleep. He has taken his painkillers and won't wake up now for some hours. He wanted you to have something, a picture that he told you about, I expect. I've boxed it up and it's waiting to go back to Jamaica with you.

Peter walked to the bed and looked once more at his grandfather. His eyes were closed and his eyes were folded across his chest as though in death. Peter laid his small hand for a moment on those hands then followed Giles back downstairs to the hall and the waiting taxi.

Term was about to begin when he got back to Jamaica. His father had made an effort to be at home for him this time.

'Peter, I'm so glad that you saw him before he died' Peter looked enquiringly and his father continued, 'Yes, he's dead; he died soon after you must have left his house. Giles said that he had given you something to bring back.' Together they opened the wooden crate . Inside, carefully wrapped, was a framed canvas. Peter knew what it was at once,' It's snow, the snow he painted on the lawn of his house. How different it all looks!' Peter's father stood back from the picture as it rested on a chair, ' Father loved the snow, he seemed to think it was saying something to him. I never understood what it was, but perhaps you do, in this picture, Peter.'

Peter looked . long at the picture; remembering the lawn; remembering his grandfather's voice and what he had said to him that last time, ' It's a very clear message, really,' he said, ' Pictures can say what words cannot, you know. I shall always remember his message now, everytime I look at the picture and at the snow just as he saw it.

❦ Concentrating the Mind ❦

The most unlikely things made Harold laugh: his shoe-lace breaking, the lights turning to red on an empty stretch of road just when he drove up, gale warnings on the radio, corn flakes, and just a few days ago, being told that he would not be alive in twelve months' time. His spluttering sort of giggle sounded to him so out of place in the white and clinical seriousness of the surgeon's consulting room. Of course his own doctor did not have the job of telling one of his patients such unwelcome news; consultants; distant and impersonal beings, were there to do that and get better paid for doing it. Harold's standard reaction to bad news in his life had always been a sort of embarrassed giggle and he gave one when he was told the outcome of the long series of tests he had had to endure before the consultant could make his final diagnosis. What else was there to do or say? Doctors did not make such predictions lightly or unless the were absolutely certain of their facts. 'Are you really quite certain?' was something Harold could just not say to the serious looking young man in the white coat who faced him across the desk. He simply and unquestioningly accepted the news, thanked the consultant in a tone of surprising warmth, shut the door carefully after him and drove home. On the journey he thought back over the scene. He was glad that he had not tried to lighten the weight of the situation in the way that he often did by telling one of his ridiculous schoolmaster's jokes, although one had immediately come into his head when he heard the consultant's verdict. He pictured the dead pan look which would have greeted the punch line,' Only two minutes to live, doctor! Can't you do anything at all for me?' ' Well I could do you a boiled egg if you don't mind it being soft.' How dutifully his third year boys had laughed at that although Harold had sometimes suspected that he had told the same joke to them before and they just wanted an excuse to hit each other in feigned paroxysms of uncontrolled mirth. Well all that was a long time ago now it seemed to Harold

Such success as Harold had achieved over his thirty five years of teaching was due, he felt sure, to his unfailing ability to to put himself in the place of any schoolboy who opposed him, treating difficult confrontations as duels of personality; battles of wit which were won by intuition and not by violence or rage. In a double lesson on Friday afternoons with the Fourth Remove when they had been doing their best to concentrate hard, he timed his comic reliefs, sensing the precise moment when the boys had most need to escape from awful seriousness of work, just for a few moments; a shared laugh; a contrived and ridiculous simile achieved much. They had returned to their studies and worked all the better afterwards he felt, for the lightening of the mood. Afterwards- there wouldn't be much," Afterwards" now for him.

He waited for the lights, always at red, to change. One of his favourite quotations came into his mind unbidden and unwelcome; " The prospect of being hanged in the morning concentrates the mind wonderfully" Doubtless it must have been one of Doctor Johnson's favourites too otherwise why would the industrious Boswell have included it in the great lexicographer's gnomic utterances? The man awaiting hanging- ' Hanging, Davenport, *hanging*; paintings and bacon are *hung*; men are *hanged*; hanged by the neck until they are dead'. Would he ever stop trying to make object lessons out of life's inscrutable events for the benefit of an imagined classroom of schoolboys?

The man to be *hanged* in the morning might have felt perfectly well beforehand, but then he had felt reasonably well apart, that is, from the occasional blinding headache, for most of the time since he had retired the previous year. In the hospital where he had waited whilst his tests were conducted, he had even managed the two flights of stairs without puffing as much as he usually did. Beforehand he had felt absurdly smug about having cut out his evening drinking, although his motives had been less concerned with his health than with putting aside something towards a replacement for his ageing car next year.

All that had been a week ago now and he had been *concentrating his mind* ever since. He was rather pleased with what he had crammed into that short time, being a disorganised and lazy person by nature. He did, however, feel galled that he would only be in a position to draw his hard-earned pension for one year more. He had some savings, his house was now free of mortgage and, in Wemmick's phrase from" Great Expectations," some "Portable P which could be realised upon. He had never been married, not out of disinclination, but owing to an accident of Geography; both the ladies to whom he had proposed in the school holidays had not wished to move and had accepted offers from suitors more close at hand.

Now he had commitments to no one and was the only surviving member of his family with no friends who might expect to be remembered in his modest will. It occurred to him to leave some small sum in his will to the school where he had spent so many years of his life, perhaps enough for a bursary or at least a substantial prize for the best comic essay each year but meantime what should he do with the rest of the money and the rest of his life? In a "Readers' Digest" in the day room of the hospital he had come across the expression, "This is the first day of the rest of your life: enjoy it." But was it possible to compress all the hopes and plans he had had for when he retired into such a relatively short period as a year? Realistically, he argued, the longer he lived, the less he would gradually be able to afford on his small pension; inflation would see to that.

He gave the matter a lot of thought and then, suddenly, it all came clear to him. If he sold his house, drew out his savings and investments, realised upon his *portable property*, particularly the antiques he had inherited or collected, over the years, he could expect an income of about two hundred thousand pounds; a fortune to be spent on the rest of his life.

The growth of his tumour could not be halted by an operation, but it might be slowed down somewhat. Harold had a list of do's and don'ts and a drug which was no doubt potent as it was in a very small bottle indeed. He was determined to live this year to the utmost as far as his health and modest wealth would permit. The sale of his house and property had gone through amazingly quickly and when prices were at the highest that they had been for some time. He paid all the proceeds into a current account and was the centre of some small interest and not a little envy in the Travel Agent's when he gave them a list of all the places he wished to visit in the next eight months. "First Class, of course, throughout" he had instructed. He did not know how he might feel and what he would be capable of in the last quarter of his remaining life; not much, he expected. But if he were still alive then, he wanted to be buried in his homeland, England and near to where he had passed most of his days.

Three weeks in the "Negresco", in Nice , a month in various superb hotels by the waterside in the Virgin Islands and then a cruise on a small luxury liner with his own penthouse suite, exploring the Greek Islands and on and on, following the sun, to the Caribbean and then back home again to Europe, to Italy and a mountain top hotel overlooking the azure of the sea in Capri, then Amalfi, where the seafood was so superb; baby squid, dripping in oil and garlic, one of his favourite dishes, to be washed down with a well chilled bottle of best Frascati. He had missed a few days only of all this delight when headaches had laid him low, but the little bottle of drug had done much to make the pain bearable.

On an impulse he had hired a car when he docked at Southampton so that he could drive over to the Isle of Wight. He had last stayed there just after the war, when his maiden aunts had invited his parents over to stay in the small guest house they ran near Ventnor. He had a very clear memory of that time, and its highlight; being bought a model boat, a small wooden sailing boat with a rudder which you could adjust so that the sails set. He would spend every morning wading in the boating pool, pushing the little boat until its sails caught the wind and it would voyage across the pool under its own power and come to harbour along the coast of the miniature Isle of Wight which was in the centre of the pool. Journeying back in time now; revisiting the scenes of his past for the last time, it seemed important to him to find that boating pool again, on the esplanade, opposite the Winter Gardens where the tea dances used to be held in the summer.

A fine mist hid the esplanade from sight until he had driven right to the bottom of the hill so that it was not until he had parked the car and walked back along the front, his mackintosh collar turned up against the wind and steady rain, that he found his suspicions confirmed: there was no boating lake now. There was no miniature island and not even the Winter Gardens remained to pinpoint the place where the pool had once been. Nothing stays the same for ever, he knew that all too well, but he had hoped . He should not have come and so his fifty year old happy memories would have remained intact.

He was the only guest in the large seafront hotel he had checked into later that day. They had only stayed open for this last week in September because the advertised date of closure was printed in the brochure and the owner felt that printed advertised dates , like railway timetables, were binding and sacrosanct.

The one waitress had certainly done her best to speed the parting guest by hovering round the empty tables a few yards from Harold. She watched him eat his indifferent meals and he had felt compelled to eat faster than he normally did; he even left a course unfinished so that she could clear his table more promptly. Her stare and her air of disapproval made him gulp his food, wipe his mouth with his napkin to indicate that the meal was concluded and look up like a child eager to placate an impatient parent by showing that he had been a good boy and eaten it all up.

On the day that he was leaving, he spoke to this frosty sentinel, 'I'm sorry the children's boating pool with its little island, and the Winter Gardens are gone. I expect that people miss them,' he said as the waitress put his coffee down in front of him and spilling some of it into the saucer, a sloppiness he always hated. She stepped back, fixed him with her accustomed blank stare and snapped, 'Nobody liked them. The kids never played in the pool- filthy dirty- I wouldn't want a child of mine messing about in that filthy water. The Winter Gardens were pulled down when the Bingo finished. Nobody wanted to hear that sort of music- Palm Court! It was out of the Ark. It's much better now it's gone There's a leisure centre there now, much more suitable to this place; the old things've . gotta go to make way for the new; that's progress. Yes, it's all different now from them days.'

On a perverse impulse he decided to leave the disinterested waitress a ten pound tip. He would not be coming again, ever, he told himself. As an exercise in irony it appealed to his odd sense of humour.

'Thanks for all you've done for me. Sorry to have held you up when you wanted to clear the table,' he said , putting the money into her hand as she moved to collect his coffee cup. He had not expected her to smile, but she made contact as best she could; 'The Winter Gardens, the pond; they had to go. Best thing all round really; make way for the new, that's what I say.' The flap doors sighed after her as she vanished into the kitchen with his solitary and empty cup. It was as close as she could get to thanking him.

Nine months and an increasing number of little bottles of pain killer later, Harold knew that he was losing the battle for survival. Much of the day had to be spent just lying down as he felt incapable of doing anything else. In his tenth month, for some reason, he had a remission; the pain lifted like a burning hot veil being taken from around his head. The probing thrust through his eye, cleaving his head in two, almost ceased or at least so reduced as to make less impossible the idea of doing something other than just lying and suffering. Part of this time he had spent in the hospital, undergoing yet more tests which both sides knew were pointless. But which were carried out notwithstanding, as part of the ritual which must be terminated by death. He was now in rented accommodation since his house and belongings had been sold months before. He still had ample money left to buy any little comforts or diversions that might take his fancy. He had kept his car, not wanting to relinquish this last symbol of mobility.

The weather grew colder.' Very seasonal' his cleaning lady had called it. On a crisp December morning in his tenth month he rose early and drove to places familiar to him from his existence before his death sentence. In the afternoon, before it grew dark, he arrived , as he had planned to do, outside the school where for twenty five years of his life he had taught English Literature and Language to the sons of those who could afford the fees and who wanted for their offspring the sort of happy school days that they thought they remembered from their childhood.

The school was closed for the Christmas holidays. The Carol Service, which all boys and many of their parents attended, would have taken place several days earlier and no doubt in its customary splendour in the local Abbey. Harold had always enjoyed the special atmosphere of that day; meeting parents of boys he taught, being *off duty*, as it were so he could relax his usual cold and professional manner and joke with his pupils. He thought they liked this and appreciated his efforts to treat them as human beings; independent and unique. ' Happy Christmas, Sir. Have a good holiday', they called and he had replied with the same good wishes. He had not accepted the invitation to former members of staff to attend and then later join the Headmaster for sherry and mince pies in the school hall. He would have met former pupils and he could not have faced their cheery enquiries; 'Enjoying your retirement, Sir? What are you doing now?' 'Dying' is what he might have replied. It was better not to go.

. The old caretaker was on duty who remembered Harold. He did not show any curiosity as to why a past member of staff should want to visit the school out of term and even want to get into one of the classrooms. Teachers were very strange people in his experience; they seemed so often to behave like children themselves; so often getting wildly upset if they thought they weren't being treated as seriously as they thought they deserved, or if a boy dared to contradict or criticize them. But he opened up and let Harold wander down the corridor to his old classroom and stood back as Harold entered.

'My goodness, George, what's been done to my old room? Harold looked at the rows of new desks, the freshly painted walls and the expensive new bookshelves.. This is where he had held court; where he had brought all his favourite books and poems to the notice of boys who had seemed, at least, to have been as much moved by them as he had been at their age when his teacher had read them to him and so had made him wish to read them for himself. Of course, they hadn't all enjoyed it, indeed some of them had wanted to read quite different books; silly bright and modern books with pointless stories, not the proper stories whose magic he had trusted, whose rolling cadences would live forever in his memory whilst he lived. They must surely be grateful for what he had done for them and how he had made the Literature he loved live on in their hearts, informing all their thoughts and days.

There had been one particular boy , brought up by his aunt since his parents had both been killed in a car accident. At the time Harold had seriously considered adopting the boy; bringing him up as his own and having him live with him as a son would have done. He had felt very close to that boy and could not help pitching his teaching and his readings in his direction. The Headmaster at the time, had vetoed Harold's adoption idea; ' Wouldn't do, Crighton, I'm sure you see why- people talk. But it's good of you to be so concerned about a boy in your class. No, Fisher will have to make do with being brought up by his aunt; she is his family after all.'

Fisher used to sit by the window, on the left, third row down. Harold could see the boy's face now with that trace of a smile on his face; conspiratorial, as though he knew that Harold was saying all this, reading all this, pointing out all this wonder in the poem just for his, Fisher's, sake . He could recognise Fisher's writing at once. He always marked his work first, perhaps longing for some sort of acknowledgement that they shared something. The writing was large, sloping backwards and with a peculiarity about the b's and c's ; they had funny little tails on them somehow. Harold remembered that writing very well. And Fisher's desk by the window; it was a much older one than the others, higher, and made from superior wood, Harold imagined. Fisher was proud of that desk. He kept it to himself jealously and would not, if he could avoid it, let any other boy sit in it. It was a special desk for a special pupil. Where had it gone now?

'George, where have all the old desks gone that used to be in my room'

'Oh Mr Newton didn't like them, said the boys carved on the wooden tops; wrote things they shouldn't, I expect. He wanted these new formica topped ones so they couldn't write anything on them, I expect.' The . caretaker swung his bunch of keys; he was anxious to lock up again and get home. Out of term he looked upon the school as being his property and resented intrusions.

Harold looked round the room, taking his leave of it and his life there. He followed the caretaker along the corridor. As the iron gate was opened for him, he saw a pile of old desks, one on top of another, against the brick wall of the playground. Seeing the direction of Harold's gaze, the caretaker dismissed any idea that these desks could possibly hold any interest now for a retired teacher and said, ' There are the old desks from your room, Mr Crighton. They look ready for being chucked on the fire, don't they? Maybe they will on bonfire night, it's all they're fit for now.'

But Harold had spotted the high desk with the superior wood; Fisher's desk. He wanted to look at it; he had never looked closely at it when the boy had been seated there. Memories, memories; his past; his life ; his special pupil. Where, Harold wondered, was he now and did he ever think about his old teacher?

'Be careful they don't all fall on you; they're pretty heavy,' the caretakers warned. But Harold was not to be stopped now by a mere caretaker's impatience to get home. He tumbled the high desk down to the ground, set it upright and ran his finger over the dusty top, a thoughtful expression on his face. If it could only speak! Then he saw some writing- letters-they had been cut into the dark wood, then emphasised with a pen. Harold could make out the words if he cleaned the top a little. Aware again of the swinging noisy keys of the caretaker who was standing with his hand on the gate ready to close up, Harold tried to hurry. He used his handkerchief. The words became more clear. It must be a message. It was certainly Fisher's writing. Fisher was trying to tell him something after all; tell him how he much Harold's lessons had meant to him. Harold was just in time to learn that message before the desks were burnt up, before he was himself burnt up. He rubbed away then saw the familiar c's and b's with tails; they were quite unmistakeable. He could read it quite easily now; " Crighton is a silly old bore. Bore! Bore'.

Watching Harold, the old caretaker felt he wanted top say something. He felt he could understand why old Crighton seemed so concerned by the old desks being thrown out . He came forward from the gate and said,

' Them old things, they had to go, had to make room for the new. It's all different now.'

Harold turned and looked at the caretaker, but what he saw also was the face of the impatient waitress, waiting for him to finish; waiting for him to get out of the hotel and her life.

'I read him wrong', the caretaker said to himself. He had heard Harold break into a strange laugh as he looked at the desk he had tumbled down from the pile. 'Well it wasn't so much a laugh, more like a sort of odd giggle, really; almost like a sob, that that's ridiculous, no one cries about seeing an old desk go off to be burnt.' He transferred the ten pound note Harold had given him to his back pocket.; worth waiting for. You never know with teachers.

Harold did not speak or turn when the caretaker shouted, 'Goodbye and have a good Christmas' He walked away from the school and towards his eleventh and last month.

☙ Love conquers all ☙

Being definite was not, unfortunately, one of Lucy Prendergast's qualities; *probably*, was as close as she usually came towards committing herself. 'Probably make it,' was her response to dinner or party invitations from her many admirers. 'Probably I'll do something about it', had had to content her parents when yet again she hadn't managed to tidy her room to their satisfaction. Falling in love had changed all that. Lucy had never been anything but totally committed, heart and soul, to .Gordon McTavish from the first moment she saw him.

In appearance, Lucy was really quite close to being beautiful, but she did have a few minor imperfections but somehow, as compensation, they seemed to gave her a special appeal which most eligible and several decidedly ineligible males found utterly irresistible. Being unattached, young, and as susceptible as the next man, McTavish had instantly fallen under Lucy's spell. Within five minutes of meeting her, McTavish had told Lucy something intimate about himself that, until then, his shy nature had hidden from the mocking and usually indifferent world. He had revealed, hesitantly, that he was a writer.

'How absolutely wonderful and exciting!' gushed Lucy, hardly conscious of what she was saying. Her gaze had taken in McTavish's burnished red hair and disquietingly deep blue eyes as he leant back on the counter of the "Crummach and Trowel", the public house McTavish favoured in his native village in the Highlands.

'Should I have read any of your books? Tell me some of their titles.' Lucy urged. This was altogether too probing a question for a young writer still awaiting a break in the unremitting cloud of his rejection slips. The power of Lucy's looks and the caress of her warm and innocent gaze opened floodgates to natural forces in McTavish which for some time he had thought to be firmly closed.

'Well at the moment I've a story out to a literary competition,' McTavish stammered, helplessly, spellbound, but nonetheless, truthfully.

'You write short stories, then?' Lucy managed to deduce despite the turmoil that had seized her mind.

'Let's just say I like going in for short story competitions', McTavish stumbled out.

'I love short stories, particularly when they end happily' Lucy encouraged, being a true romantic who held that in an ideal world, all things should end happily.

'You know, I've never actually written a story where it all ends happily, as you put it,' McTavish had to admit. He was still struggling to keep his speech and senses under control.

'Well do you still get them published? Do they win prizes, even though they don't have the happy endings everyone wants?' probed Lucy. McTavish felt that it was time to take a slow and very long pull at his pint of bitter. Then he ventured a defence.

'People don't want "Happy Endings" nowadays. They want serious and cynically witty, or wittily cynical insights into the general mess and confusion of values which passes for human existence nowadays.' Lucy said nothing.

To be fair to McTavish, what he had just uttered was neither original nor his personal belief, but part of a speech in the story which had just won the £1000 first prize in one of the writing magazines to which McTavish, with diminishing hope, usually sent his stories. He had memorised the words rather as a bank clerk might memorise the combination of the safe deposit vault; both could unlock doors to worlds which haunted the subconscious.

'I'm impressed. That sounded important – I didn't understand it, but it sounded most important', Lucy admitted. McTavish could have cried; he wanted at once to kill at least five dragons for the adorable Lucy and then take her in his arms for a very long time indeed. Instead he merely informed her that he had not seen her in that pub before.

'No, I've never been to Scotland before. It's everything that dirty overcrowded London isn't,' said Lucy, her soft voice imparting a glow to each word in a way that the enslaved McTavish found set his very being on fire. London! London was the home of the publishing world! It was to this intimidating metropolis that his short stories were usually sent. But to McTavish, because Lucy lived and possibly even worked there, if angels ever lowered themselves to work, London instantly became a place of wonder and miraculous possibility.

'Do you live in London, or just work there?' he had to ask.

'Both', was the reply. I *just work*, as you put it, in a big publishing company. I don't do anything important, I don't suppose I'd even recognise the writers we publish. It's a very big place. I just type letters, that's all', Lucy confessed.

'Have you ever come across a little magazine called, "New Ground" asked McTavish?

'The name's familiar, it's one of our subsidiaries, I think. Yes I'm sure I've typed letters about it. Why do you ask?'

'It's the magazine to which I send my short stories. I've read all the past winners and I try to make my stories fit the formula they seem to like at "New Ground".

'But you must write in your own way; I'm sure that's very important. What is their formula anyway?' Lucy asked. McTavish clearly disliked the idea of there being a formula to which his stories must conform if he expected publication.

'They are all a bit gloomy and there's lots of sex of one sort or another in them. Nobody ever acts naturally and the endings are always very unhappy ones.'

'Well that's just horrible,' Lucy exclaimed. 'If you're interested though I think I can tell you how they decide on the winners of your competitions. Sometimes there are heaps of manuscripts on the table in the office next to mine. The competition judge pays various people to take bundles of the stories to read and choose ones they like. He once asked me if I'd like to take some to read.'

'And did you?' McTavish, aghast, had to enquire.

'No, of course not. I said I thought that was a job for people with proper training in judging writing. The judge just laughed. I was jolly angry when I found out he used to pass the stories round in his pub for people to read. 'Throw out any with happy endings,' he'd say.

'How did they decide on the winner then?' McTavish was eager to find out.

'When they came back from the pub after reading them, the stories were put into two piles. One was labelled, "Rat Food" and the other just had a question mark on it. He gets angry if there are more than about three stories in the question mark pile. He would just take those to read and decide on which he thought was the best. It's all very haphazard and quite unfair, I'm afraid.'

'You're saying that any story with a happy ending has no chance of winning the competition,' McTavish exclaimed. and his depression at what he had just been told was obvious to Lucy. 'I really thought my last story stood some chance. It's the best one I've ever written, I'm sure. It's my only attempt at a love story and it's got an unhappy ending. If it's just going to be read by any old drunk in a pub, I'm wasting my time! What chance can it ever have?'

Over the three days of the Easter Holiday, Lucy and McTavish would meet each morning and spend the day together. McTavish worked for the Highlands and Islands Tourist Board and had a pleasant enough job travelling round the country seeing that all that could be done, was done to show off his beloved homeland to advantage. Lucy returned to London and *just work*. She faithfully promised to keep in touch with McTavish. Back in her publishing office she decided to strike a blow for aspiring short story writers and in particular, a disillusioned young Scot in whose fortunes she now felt so involved. The two piles of manuscripts for the Easter Short Story Competition were on the table as usual in the judge's room along the corridor. The judge was still on holiday and Lucy took the opportunity to sort through the hundreds of manuscripts until she found "Love's Reward" a story by Gordon McTavish. She read the story and was impressed, but the ending was wrong: two lovers had miraculously survived tragedy only to be separated in the last line. It was a betrayal she felt.Lucy firmly believed with the poet that love must conquer all and when she had found a typewriter with the same type face as McTavish's, she made sure that in his story, love did finally *conquer all*.

His last line had read, "And it was in a pea green boat that he drowned that very afternoon". Lucy replaced this with, "And they were married next day, by the turtle that lived on the hill." She put McTavish's now altered story at the bottom of the three manuscripts in the question mark pile and awaited results.

McTavish's belief in himself and also in short story competitions was restored when he read in the letter from the editor of "New Ground" that his story, "Love's Reward," had won first prize – a thousand pounds – and would be printed. He phoned Lucy at once. They were married next month and Lucy went to live in the Highlands with the man for whom she had sinned. McTavish had his suspicions about how the last line of his prize-winning story had come to be changed. 'Just a typographical error – basic mistakes in spelling and type-setting happen all the time. It's because printing is now in the hands of machines not people,' Lucy explained.

'Yours was a story that just had to have a happy ending,' she insisted. 'I've always believed that love conquers all – "Amor Omnia Vincit" – it was my old school motto. All lovers want to be married by the turtle that lives on the hill, you see, and the computer that printed out your story was just doing what it had been programmed to do; it provided the standard happy ending suitable for all love stories'.

McTavish was unconvinced, but said nothing. He felt very moved by the risks and lengths which he guessed his beloved Lucy had been prepared to go to make her loved one's dream come

He never wrote another story for a competition, but kept his storytelling for winter nights in their Highland cottage when, tucked up snug in bed with his beloved Lucy, he frequently and fully appreciated the truth of Lucy's old school motto;

Love Conquers All.

 **Outcasts**

'It seems you lacked gravitas, Terson's favourite ingredient,' was Bill's reading of my failure in the interview for the Head of Liberal Studies post. Bill Onslow, my fellow lecturer, perhaps felt some sympathy. If he did, I didn't recognise it.

'Gravy, gravy,' I muttered, not quite under my breath.

'That's the sort of thing that Terson would be thinking of I expect; the way you never take serious things seriously.' Bill remarked.

'Ars longa;vita brevis, meaning he's got a fat arse and his feet are short, that's why he always sits behind a big desk.' Was my reaction.

'There you go again, Jim-no tact. Don't you want to get out of the classroom and lurk in an office of your own, get everyone else to do all the grind, have *working* lunches, ha, ha, claim some expenses creatively when you are waving the college flag at conferences? And don't forget all those unappreciated women lecturers who haunt all the conferences!'

I broke in here with a song:

'My brother's a church missionary, a saving young women from sin, he'll save you a blond for a shilling', here Bill joined me in the chorus to harmonise,

'My God how the money rolls in, rolls in,
      My God how the money rolls in '
Our laughter made me feel less self conscious; I was all too aware of my inadequacies at interview or in the classroom as well for that matter.

For the last eight years, ever since I had taken my degree, The West Hampshire College of Further Education had been my uninspiring employer. It was not my first, second or even eleventh choice as a place to earn a crust when I had felt an urge to bring the joys of literature to bored teenagers. That urge, like wind after a curry, soon passed . Now at thirty I knew that I must get out of my life's present empty routine or stay forever in its depressing rut and became indistinguishable from all the other downtrodden junior lecturers in that wretched college. These sad eyed disillusioned men spent their free time in the nearest pub or else trying to palm their duties off onto the youngest and most recent additions to their departments . I had been in this unenviable position until this year when Tabitha, just down from Oxford, had joined the Humanities Department. Tabitha, so far had managed to avoid being put upon as I had been by the older lecturers. She just raised her elegant eyebrows at such suggestions and then laughed, as though at a good joke.

Amongst the various fantasies I secretly nurtured regarding Tabitha was a longing to hug her for the way she so effortlessly outflanked them. I hadn't managed to side step any of the trivial duties that had been lumbered onto me. My only hope was to gain seniority, that was why I had made my half-hearted application for the post of Head of Liberal Studies.

In the interview Terson had asked, predictably, all too predictably, how I would define Liberal Studies. I had replied, 'Oh anything generally useless, indefinable and regarded by other departments as a suitable dumping ground for any work that they can't or won't do.' The predictable silence followed. Perhaps to make the farce of the interview seem slightly less obvious- he had already decided that the post should go to his protégée, Davenport. Terson had put the stock final question, 'Have you any question, Mr Clements, that you wish to ask me?'
What I knew I was supposed to say here; what any serious contender for promotion would say here was, 'Yes, Mr Terson,' (leaning forward here in eager motivation) 'What latitude should I have, if appointed (modest smirk) to initiate new courses, consolidate excellent existing work, of course, but being free to build on that secure foundation?' That is what any sane, ambitious and normal applicant would have said. None of these descriptions applied to me. I could only react to what was happening to me as though I were in a Marx Brothers film, writing the dialogue as well as acting all the parts and the last thing wanted here was any note of seriousness or *gravitas* , as Terson loved to call it.

What I did find myself saying was, ' What latitude should I have, Mr Terson, for instituting advanced courses of study in flatulence, where your own pre-eminence in that field would be so valuable, also, I assume I should be free to get stoned out of my mind at the college's expense at any and every open day or conference to which I managed to find some excuse, however far-fetched, for attending. I assume that my own personal tastes in the furnishing of my new office would be considered; a Swedish reclining couch in off white leather, like your own, might be on the cards, perhaps? Those would be my terms of acceptance and I should expect that they be fully honoured in all respects. The rest, as Hamlet put it, "Is silence." '

Silence indeed there had been for a few seconds, then Terson had croaked something about not needing to detain me from my duties in the classroom any longer. I paused only to click my heels, give a Hitler salute, and leave. The standard form of rejection was in my pigeon hole the following day. Under, "Reason for non appointment", was written, " Inappropriate qualifications." There was also a memo from Terson in his own spidery hand. He had written that he was prepared to overlook my outrageous behaviour at the interview as I was no doubt suffering from stress, but he advised that I take a week's sick leave and consult a psychiatrist as a matter of extreme urgency. Well, I thought, it's an ill interview that blows nobody a week away from the treadmill. So, at once, to the helpful pub, "The British Grenadier" opposite the college to celebrate.

I have a clear memory of standing on one of the tables. The public bar was about half filled, mostly with college staff all enjoying the free cabaret of one of their colleagues making a fool of himself and I was giving my best performance in that, my only real specialism.

'Why do we do it? Why, I ask you, do we give the oyster of our years to these evil smelling, barely literate little hooligans who only learnt to read so that they would be able to claim their dole, find out what rights – *rights*! they are entitled to. Who foul up our places of education on day release swindles and sit in the warm and mock and deride those who are fools enough to spend our time in the lost cause of trying to improve them.!'

Cries from the non college drinkers of, 'You get paid for that bloody rubbish, don't you?' and ' You lot don't know what work is. Have you ever been down a mine?'

Something must have snapped for I threw my empty glass at the heckler, kicked the ashtray and danced on the table until I was dragged screaming from my perch then held by two barmen whilst the police were called.

The college was informed of my distinguished action by one of my well wishers. Terson must have made some reference to stress and my being advised to see a psychiatrist because after being kept overnight in the police station, I was driven to a hospital a few miles away which was generally known as the "Booby Hatch."

If you saw the film, "One flew Over the Cuckoo's Nest", you will know that Group Therapy is done in most mental institutions, including the one to which I was committed. About fourteen of us would sit round in a circle. There was a young psychiatric worker in charge and we were encouraged to talk about ourselves, our problems, our fears and frustrations. I refused to utter. I was kept in bed the next day and given an injection, a sedative, I imagined.

'You are all valuable people. We need you; the world needs you. You're wanted; you're needed. Mr Jackson there repairs cars. Not many of us know how to change a wheel let alone change an alternator when it breaks down. Mr Jackson can do that; he can fix anything on a car. I want you to clap and cheer Mr Jackson,' said the psychiatric worker. And clap we all did. Next was a dinner lady from a big comprehensive school who had thrown a wobbly in front of the children because her husband had, 'Gone off with a bloody little dolly bird!' Would it have been better if she'd been a 'Bloody big dolly bird', I wondered, but I said nothing. I knew that I should again be asked to say something; to tell these deadbeats what had led to my being there sitting amongst them

The dinner lady did a lot of really good heavy duty weeping; plenty of artistic flourishes, snorting inhalations and gurgles, but she gave no explanations. I was kept to last, after an evil faced traffic warden who had been mugged by two youths whilst "Going about" what he kept calling, "My proper duties. Then it was my turn,

'And Mr Clements, you have such a rewarding job; helping students to like books and reading. I'm sure you love children otherwise you wouldn't do so much for them. Did you get worried about there not being any jobs for them when they'd worked so hard to pass their exams?'

It happened again. I stared a long time at my shoes, then began to recite this dialogue written by the lodger who lived in my head,

'I have worries, about pupils, yes. I'm worried that there aren't enough prisons to keep them rotting in until they turn to manure, then they might make some sort of contribution to the land, that's the best you can hope from them. If we all contribute our little bit, in whatever way we can, however small or insignificant, we can build bigger prisons, more prisons, more bolts and bars and there won't be any central heating and colour televisions either. Bring back the thumbscrew, the rack, the "Iron Maiden."

I then found that I had so much to say and that the words were bunching together to get out. I stood up and talked and talked until at a sign from the psychiatric worker, two male nurses moved in and I felt that sedating needle again in my arm.

That must have been a year, maybe two years ago now. Yesterday five of us were told we were free to leave, that the community would assume responsibility for us now. We didn't need a special place and special care anymore. We were given some money and the address of a sheltered home where we would find a bed. We could go. We did.

I slept under a bush in the park. It is summer still, I think, and anyway, it was quite warm and I'd lost the address to go to that I'd been given. But I had found a use for the money they gave me. You can get a lot of drink for a fiver; Buckfast Abbey Tonic Wine, 17 percent alcohol, is best, if you can find it.

Whilst I was sitting on one of the park benches, a figure I thought I recognised sat down next to me. I saw that it was Jackson, the car mechanic. He'd been let out at the same time as I had. He smelt vile and kept coughing. I decided to speak to him, ' No cars to mend today then? No one burnt their clutch out? No one's big end need replacing, or a cut price service or computerized tune up?'

I expect that they had been glad to see the back of Jackson at the booby hatch; he was always getting into fights and shouting at the staff.

'Give us a drink for Christ's sake and shut up about bloody cars, I hate them. No one wants a bloody mechanic unless their car's buggered. They hate you. They won't believe you're not trying to rip them off- tighten a screw and charge you for a head gasket job. At least you did something half way useful- teaching books and writing and that.'

I had to tell him how wrong he was. I was useless, had always been useless, a worse con man than the worst crooked mechanic or double-glazing swindling cowboy that there had ever been. I could see it clearly now.

'Listen,' I said to Jackson, handing him my half empty bottle,' you did something; you mended a piece of machinery, you got people back on the road, back to work, back to their homes or off to their holiday. You made things possible; made things work again. You didn't write the bills. You're not to blame. But me! Oh listen. What I used to do, that was wrong-bloody evil, if you think about it. I never explained how something might be mended. I didn't teach History and how to avoid the cock-ups of the past, or Geography and how to understand what makes the weather and where to find Australia, or Physics or Chemistry so that they could understand how a vacuum flask works. No, I spent all my time telling people about books- novels, plays and rhymes. It was all about people who had never lived doing things that never happened. And bloody , poetry! I tried to make sense of words which never made any sense to the kids. It wasn't written to be UNDERSTOOD, if it was understood, it wasn't good poetry. I was supposed to tell them what they were *supposed* to feel- the poem should have done that!
" Alterwise by owl-light in the half –way house,
The gentleman lay gravewards with his furies".
Or
"None worse there is none, pitched past of grief, more pangs will,
Schooled at forepangs, wilder ring"
How about that? What's it supposed to bloody mean? I ought to have been locked up-I was bloody locked up!'
Here we both laughed.
' I should never have been. Why couldn't I tell them about the real world; tell them about real things?'

Jackson seemed moved by this. He passed my bottle back without drinking the last inch.

'I like a story from time to time, takes your mind off your worries, but I like a song too. Know any songs?' he asked. I took off the cap they had given me at the booby hatch, placed it on the path in front of us and started to sing. What I sung was clearly well known. Jackson joined in at once and we managed to harmonise a bit A few passers by slowed for a moment, smiled, then threw a coin or two into the cap. We sang,
'My brother's a church missionary, a saving young ladies from sin,
He'll save you a blond for a shilling, my God how the money rolls in.
Rolls in, rolls in, my God how the money rolls in.'

When we finished there was enough cash in the cap for another bottle of Buckfast Abbey Tonic Delight for outcast souls.

"Time For a Change"

The afternoon bus was slow as it wound its way through the sleepy South Wales countryside. At the end of the route it stopped, the door swung open and the only passenger, a middle-aged man, alighted. He had been in the bus for a long time so that a farewell wave to the driver, lighting up a cigarette outside, seemed appropriate.

The passenger swung his small holdall in his left hand and walked purposefully towards the line of shops that he saw further down the road.

'Somewhere to stay?' the lady in the Post Office store asked.

' Yes; a guest house, B and B, a simple place, just for a few days, I'm not really certain for how long,' The bus passenger enquired.

'Well, we don't get many staying 'yere, you know, not on the road to anywhere; nothing much to come for, know what I mean? You could always try "The Larches" with Mrs Di Evans, she used to have people to stay.'

The passenger thanked her after getting directions and walked up the hill, ticking off mentally the places and signs he'd been given to find "The Larches".

The door, when he found "The Larches," was opened immediately, as though his arrival had been observed, even expected.

'Mrs Evans?' he enquired.

The woman who opened the door to him was about forty with a slow smile that seemed to spread gradually to every part of her unlined face and then to light up. The passenger warmed at once to that smile. There was a room vacant. They went up together to inspect it. The cost was stated and the terms- half-board only, 'lunches being such a tie midday, you understand,' accepted,. Then the traveller was left alone in his temporary home. His holdall unpacked, he went over to the big bay window and looked out. He could see the side of the garden from his room; neat lawn, garden shelter with deck chairs stacked inside; distantly the shoreline and a small harbour, all very peaceful. The traveller liked what he saw. He sat in the high-backed wing chair and sighed. He somehow felt that things, at last, might be going well for him, but he dared not hope too strongly for he'd been disappointed so much over the years, really more often than not, now that he thought about it. Yes it was time for a change.

———————

'My name? Palmer, Sidney Palmer. I expect you need that for your records,' the traveller told his landlady after he had finished a thorough breakfast.

' Not really, I hate keeping any records but I don't have many people to stay; there's nothing to bring them here, you see,' she answered. What, in fact, had brought him here? Perhaps she was fishing to find out. He could not have provided an adequate or sensible reason for being in this tiny Welsh village at the end of September. He was not a "Commercial", he was not visiting friends or relatives nor researching anything for a study or book and the village, from what he had seen of it, was certainly not the sort of place one would come to for a late holiday. She collected some of the plates he had finished with then stood holding them as she looked out of the window.

'It's a good day; good for walking, along the beach or across the moor would be my choice. Do you like walking, Mr Palmer? Is that what brings you here?' He said nothing. ' Sorry, I don't want to pry into your affairs, but I can't help being interested, you see there's not much to do here except poke our noses into other people's business, it's a national hobby really in Wales.' He laughed and she joined in.

'There are worse' he said, 'and certainly more dangerous hobbies; there's fishing and golf, for a start. You can't do the first without lying about it and the second one's destroying our countryside so that people can spend a fortune for the pleasure of hitting balls into the air and sometimes hitting quite innocent people.' She smiled again, she loved to hear a man with prejudices sounding off about his pet hates.

'I expect you dislike certain people, people who you know who do one or the other. I'm not fond of dogs myself. People who have them think that every one likes them, that every one wants to pat their dog and talk to it. They shouldn't presume. But then I've never owned a dog. Now that I'm alone people say, "Why don't you have a dog? It would be company for you". The proper company for a dog is another dog, that's what I think.'

She finished clearing the table but still hovered, wanting to say more and to hear her guest talk about himself. The traveller remained in his chair although his breakfast was over. It seemed to her that he wanted to say something else, something important, not just small talk about things of no consequence. She waited for him to speak, busying herself with rearranging the ornaments on the sideboard to justify her presence. He spoke again, at last.

'You asked just now what I was doing in this town, well the strange truth is, I just don't know. I don't know why I got off the bus when I did or why I decided to stay. I keep thinking that I shall find out. Maybe there is something special for me to do, but I don't know yet what that something is.'

She stopped her rearranging and stood watching him. She spoke with some hesitation after a minute or two.

'I've always wanted to do something like that. All our lives we have to be sensible; make the right choices; be responsible; do what's expected of us... or what we think is expected of us, but what room is left for doing what we really want to do, just for ourselves, that is?'

The heavy mantelpiece clock chimed nine. The sound hung in the air with the force of a signal. The man got up from the table. He smiled at the woman, thanked her for his excellent breakfast and went up to his room She cleared the table and went back to the kitchen, stopping once on the way as though she had remembered something, something she had wanted to say.

The traveller decided to explore the coastline. It seemed that the beach was in walking distance of the guesthouse and he liked walking, especially if he was not in any hurry. The landlady looked up as she heard the front door close after her guest.

'See you later. Walking are you?', but he was already down the path and did not hear her. He asked the way a couple of times but at last found himself trudging- the word suited the effect of his laboured pace- trudging, trudging across the flat sands of the estuary. There were no other footsteps to be seen anywhere; he liked that, it emphasised his isolation, his detachment from a world that he had left behind him. The tide was a long way out, the little waves turning in a slow rhythm at the edge of his view. He felt no wish to go closer to them as he had always felt compelled to do when a boy. Then it was the essence of fun to slap his bare feet in the oncoming wavelets, it made the sea more real to him. Her would walk to the end of the beach, not for any reason, but he suddenly felt the need for some objective in his day and in his activity.

Memories arose; of walking on other beaches, as a child, on holiday by the sea and later , when he was a student, working in a seaside hotel as a waiter in his long vacation Then he had clear objectives; to get the girl who walked beside him up into the marram grass in the dunes and see how far she would let his wandering fingers explore, under her sweater, under her guard. The chase had a beast in view then; sex was always an objective in itself; a conquest. What a ridiculous and selfish attitude he now felt, but then he was a different person with so much to fill his days, and his life.

And when he got to the end of this beach, what then? Nothing, of course, but the retracing of his steps, even stepping in the same footprints as on the outward journey. But one could never exactly repeat the same steps in life, only approximations. So it had been with so much of his attempts in life; approximations only; nothing ever rounded off, complete, perfect, finished

Walking on sand is far more tiring than walking on a road or on grass, much of the forward impetus of the footstep is absorbed by the sand's give under the weight of the body, like going uphill; *trudging* uphill. Would there ever be a time in his life when he would feel that his life was "Downhill all the way?" He said the words out loud to himself, ""Downhill all the way." That road, lined by cheering, waving, smiling, eager crowds, would stretch invitingly, easily, ahead. "Keep right on till the end of the road, keep right on to the end. Though the way be weary, still journey on, till you come to your happy abode. Keep right on till the end of the road..." He walked in time to the rhythm of the old song and sang the words under his breath, only singing out loud at the line, "Till the end of the road." The old songs; any *old* songs, brought him always close to tears, "Tears, idle tears, I know not why they fall. Tears from the depth of some great despair"... he could not remember the lines now. Some words, just by themselves, quickened the tears under the lids; "Old Times" "Bygone Days", the words alone could do it , said in the head when he was alone, or worst of all, when he was surrounded by happy , laughing, bright people, but he, locked in his melancholia, saw only the setting sun and lived only in those "Old Days".

It took some time to reach the end of the beach and when he sat at last on the rock which had been his target, he felt the wind growing colder, now that he faced into it. The clouds had faces, all upturned as though borne on a bier, with eyes closed, beard jutting out, nose high and bent and dissolving away to nothingness as he watched. He got up suddenly and set off on the long trudge back.

He took a different road when he reached his starting point once more at the edge of the beach. He remembered seeing a little pub in the village, before the coach had deposited him. It wasn't difficult to find. There would be pickles, freshly baked bread perhaps and certainly local cheese. And beer. He discovered that his walk and the wind had given him an appetite.

The "Captain's Parlour" in the pub was empty, clearly the "Fo'csle" was where the locals gathered. He was about to go there when the landlady appeared and asked what he would like. Having ordered, he felt that it would be silly to leave to eat his lunch in the other, more welcoming public bar. But why didn't he do what he wanted? Again he found that his conformity, his reasonableness, his fear of being any sort of trouble had forced him into taking an action against himself. What possible difference would his change have made to the landlady? He was tempted just to leave the place, abandon his lunch and go somewhere else and get things right. But he didn't. When he had been a smoker, this would have been the time to light up and occupy himself with the business of smoking. He missed that aspect of the habit; its ability to keep you occupied when you had nothing to do. He found yesterday's local paper on one of the tables and tried to find something to distract him from his introspection, but the accounts of fines for traffic offences, dates of cattle auctions, details of houses for sale and other such matters held absolutely no interest for him.

The plate of bread and cheese and pickles and the pint of beer he had ordered were placed in front of him. As he took his first sip, the door opened and a man of about sixty came in. The landlady bustled back into the lounge bar to take his order. Something had to be said; ' Lovely fresh day', the traveller said to fill the silence.

'You just passing through,' the other man said; not a as a question but as a statement.

'Well, in a way. I'm looking up an old friend as I had business in these parts. I've never been here before but I knew that my friend had moved here some time ago, then we lost track of each other, as you do. I've been wanting to look her up again for a long time. Just found myself here by chance and so I decided to stay and look her up.'

What was he saying? Why fill the emptiness with his silly lies? He was bound to be bowled out, made to look silly. He cut off any more communication by giving the food his entire attention; the precise cutting of the bread and the cheese then taking a great draught of beer. The other customer stared at him, his eyes following his every bite and swallow.

How often in the past he had found himself inventing a story, a pointless rigmarole of lies, no not lies, nothing so contrived, but more an alternative history; another life; a path not taken. At once he wanted to be free of this place and of the polite interest the other man might take in his fabricated account of "looking up an old friend," a woman, at that, therefore provoking, logically, an idea of an old flame, a past affaire, a youthful romance; something, perhaps, clandestine about which, in a way he was boasting, or if not that, at least giving himself some sort of glamour.

It was his own fault that the other drinker saw his cue and started to tell his own story. He had, he said, always wished he'd kept track of some men who were in hospital with him a year back.

' You been in hospital, at all?' he asked.

The traveller feigned not to have heard. He did not reply.

'I said, you been in hospital?'

This time the eyes of the other man forced a reply, 'Yes. Yes I have been in hospital since you ask.'

Idiot! The dialogue was writing itself again; creating bridges; showing interest; following through. He must get out, but the man was warming up for his story.

'Well I was in for a couple of weeks and I really got to know two of the other chaps in the beds next to mine. Thing about a hospital is that you can't just leave when you feel like it and there's no privacy. They've seen you come back from your op. and seen you come round, seen who comes to visit you, overheard a lot of what you say to each other. They've got to know more about you and your private life than anyone else could, even your wife, perhaps.' He wanted me to respond; tell him my story about being in hospital; confirm his findings; reassure; open out. All that he had said I had found true; most people do behave as he did. Most people do take the strangers in the beds next to them into their confidence and tell their life stories, confess their secret fears and hopes. The traveller had been no exception to that pattern, but the story he found himself telling in reply, inventing as he went along, bore no relation to what had in fact been in any way his actual experience.

' I was in hospital in France; heart problem, almost died, would have died, in fact had I not had the heart attack just outside the hospital and they rushed me in and used the defibrillator at once to restart the heart. I was lucky. If it had happened anywhere else, I should not be here drinking this pint and enjoying chatting with you. But when you talked about the people you meet in hospital, I thought back to that time in France because the man who was in the bed next to mine was dying, or at least he believed he was dying and he told me that he had killed his wife years ago. He had deliberately set out to kill her, he said, and he had been successful and no one had ever known or even suspected what he had done. He wanted to confess, I suppose, as people do to their priests in the Catholic Church. I was the only person he could tell his story to. He did die, otherwise I might have wondered if I should tell the police or someone about this.'

'No, you wouldn't have said anything, no one would. What people tell you in hospital is like being in a confessional, it's sacred; you trust them, absolutely. I know I did . '

There was going to be more; a long account of how the man's life had been changed, intimate details of his private life, then they would be buying each other drinks, losing track, wasting the day. The traveller was not prepared to be swept up in another man's life so that his experiences and thoughts would become part of his own consciousness. There was enough in that cluttered record already.

Sidney finished his drink, pushed the now empty plate away from him and just left. He gave a blank stare at the other man who looked amazed that his audience should be leaving before he had got to the actual nub of his story, like someone leaving a theatre as soon as the first lines of the play had been delivered.

Now what? Outside the promising bright morning had given way to an overcast afternoon with the possibility of rain. He walked into the town itself and when he reached an estate agent's window, he stopped and peered intently at the photos and details of houses, shops and commercial properties for sale. "Fish and Chip business.

Good site, good turnover, small two-bed roomed flat above. Just on the market." Is this what he should do? He could already feel his frustration and intense irritation with everything; the omni-present smell of much used oil, the constant whine of the automatic potato peeler, the difficulties in getting the right sort of fish, the complaints about portions, the cutting up of old newspapers as outer wrappers, the patina of fat and grime over, in and on everything and in his hair and clothes, the insolent children poking their heads and money above the counter, ' Cod and chips twice and Mum says your chips are too soggy, not like Mr Jones used to make- nice and crispy. And he always gave us a bag of crispy bits for nothing and. and..'

Why did he do this to himself? But he went into the office, paused and then was directed to a chair opposite a woman with a permanent and empty smile,

' How can I help you?'

He almost heard himself actually saying the words which bubbled in his imagination; 'I would like you to tell me which of all the uninteresting properties you have on your books I should buy so that I could live out a life of misery, boredom and squalor with neighbours who make my life a misery, with barking dogs, screaming children, leaking pipes, crumbling foundations, lethal wiring, leaking roof, rat infested cellar, wet and dry rot in every floor board, and absolutely and positively no hope of ever selling the place even though I reduced the price to almost nothing?'

He actually said, ' I saw in your window a Fish and Chip shop advertised. Can you tell me something more about it, please.?'

She went to a filing cabinet, the smile still fixed, and after looking through several files. she pulled out the details of the shop.

'"The Fishy Plaice," just the name for a fish and chip shop, eh?'

'Perfect', said Sidney. 'I'd never have thought of that.' The details were passed to Sidney and he smiled as he read, as though reassured by everything he saw.

'Sounds just like what I've been looking for. When can I view the premises, please?'

'I'll just give the vendors a buzz.' More smiles. She phoned , spoke briefly and put down the phone.' You're in luck, Mr and Mrs Carter can show you round the property now, if you're free.'

He found the shop easily from the directions he'd been given and rang the bell on the door next to the shop.

'Mrs Carter? I've been sent to have a look at the shop; your "Fishy Plaice".'

'Do come in. You'll have to take us as you find us, I'm afraid.'

Mrs Carter was not just large, she was vast, extending in all directions and towering several inches above Sidney. He followed in her wake as she led him through a door in the passage into an empty shop. The usual stainless steel fryers and tables, till, stack of wrapping paper and drums of oil faced him.

'New potato peeler,' Mrs Carter shouted, pointing at a complicated machine against the wall. 'Everything depends on that. It chips the potatoes as well; different sizes by adjusting the cutters here. Never gone wrong yet.'

'Plenty of time for that, eh? Are you open every day?' Sidney asked.

'Wednesdays, Thursdays, Fridays and of course, Saturdays. We open midday on

Saturdays too , but not otherwise.'

'Not otherwise?' he repeated as though it were an expected password in a secret message. 'Not otherwise? I thought all fish and chip shops opened otherwise.'

Mrs Carter blinked as though she'd been insulted, but then decided to ignore the insult in the interests of keeping on good terms with someone who might, just might, take the unprofitable, smelly establishment off her hands. 'I like that, good one, that,' she said and then ushered Sidney upstairs to look at the "Flat over". Here one or two people could pass a life of intense discomfort in the cramped little rooms with rusting metal storage heaters hanging off the walls, a definite sense of damp and the sour smell of old frying oil everywhere.

'Perfect, he said, 'quite perfect. My wife and I – if she came back to me, that is- could really be extremely fulfilled here, as I expect you and your hubby are, are you?' A basilisk stare from Mrs Carter was the only response.

'Mr Carter and me have had a very successful four years here, and if it hadn't been that his back has given out on him, we'd never be selling this place,' she said.

'Place or plaice did you say, Mrs Carter? I just like to get things clear in my mind. So, let me see; four years of success have given your husband a pain in the back and now you want to unload this fishy place, plaice on to someone else's plate. I could be your man, but you can't be sure yet. Can I see the garden, please? My wife – if she came back to me –wouldn't think of moving to a place, plaice without a nice garden where she could lie out and take her ease, or g's or f's , if you get my meaning

At this Mrs Carter looked at Sidney very intently. She did not smile or register any emotion whatsoever. Then she said,' Follow me' and led Sidney down the stairs until she stopped in front of another door.

'It's out there. Have a look.'

Outside was a square of ground with a stack of rusting containers which had once held cooking oil. There were the remains of a large piece of equipment in the middle and the abundant weeds grew over and around the various bits of debris.

' My wife likes a challenge; she could turn this into something special; ornamental pool, water feature, gazebo, bit of lawn perhaps and over there a porch glider where the old potato peeler is. Yes, this has certainly got a lot going for it. It just takes a bit of vision to get it into perspective-know what I mean?' The large woman simply stared at Sidney, but said nothing.

'What I shall do is see a surveyor, and an architect, the planning people, my bank manager, the Inland Revenue, a psychiatrist, a chiropodist, a heart surgeon, an undertaker, an over taker , the Pope, the Queen; everyone whose opinion I value.' But Mrs Carter's heavy hand was already propelling him through the garden door and into the street.

Now where should he go? He decided to return to "The Larches" and perhaps have a rest. It had been a demanding day.

As he opened the front door as quietly as he could, he heard the voice of his landlady, 'Is that you, Mr Palmer?'

'Yes, Mrs Evans. Would it be possible for me to have a bath, if it's convenient?'

'Of course. Go right up. The water's always hot. Have a nice long soak. And I wondered if you'd made any arrangements for your evening meal at all.'

'No, I haven't but I expect I could get some bread and cheese at a pub I saw in the village.'

'No need to do that unless you really want to. I like cooking and I could have a nice supper ready for you after you've had a soak and a bit of a rest.' It sounded like something from his childhood; "a hot soak and then a cosy supper by the fire." With a story, perhaps.

He said, ' That sounds just wonderful, Mrs Evans, if it's really not too much trouble.'

'Not in the least. I'll just pop down to the shops to get a few things whilst you have your soak. Shall we say, seven o'clock?'

There were two candles flickering invitingly in a shining silver candelabra when he came down later after his bath. The table was spread with a starched linen tablecloth and on the sideboard he saw two bottles of wine; one red and one white. The red was opened and the white was in a bucket with ice. Sidney's appetite sharpened at the aroma of cooking. Mrs Evans called out from the kitchen, ' Seat yourself, Mr Palmer, and I'll bring in your soup'

The soup had mussels in it and was accompanied by a glass of the white wine. The soup bowl emptied and removed, Mrs Evans's magical hands eased a silver chaffing dish onto the waiting trivet then handed Sidney a serving spoon. ' This is what I call my speciality, I do hope you like it,' she said and stood back to watch him as he pressed the spoon through the paper thin pastry crust releasing a waft of the most exquisite savoury steam. The spoon dipped and came up laden with tendrils of green and brown frills, globules of a rich dark substance, an enveloping and enfolding silky sauce sustained all. But what was it? He helped himself liberally then added two spoonfuls of frothy mashed potato, or was it mashed potato? The texture seemed too subtle and light for that familiar homely dish. Mrs Evans went to the sideboard and came back with the bottle of red wine. It had a black label and made wonderful glugging sound as it slipped into the large crystal glass awaiting it. Sidney's mouthy was full of nuggets of exquisite textured bliss. He closed his eyes in ecstasy. Mrs Evans smiled.

And so the meal progressed; the main course remained a mystery to Sidney and he could not bring himself to ask just what it was that he had been eating. But the pudding he recognised instantly as one of his childhood favourites, Spotted Dick and cream. At last he sat back in his chair and drained his glass. He felt replete and satisfied. Mrs Evans cleared the plates and looked questioningly at him.

'That was a truly magnificent meal, Mrs Evans and one I shall not forget, nor indeed my whole visit to you and this charming little town,' Sidney spluttered out.

'Did you discover anything? I'm sorry, that sounds a funny thing to ask. Maybe you know what I mean,' she said.

Sidney was not sure what to reply. He was tempted to tell her of his walk to the end of the beach, to look for an objective of some sort. Or he might tell her of his invention of a past history to the man in the pub. He felt that she might well not have approved of his perverse game with the lady in "The Fishy Plaice"

He was aware that the impression he was giving was ambiguous, but what impression did he want to give? Did it matter to him what she thought of a chance traveller who stayed only two nights? Was he then going to stay another day? He longed to speak to her of the things that were buzzing in his mind; things that never left his consciousness, day or night; things that were always there when he woke and which never leave him even in his sleep. But what possible point could there be in unloading so much of the traffic of his subconscious on to this inoffensive woman who had cooked him such an excellent meal?

He put down the knife he had been using to cut a piece of the cheese that Mrs Evans had placed in front of him. He must consider his next move carefully. He helped himself to another glass of wine then spoke, ' Mrs Evans, does your wonderful hospitality in this , your delightful home, extend as far as providing such travellers or guests as you think might value it, the comfort of your body in bed?'

Was this, in fact, what he meant to say? He had allowed his inner voice to get out of hand, as it had done several times already that day. He thought of many other questions that he might have asked that would not have brought a blush of embarrassment to the cheeks of the good Mrs Evans as his actual spoken words had just done.

It was clear that he was not in charge of himself; some malign force had taken control of him and was using him as its creature. Was he capable of any independent thought whatsoever? For example, could he possibly salvage something,anything,from the havoc he had wrought in the otherwise civilised and amicable relationship he had taken for granted between himself and Mrs Evans? Perhaps secretly she had been longing for him to crash through the fragile and artificial constrictions of accepted behaviour and seize the hour. He got up, faced Mrs Evans and held out his hand. For a full minute they looked at each other without moving or speaking. Then Mrs Evans suddenly took Sidney's hand in hers and smiled.

'I was so hoping you might say something like that ; "the comfort of my body." There are other and unnecessarily coarse ways of asking what you have just asked and I would not have wished to hear such things, but how could I refuse such a delicately expressed invitation?'

Sidney remembered having read something about the importance of timing in our life . Had his whole unprepared , unpremeditated trip to this place led up to this moment he wondered. The next step depended entirely upon him. He was not clear what that step should be. The scenario following his invitation to Mrs Evans, and her acceptance, without provisos, conditions or any terms at all, had left him at a loss.

She took his hand and he followed her out of the comfortable little dining room, along the corridor and then up the stairs. Would she want this scene to be played out in the neutral territory of his hired room where she would, inevitably, become part of that financial transaction; a sort of *room service* in the way that jokes had traditionally been made on the subject? But she led him to her room. She stood outside and motioned for him to open the door.

Inside the room seemed much smaller than he expected. There was no view of the garden and there was little for him to take in. Against the wall opposite stood the headboard of a double bed. Beside the bed there was a small bedside table with a lamp on it. There was a book on the table, a small bottle of pills, perhaps sleeping pills, he thought, and there was one pillow. This was not a *love nest*; not a room dedicated to dalliance or anything except its purpose; a room in which to sleep; a room where one could, "Knit up the ravelled sleeves of care", such care as had been demanded of her during a day filled with domestic tasks. She looked at him when the door was open, her expression registered hesitancy and enquiry.

'This is just the sort of room that I should have imagined you would have chosen for yourself. You've given the one with the view to your guests; this is a place for resting only. I think that you must sleep well here. Do you read much before you go to sleep?'

'That book has been there since my husband died. I have never felt like reading any more of it. If you were to ask me what it is about, who wrote it and what was the last thing that happened in it, I should not be able to tell you. Yet I can't bring myself to start reading it again or putting it back with the others in the bookcase. I seem to live the life of another person entirely now. And that's funny because my husband and I never really talked about serious things, things we had been turning over in our minds all day. He worked hard and when he came home, he wanted only to have a simple meal, watch the television a bit then go to bed. He never read a book to my knowledge . When we had sex- I won't call it "Making Love" as that was not what we did; we satisfied each other's animal needs. He never asked, I just knew what he wanted and I gave myself to him. It was all very mechanical. Something in his eyes used to tell me when things at work had got him down and he felt bruised, unloved and unimportant. I did my best in bed to give him back himself, to make up for the hurts that life sometimes dealt him.'

'Mrs Evans,' the traveller said. 'You are a considerate and a loving person. I know exactly what you did and how you both felt.'

He thought of the only occasion when his wife had taken the initiative or shown any interest in his sexual needs, and then it had been empty, a mere ritual. She had just wanted him to fill her with seed so that she could fulfil her basic female need to reproduce; to become a mother and then devote herself oh so justifiably, entirely, day and night , to the selfish insistent needs of the little stranger's life . He had never since that time been sought for as lover, as a husband. Such "Comforts of the bed" as he had been granted had been entirely offered "in the line of duty", with her eyes clenched tightly shut and the impatience for the ending of her trial all too apparent so that he would lose enthusiasm and just give up on the whole charade. Sex with her had always brought to mind references in Victorian novels to "The cross women must bear".

There had never been between them a sharing of bodily pleasure; no giving and taking, no communion of beings. This he knew was what Mrs Evans had given her husband and this was what she missed now that he was gone. The responsibility of trying to make up for that loss; of attempting to play someone else's part was beyond him. He knew , without a shadow of doubt, that no other male had stood in her bedroom since her husband had died. He took her hand and just stood, looking at her until her eyes came up to his then he broke the silence, 'I don't think it would be a good idea, however much I should value and enjoy "the comforts of your bed." There is something about a dear memory that demands that it remains unchanged, and holy. I'm sorry.' She smiled a little, then nodded and they went to their separate rooms.

In the morning all vestiges of the previous night's meal had gone and the table had been laid for two.

'We shall share one simple pleasure together, Mr Palmer, I have cooked us my husband's favourite breakfast, in his honour and in his memory and in my gratitude to you for allowing things to remain as they were. It's poached eggs on haddock with field mushrooms'

' I think that's quite enough indulgence for me this trip,' Sidney said as he took his place and unfolded his napkin.

Sidney was the only passenger waiting at the bus terminal. As the bus was about to pull out, a man jumped on board breathless with his haste. He collapsed in the seat in front of Sidney. During the journey they caught each other's eye from time to time and when the other passengers had all got off, they remained and this established a sort of bond. It was only in the last mile of the journey that the other passenger actually spoke.

' I never normally travel by bus, it's a funny thing but today I just felt like a change, a bus journey,for no good reason. They say that a change is as good as rest and now I feel rested. Do you understand what I mean?'Sidney said nothing, but he nodded; it had been time for a change for him also. Tomorrow he would return to his world; the world of conformity and example setting, and dog collars

The Sensible Thing

My wife's one joke was to tell people – usually uninterested strangers – that it was Bruckner who brought us together. Gwen, my wife, just took it for granted that everyone had heard the music and was familiar with the name of that Austrian organist, His symphonies had such a dedicated following of enthusiasts that if the Eighth was being performed, we would pack into the Festival Hall with all the fervour of Mohammedans resolute on getting to Mecca. It was a deeply spiritual event.

"They", that is people who make a study of some subject and then produce a book of their findings, say that the sharing of at least one real interest is absolutely essential if a marriage is to be successful. Our interest was music, and in particular, the music of Anton Bruckner. Before I was married I used to go to concerts at the Festival Hall pretty frequently. The acoustics are so superb so that it doesn't really matter where you sit in the auditorium of that great ugly building, however, being a creature of habit, I always chose to sit in the same seat,- M24, if it was available, the lady at the ticket office had got used to this and recognising my name, which is an unusual one, she would say, 'M24, as usual , Mr Sanderstead?' She said that she remembered my name because it was the name of the place where she had been born. I decided never to visit the place, if I could possibly avoid it as it would undoubtedly lead to confusions, and in any case, I'm a believer in omens, especially ones connected with place names. If your name were Hamburger, a visit to Hamburg might cause you problems and you'd probably be sensitive about being born in Oldham if you were an actor,

Fortunately Gwen, was also at the mercy of about as many superstitions as I was and felt a fellow feeling rather than irritation or disbelief when, for example, I refused to board a boat of any sort if I had seen that one of the passengers was wearing green, or I would avoid going out if I possibly could if I'd glimpsed the new moon through glass the previous night. It made not the slightest difference to be told that such fears were quite irrational and were based on a totally irrelevant religious of tribal dogma, which, in any case, was somewhat suspect. My prejudices were strengthened enormously when I happened to find out that a teacher who had tried to cure me of avoiding stepping on cracks on the pavement had died of a poisoned foot. Apparently she trod on a sewing machine needle sticking up between two pavement blocks, The needle had gone through her shoe, pierced her foot and septicaemia had set in. The leg had been amputated, but the poison had gone too far and, within a month of her breaking one of nature's strange laws, she was dead and buried.

To return to Bruckner and my marriage; Gwen, it seemed, also had a special preference in seats at the Festival Hall. Hers was for L24, and since we both attended regularly, certainly never missing any Bruckner night, after some years we became aware of each other. We struck up a conversation over coffee in the interval and very soon found that we had much in common. I worked, and still work in the cataloguing department of one of London's big museums, Gwen, it turned out, also worked as a cataloguer, but in another famous London museum, The hand of fate, we decided, must be at work and we took to meeting in other places than the coffee area of the Festival Hall. Gwen knew of an Italian restaurant which a colleague had recommended and we visited this place together each Friday for a year, unless there was a concert for which we both had tickets at the Festival Hall.Because we were both very wary about departing in any way from long established habits, we continued to sit in our usual seats at the Festival Hall – she in L24 and me in M24, immediately behind her. Sometimes I would lean forward and whisper to Gwen, sitting in front of me.There was an occasion when my whispering caused a lady sitting on my left to caution me against molesting a female just because she was on her own. I at once protested to this militant feminist that the person in front of me was in fact my brother, but because of his awful disfigurations, he insisted on sitting separately, The long hair, I claimed, was a wig which my brother used to hide the plastic surgery carried out after being slashed in a dreadful riot in Broadmoor.

Gwen seemed to enjoy my humour and we got on famously, indeed so famously did we get on, meeting three or four times a week for dinner or a concert or film, that we both became aware at the same time of the strength of our friendship. It was perhaps not love; I don't think either of us knew with any degree of certainty quite what that dangerous emotion involved, having never experienced it to our knowledge, but if "they" were to be believed, then the various feelings, prejudices, superstitions and preoccupations which we had in common seemed to suggest that a more formal relationship between us had a better than average chance of succeeding.

Although the 1st of April fell on a Saturday and was the first day of the Spring holiday, we unhesitatingly forfeited three days of our honeymoon so that our marriage should not bear the curse of having been initiated on such an inauspicious and fateful day as All Fool's Day. Having led single lives for over thirty years, neither of us felt any necessity to rush into matrimony, indeed had it not been that the administrative machinery of state museums and art galleries had undergone radical changes, none of which was likely to please creatures of habit, accustomed to and even dependent upon following a set pattern of behaviour, we should probably never have even considered marriage.

When we met for dinner in the Italian restaurant where we had first dined together, several years before, we both felt unsettled and quick to overreact. The restaurant was now under new management and the dishes which we had always plumped for were no longer available. Worse, the Bruckner Concert scheduled for the following month had been cancelled and replaced by some sort of Pop concert, or so it seemed to our outraged sensitivities.

'And it was to have been the Eighth! Gwen moaned and it was very clear that she was close to tears.

'I hope with all my heart and soul that every single stupid person who goes to this wretched, stupid Pop concert suffers chronic headaches as a result of being exposed to the fiendish noise that these Pop people make, and they even dare to call it "music!" I said as calmly as I was able, under the circumstances.

'I wish I could just give up working for the museum, it'll never be the same after all they are planning to do', Gwen complained, still dwelling on the impending upheavals to her ordered life.

'Exactly how I feel. I've given thirty years to my place and now they turn round and change everything – all records now have got to be put onto a computer and be set out in a new order. The hours I've spent getting everything clear and ordered! To hell with the computer!' I raved.

'Same with my place – new, new, new everything! Damn them! Damn them! I wish I could just go in and tell them that I'm leaving and they can get some new person, preferably without any qualifications whatsoever or any sense of loyalty either who will do their dirty work. But what should I live on? ' Gwen added as an afterthought.

I was as close to putting my arms around her to comfort her as I have ever been, but I've never been keen on making demonstrative physical expressions of emotion. As it was, I took Gwen's hand and squeezed it and she squeezed mine back in return.

'Look, why don't we look into the business of early retirement, I'm sure it's possible, lots of people do it, and... 'And here I suddenly hit upon the obvious solution to our respective problems.'And what do you think of sharing expenses – one of us sells his, or her, flat and moves in with the other; costs are halved and income is doubled and..'But it was Gwen who finished my sentence by saying,

'And we do get on pretty well and see eye to eye on most things. But you realise we should have to be married?'

'Goes without saying', I replied, and quite uncharacteristically for two such cautious people we ordered two more glasses of the house white wine to celebrate our joint decisions and our new plans.

We were both fairly surprised at how easily our respective employers fell in with our new schemes, I think perhaps it might have been because they were secretly glad to get shot of two such obvious opponents of the new order. We had both been very cautious in financial matters and each of us had several little insurance policies and endowments, so with the enhancements we had both been granted, our joint pensions together with our investments meant that we should be relatively comfortably off. I considered the chivalrous thing to do was to offer to sell my flat so that Gwen need not have to move. I thought she would be appreciative of my sacrifice since my flat was clearly the better decorated and the more interesting of the two, but she never once acknowledged my sacrifice. We didn't even try to get used to sharing a bed and by tacit agreement, we slept in different rooms, but we did share the one bathroom.

For six months all went well. We looked out for Bargain Break holidays out of season in places which neither had visited and which looked appealing in the brochures. "It's the sensible thing to do" became our catch phrase, whether shopping for meals to stock away in the deep freeze and eat when convenient, or deciding which car we should jointly own. An economical little low maintenance car served us well until an articulated truck backed into it on the docks as we were waiting to go on an economy Autumn trip to Brittany. Gwen wanted to replace the car with one which had a soft top as she had always wanted an open car, it appeared. I argued her out of that by pointing out the number of thefts of and from such cars because they were so vulnerable. Gwen won over the buying of a dishwasher. I said I had always enjoyed the simple relaxing therapy of washing up. She said the cleanliness of the dishes when I washed up left much to be desired. A stubborn fried egg stain on a plate proved her point and a large and noisy dishwasher was installed.

I was leaving all the week's washing until a Friday and then making a day of it. Gwen said that Monday was by tradition washing day, and acted accordingly. I partly scuppered this by finding out that there were always theatre ticket returns to be had on a Monday, if one was not washing, but free to queue up early outside the theatres. It was, after all, the "sensible thing to do" if we were going to afford to visit the theatre as frequently as we hoped. Other little differences between how we had been accustomed to ordering our lives before marriage began increasingly to crop up. Gwen objected to blue towels; I said I hated the pink ones she invariably chose. I wanted a push along Hoover as my mother had always used and sworn by one; Gwen said they took up too much space and were less powerful than the cylinder ones. We disagreed on whether the best soap was scented or simple, whether paper napkins or cloth ones were the "sensible things", whether toilet paper should be green – auspicious I argued- or white and clinical looking, and good ecology, as Gwen contended. Baths in the morning or baths in the evening was a real battle, but perhaps we might have weathered all the numerous trivial differences if it had not been that Gwen went to a concert on her own on one occasion. I had flu at the time but pressed her not to waste the ticket. "It's the sensible thing", I insisted; my flu would not improve by her presence and I thought it would do her good to get away from the sneeze ridden flat for a bit. I didn't say that I was secretly relieved not to be going as the programme included a piece by Shostakovich, a composer that I have never been able to stand, let alone sit through. You can imagine how I felt when Gwen came back from the concert that night bubbling over about Shostakovich's Ninth Symphony that she had heard. She bought the record and played it almost incessantly, or so it seemed to me. I used to have to go out until I thought she had finished listening to it. Insult was followed by injury when she said she had a headache on the night that Bruckner's Eighth was being played at the Festival Hall. I felt deeply hurt and upset that the very piece of music that had once meant so much to both of us and which, indeed, had really brought us together, was being missed, just for a headache, a silly little headache!

For three days we did not speak a word to each other, then over breakfast, Gwen suddenly said she'd been thinking and had decided that the "sensible thing" was for us to part and call it a day. I agreed and we got on again as famously as we had before marriage had separated us. By chance my old flat had become vacant. I had enough money left to buy it and so I returned to my old way of life and my old habits again. I even went back to working, part time, in my old museum – in a "consultant capacity" as they grandly called it. But I could see that the computer hadn't been quite the miracle worker they had expected.It was nice that Gwen also had the chance to go back to her museum, part time – probably for the same reason that they took me back at mine.We still meet at the Festival Hall – she still sits in seat L24 and I in seat M24 The only thing that has changed, I suppose, Is that Gwen no longer tells people that when we were married, it had been Bruckner who had brought us together.Nowadays, I always get my word in first and say that when we had been married, it was Shostakovich who had driven us apart.

Lobsters and lust

Try this one with a "Camp" voice for Johno and Den.

Johno and Den were *snugglers* . They shared a snug little flat in a nice, snug little corner of a nice part of North London They felt very smug about their postcode; 'NW3 is definitely OK, Johno. It's old money, new artists and the odd writer or two, I understand,' said Den.

'*Odd* writers?' Johno queried the term by raising one eyebrow. Den explained, 'Writers are all *odd*, in that sense, but I was merely saying that there were bound to be quite a few of them here, dotted about like, you know. You'd expect that in a place like this, wouldn't you?'

'Just as well there's only a few', said Johno, 'We don't want anything *odd* in our neck of the woods, do we; spoiling the air, stirring people up and making changes. I want everything to stay just as it is, as we like it; you working away in your nice gents' outfitters and me barbering away in my little barber's shop; same customers; same haircuts; same small talk. You fitting your gents with nice three piece suiting, happy as a sand boy, whatever that is, so God's in his heaven; all's well with the world and isn't it just lovely here in NW3?'

It was indeed a very ordered world that the two friends had created for themselves over the years they had lived together. Den did all the cooking because he liked cooking and was very good at it He specially liked creating new dishes which he had thought up in those fertile moments between sleeping and waking. But Johno had always been just a little bit wary of some of the more extraordinary combinations of ingredients which characterized Den's culinary style. Wafer thin slices of celeriac with ribbons of fillet steak marinated in all sorts of strange herbs and then seared lightly in an olive oil into which garlic had been soaking for a day, then oyster mushrooms, crispy dry cured bacon with just ripe slices of mango added at the last moment had proved to be an "absolute poem", as Johno discovered. Den was pleased; he liked to have his creations appreciated. Another of Den's delights was roasted red peppers, tiny shallots, and aubergine fritters as a starter followed by crab risotto with sushi slivers of raw scallop. Den loved this but Johno said nothing. Den could never get interested in cooking the cheap and cheerful, simple dishes which Johno, in fact preferred so the extra housekeeping costs relied heavily on Johno's occasional helpful cheques from his wealthy maiden aunt.

After Sunday breakfast, always a long drawn out affair, eaten whilst they read the papers, Johno put down his coffee cup and informed Den that he would have to go away the following Saturday as it was his aunt's seventieth birthday. Duty and family ties demanded that he be with her to take her out for dinner, mend any household appliances that his aunt regularly broke and generally to show himself to be a grateful and affectionate nephew. Den said nothing. He hated any and all changes to their domestic regimen and would miss Johno's warmth in bed, his amusing re enacting of conversations with his customers during the day and the way that Johno patted Den's head before they both dropped to sleep. Theirs had never been an overtly physical relationship in the way that most gay partnerships seemed to be, neither man having either the taste or the libido necessary for such activities.

Johno caught the coach from Victoria to Bournemouth early on the following Saturday and Den was left to his own devices for the day as Johno would not be returning until Sunday afternoon. Having spent the morning doing some overdue cleaning and tidying, Den went out to do some shopping against Johno's return the next day. A thin and depressing drizzle had set in by the time he returned in the late afternoon and it had grown suddenly darker; after all, it was February.

Den stirred his scrambled eggs very slowly- eight minutes in unsalted at the lowest temperature- Mrs Beeton had decreed. The doorbell rang. Den screwed up his face in annoyance and hoped that whoever it was would go away, but the bell rang again and again. He turned off the heat under his supper dish, moved the pan onto a cold part of the hob and went to the door.

'Awfully sorry to bother you, but we've got a problem and we hoped you might be able to help us. Please.'

Den had registered that there were new tenants in the flat above and had glimpsed two young women from time to time as they installed themselves but he had not met either of them face to face

'Oh very well. I'll just have to check that things can be left in the kitchen and then I'll come up. Oh, by the way, I'm Dennis and my friend, Johno, er John, lives here too, but he's had to go away to visit his aunt until tomorrow.'

'I don't want to be a nuisance, but we're a bit stuck. I'm Sandra and I share the flat upstairs with Penelope- Pen. Glad to meet you' Den took a quick look round the flat then followed Sandra to the flat above.

Sandra's flat, although identical to Den's in layout, was totally different in décor, furnishings and atmosphere. Decadent was the word that suggested itself to Den when he looked round at the piles of cushions everywhere, the thick and brightly coloured rugs strewn about and the muted lights that left much of the room almost in darkness. There were no books to be seen, only a vast television and two laptop computers on separate tables. Computers were a closed world to Den and Johno, they watched their *soaps* on the box and that, with their book, was all the diversion they wanted.

'And this is Pen. Pen, this is our kind neighbour from the flat downstairs. He's going to fix our cooker.' said Sandra. Pen and Den shook hands very formally and then laughed self-consciously at the formality of the action.

'I'll do what I can. I'm quite good with electrical things, but not as good as Johno, still, I'll have a go.'

The kitchen to which Den was led by the girls was Spartan compared with Den's well stocked and orderly arrangements downstairs. He saw no sign of any saucepans, cook's knives, jars of herbs and spices and all the various things that Den considered vital and which were all conveniently to hand in his kitchen.

'I've turned all the switches on the cooker and nothing at all works,' Pen pointed out. Den put on his glasses and gave the cooker a close inspection.

'I'll just look in your meter cupboard, I expect it's that one over there, like it is in our kitchen. A minute later he closed the cupboard door and said, 'That's your problem; the master switch for the cooker is separate and it's been tripped out. I've put it on again. Should all work now.' He turned the knob on the hob and the light lit up.

'Wonderful! You're a genius, Den. We wouldn't have been able to sort that out or cook anything if you hadn't fixed that for us. Can I give you a kiss, Den?' Sandra asked and not waiting for an answer, she kissed him noisily on the cheek. Den put his hand up to the place as though he might feel a difference. He smiled. . He couldn't remember being kissed by a girl, before, even just on the cheek. A whiff of her perfume, musky and exciting, came to him.

'Well it was nothing really, not when you know what the problem is. I'm no electrician, that's more Johno's line; he can mend anything. I just do the cooking, that way we seem to work out getting the jobs done in the flat.'

'Tell you what,' said Pen, 'you're on your own tonight, aren't you? We haven't had a flat warming party yet, why don't you come and join us here for dinner tonight?' Den thought of his scrambled eggs; cold, congealed and unappetizing downstairs and wavered.

' A friend of Pen's brought something round as a gift for her birthday. It sounds an odd thing for a birthday present but he has his contacts and is always being given super foody things which he often passes on to us. Look, aren't they marvellous, but we've absolutely no idea what to do with them and then the oven didn't work so we thought we might have to throw them away,' said Sandra and held out a wooden box in which two superb lobsters nestled , packed round with seaweed and dry ice.

If there was one thing that Den loved more than anything else in the wonderful seafood line, it was a lobster. Once he had treated himself and Johno to one on his birthday. He had used a classic recipe he found which involved searing thick slices of raw lobster tail in hot butter, with garlic, then boiling the claws and the rest, The roe he had crushed into a savoury paste and served the flesh from the claws and legs in a separate sauce, involving flambéing in cognac and stirring in double cream, capers and fennel fronds. They had drunk champagne and then watched Johno's favourite film, "The Sound of Music" on the video. On Johno's birthday they had gone out for fish and chips, not very memorable, but it was what Johno wanted.

On the spur of the moment Den decided to accept their invitation- it would be criminal to let the lobsters go to waste.

' Pity Johno's visiting his aunt and won't be back until tomorrow,' said Sandra. Was it Den's imagination or did he catch the girls exchanging a wink?

' Tell you what' said Den, 'I love cooking and I've got a really super recipe for lobsters, you'll absolutely love it, but I'll have to pop down to my kitchen to get a few things. See you in a tick.' And he shot off excitedly, impatient to be starting on the preparation of his masterpiece. When he came back, he was laden down with ingredients, his best saucepan and a bottle of champagne he'd been saving for Christmas. He found the two girls sitting in the lounge sipping champagne.

'I always buy Pen champagne for her birthday. Gosh, you've brought another bottle- this could be an amazing night,' Sandra giggled.

Den could never remember, or probably he chose not to remember whether it was the perfection of the exquisite meal, the seven glasses of champagne he had drunk, the songs that the three of them had sung together, the old armagnac and petit fours or just that he had suddenly felt cold but somehow he found himself trying out the girls' new water bed, with one of them on each side of him and none of them wearing any clothes whatsoever. The giggling and singing continued into the night. They drank some more armagnac, then just lay back, all three wrapped together,' Like a sandwich,' Den had said at the time and started the giggling all over again. The water bed had picked up the rhythm of his laughter. The girls added their own laughter and their own rhythm. Den found that he enjoyed the nearness of the girls; their hands around him, their lips on his, again and again, each in turn. Then his hands found their way to the special warmth of the girls in a most exciting way. He was lost He just gave himself to the interlocking rhythm and felt his manhood assert itself deep inside first Sandra then Pen. They all laughed some more and encouraged Den to try his tricks again. And miraculously, he could. And he did. Then they all slept, lulled by the rocking of the bed

Den woke first and freed himself from Pen's arm which was still around him. He made his way to the shower then dressed hurriedly. The girls stirred then blinked awake.

'Now that's what I call a real birthday party,' said Pen and got out of the bed. Seeing her naked now that he was sober, Den blushed and stammered something about, 'Wonderful party, wonderful lobster and wonderful-' Then he fled; back to sanity and the safety of his familiar snug home a floor below.

Johno returned the next afternoon, a bit irritable after having to be so very nice to his dear old deaf aunt. Den had cooked a special welcome home supper- Toad in the Hole, onion gravy and afterwards, Queen of Puddings, Johno's favourite menu. He said nothing to Johno about the lobsters or the champagne or anything about his activities the previous night with the girls in the water bed. Mercifully, Sandra and Pen seemed to have decided to forget it all too; they merely waved and smiled when Johno and Den passed them on the stairs

Afterwards, in the days and years that followed that best forgotten night, Den was never really certain whether he had or had not heard or just imagined that he heard Pen's laughter as he left their flat that morning. Sandra had been shouting to Pen, 'That's twenty quid you owe me, Pen. I said no guy, straight or gay, could resist two birds, two bottles of bubbly and a water bed on full power.'

'And two lobsters', Pen added, laughing, 'don't forget those lobsters!' and they had both collapsed in laughter again.

≋ Addiction ≋

For two whole seconds Elsie's plump fingers were poised before forcing another coffee cream into her waiting mouth. Delia, holding out the box, smiled reassuringly at her aunt. Catching Delia's eye, her fat aunt made her usual apology, 'I have to watch my weight, you know'

John, Delia's husband, looked over the top of the paper he was reading, took in the scene and did nothing to stop himself remarking, 'Why not? It's what everyone watches you for, isn't it?' The effect of his words on his wife's aunt was instantaneous; Elsie's face just caved in and soundless sobs shook her many layered cheeks. Delia looked hate at her husband before going over to put her arms round her rotund little aunt.

'John was only making a silly joke, of course he didn't mean it, did you, John? You wouldn't dream of saying such an upsetting thing otherwise, would you?' But Elsie shrugged off her niece's comforting arm around her shoulder.

'I can't help the way I am; I was just born with an inclination to fat. There's nothing I can do about it' John was incapable of standing against it; the words forced themselves from his mouth,

' Some are born fat, some achieve fat and some have fatness thrust upon them.'

'That's it,' Elsie snapped, all self pity turned now to fierce anger, 'I will not stay another minute in a house where I have to listen to such horrid insults.' By five that evening, as good as her word, Aunt Elsie had packed and was gone. Delia's tears had been heartrending at this departure of her only relative. John knew that he must keep out of his wife's way and had gone on a long and aimless walk ending up at the municipal park where he sat down on one of the benches to think things through, but thinking only increased his depression. By six he had found himself in a sad little pub which he had never seen before in a neighbourhood he hadn't known existed. He was the only customer and the doleful publican was being as busy as he could be with nothing to occupy him. 'Turned out nice again, hasn't it?' the publican remarked in the time honoured way that bored publicans use to force themselves to make conversation with taciturn customers. He watched as John took a sip of the pint he had ordered. The words created a pressure in John's head; he struggled to stop them finding their way out past his lips. The sad eyed publican's desperate situation and worries about the poor business his wretched little pub did was obvious from his face and the "Happy Hour" offers which ironically had failed to tempt any homeward bound commuters walking from the station. He must surely be living below the level of basic subsistence and so was pathetically eager to encourage his one customer; even the obviously preoccupied and melancholy John. There were only two beers on offer and John was drinking the more expensive of the two. He longed to be able to answer in the role that the landlord would have wished and say something like,' Nice little place you've got here, I've not been in before but I'll certainly be back. I'll tell my friends about it; they'd love the quiet atmosphere here.' What he in fact did say caused him as much pain as it did the only other human being in the room, separated from him by the bar.

'Weather's turned out nice, yes, that's more than I can say for this swill. I see there's no one else come in here to drink it- swill! Word must have got around.' He banged the half full mug down on the counter so that it spilled and he left, the door clanging to behind him. The picture of the forlorn landlord, who looked close to tears. filled his mind and he could feel his own tears rising. Why had he done it? Why had he again gone against his natural inclination to be pleasant; to make his fellow men feel comfortable? Why had this *thing* come upon him; a man who up until recently was known for his unfailing kindness, tact and consideration for others? 'You're just a pushover for every sponger going, do you know that? Why don't you ever, just once, tell some of these free loaders where to get off?' Delia had been saying things like that to him ever since they had been married, and now, horribly now, he could not help himself; there was no standing up against the remorseless imperative of the alien being who had taken possession of him and who determined what he said.

The next week Delia tried to avoid having to say anything at all to John and when she did at last bring herself to addressing him to ask when he had put down for his annual holiday, her husband had just snapped out, 'The day my holiday begins will be the day I can get clear of you and your incessant and infernal whining' Her attempt to end the silence between them and so recover his pleasant friendship had failed. She had been softening towards the man who, up until now, had been a devoted, selfless and caring husband and companion for eight years, but now that warmth was cruelly cut off; her need for him was suddenly gone as were her memories of what had been before. She did not want to give him the satisfaction of seeing her cry, but she could not stop the flow of tears. John's need to hurt receded only when he saw the tears coursing down her face, the face of the only woman he had ever loved. It was the sight of those tears that this inner, Mr Hyde-like demon craved. He knew that if he could go to her and say all the comforting things that now came into his mind so easily, she would weep again, incapable of reconciling the incompatibility of his two attitudes towards her. He might be uncontrollable again and say even worse things; she would weep again and he could not bear to see that. He left, found a small guest house not far away and sent for his clothes.

In the stark, functional but comfortless bed-sit he wrote Delia a letter. He told her that he was sorry for what he had done to her, to Aunt Elsie, to the landlord of the little pub and to the other people who had been their friends but who now never came near him. He was ill in the mind ; he would see a doctor, see a psychiatrist. He would not attempt to come back until he could stop hurting everyone with whom he came into contact, but above all, hurting his own dear, darling wife whom he so much loved.

At the office that week there had been a little party for one of his colleagues, a man several years older than John who had given John a great deal of help and useful advice over the years that they had both worked together. Bill wanted those in the office to believe that he had been given early retirement and on such favourable terms that only a madman would have insisted on staying on until the normal retirement age with all the stress that involved. Only John had been taken into Bill's confidence; only John, of those in the office, knew that Bill had been diagnosed with an inoperable and malignant tumour and wanted to stop work to spend as much time as possible with his family. The false bonhomie, the toasts to Bill's "good fortune" by those who had no idea of the real state of affairs tore at John's heart strings. When Bill and John were in the lift together, the party being over, Bill spoke,

' I'll miss you, old mate; miss our chats, our bits of fun, like when we had those damned auditors prying about and you sorted them out. But thanks above all for being a really good friend; I don't know how I would have stood being here if it hadn't been for you and your support and good company.' John's tears were very close; he knew what he wanted and needed to say at this sad time but to his absolute horror he found that the words he actually said were not what he had in his head to say but were the words of another; the were Mr Hyde's words,

'Well now that you can't do me any harm with the powers that be, I shan't have to listen to your inane jokes, your wretched moaning about every damned thing under the sun, let alone your feelings about auditors- you were bloody lucky there that they didn't winkle out all your devious little expense account fiddles, but above all life will be the better for not having to see your flabby chops and put up with your stinking breath every working day here.'

Bill had held out against breaking down and shedding the tears that he had wanted so long to shed for his miserable fate ever since he had learnt the truth, but now the flood gates opened and he sank down on the dusty floor of the lift and let his tears fall; he wept for himself; he wept at the hateful words he had heard from a man he had thought a close friend; he wept that he must leave his family and give up all the joys of life before his time was ripe. When the doors of the lift opened, John rushed out . It would just not have been possible for him to explain to Bill that it was not him but another man within him who had said these awful words and hurt his friend so much.

John stayed away from work, lived on in his bed-sit and went nowhere. He had not given Delia or anyone else his address, he wanted to stay anonymous, pinning his hopes on the psychiatrist with whom he had an appointment.

The psychiatrist looked more like a gardener than an eminent manipulator of minds. He listened expressionless to John's account of his problems and his confession that he seemed to have become addicted to hurting people and reducing them to tears; the more he cared about them, the more he felt an irrepressible need to hurt them. The doctor listened without comment or reaction until John had finished his account then he touched the ends of his fingers together in a formal gesture and leant forward to address John,

'Lacrophilia; it's not as rare as one might think, indeed, in people who do not have your normal kind nature, it can often go undiagnosed; put down as the inevitable concomitant of a having the currently valued tough business sense. The late Robert Maxwell almost certainly suffered from it. You will, I'm afraid, not like what I'm going to say to you, but you must come to terms with it in the best way you can. Your condition; your addiction, is, to the best of my knowledge and researches, quite incurable. The effects are less distressing for the sufferer when no one any longer expects or looks to him for a kind word. Possibly you might even be able to tell some of your friends and your wife, about this problem and your need to hurt and reduce to tears everyone with whom you come into contact, particularly, and this is the worst part, with those whom you most love. I'm very sorry. I wish you luck with what nature or destiny has seen fit to visit upon you. Now, if you'll excuse me, I have another patient waiting.'

If it had only been a normal, run of the mill addiction like good old alcoholism-drunks still managed to have a lot of friends, John had noticed. Or if it had been for drugs; he could have got by; even had treatment for heroine, cocaine or morphine addiction. Such things were part of the fabric of normal human existence now, but to be the martyr to- what was it the shrink had called it? Lacrophilia. It was something which he did not think he could ever *come to terms with*, as the doctor had suggested.

It sometimes happens that the mind or. spirit works at cross purposes to the dictates and interests of the body; the spirit can crave that which it hates and which will destroy the body. Diabetics long for sugar, obese people cannot resist chips or chocolates and everything calculated to swell their grotesque proportions which they so hate. For the alcoholic there is never enough booze; for the drug addict the thought of the next fix entirely dominates every waking moment. An addiction cannot just be put aside like an uncomfortable garment. John would have to face a friendless and uncertain future.

On the few occasions when he left his bed-sit retreat; to draw money, to pay his rent, collect a take away or change a library book, he would find some means to humiliate and hurt someone with whom he came into contact. There had been the lame library assistant whom he questioned about the works of Victor Hugo, saying she was bound to have read "The Hunchback of Notre Dame", it would be "right up her street," if only for Quasimodo. Then there had been the old lady who had dropped her shopping as she was crossing the street and had almost caused an accident. She had been subjected to an inquisition from John as to what right she felt she had to got to, ' burden humanity with her decrepit presence when clearly her continued existence was an offence to every one around her who had to put up with her clumsy, stupid existence.'

The awful things that he said, the tears and misery he had caused made him want to die with shame and remorse, but even as he felt this compassion, the evil thing within him was at work stage managing further hurtful scenes and writing scripts to use on the last few friends he had somehow not yet sacrificed to his cursed addiction.

The misery that overwhelmed John made him, at last, decide to escape from the pernicious effects of his addiction by killing himself. He devised a simple plan, He would find some excuse to get his doctor to prescribe him some sleeping pills and then he would go to some remote and lonely spot and consume all the pills and so put an end to his misery and all the hurt he was causing everyone.

It is often not until things are at their very worst that they begin to change for the better. Maybe it was fate, maybe the Gods were relenting, but circumstances finally led to John being cured of his affliction and it happened in a very strange manner. .

In the doctor's practice, of which John was a patient occasionally, there were seven doctors. The waiting room was entirely full of an assortment of people coughing, twitching or suffering in some way. John went up to the reception desk and waited patiently for the attention of the one lady on duty. He had a long wait as the man in the queue in front of him was very deaf and the receptionist was having to shout everything she said to him at the top of her voice and then to repeat the message several times. It was wearing. The waiting patients had begun to giggle as this performance continued and the receptionist shouted even more slowly and pedantically at the deaf man. When it came to John's turn, she was still in the habit of shouting and boomed at John,

'Which doctor do you want to see?'

A witch doctor! Is that the best the NHS can do, then I'll go and see my vet' John shouted back at her in reply.

Everyone in the room heard this exchange and everyone the room burst into laughter. Those with asthmatic coughs gave out great whooping splutters between bouts of uncontrollable laughter, girls shrieked, bent old women, their faces cracked open in hilarity, clung to each other. The room shook with merriment. Doctors looked out of their consulting rooms, were told the joke and then they too joined in the general chorus. Even small children, too young to understand what had been said, picked up the vibes and joined in with their own throaty gurgles and screams. John stood and listened, watching the faces around him and sensed a deep satisfaction spreading through him. Suddenly he felt different; his mood lifted and he felt for the first time for months, quite light hearted. He knew that from now on it was not to be tears but peels of laughter to which he would be addicted in the future.

Perhaps, deep within us all, there is some need for an intense human reaction against a world pasteurized and militantly rationalized. Perhaps it was this that caused John to develop his strange addictions, first to tears and then to laughter, but whatever the driving force, it eventually and logically led to John becoming one of the best known and best loved comedians of his time. He was able to return to his own home, reconcile himself to his beloved wife whom he had so missed during his dark period. He even made his local the sad little pub where he had so offended the landlord and simply by dint of it being the favourite haunt of such a well known figure, it prospered . John's success on the stage and on television allowed him to afford to pay for special treatment and a long remission from the tumour for his old friend, Bill. Life was no longer a burden, nor was he any longer a social pariah.

It was in an interview on the "In The Psychiatrist's Chair " programme that he was asked how he had become a. comedian.. John paused a long time before replying,

' I happen to suffer from an addiction. We may all, in fact, suffer from an addiction of one sort or another. It's like being in the power of a mighty river in spate. The gigantic force swept me along. I was powerless in its clutches and there was nothing I could do to free myself from its grip My life seemed at an end but it was just by chance, by sheer luck that the river changed direction suddenly and carried me towards a helpful shore rather than out to my death in the great open sea and the rocks that would tear me to shreds.'

The psychiatrist nodded and remarked,

'I've heard that it's almost impossible to save a person from drowning unless that person wants to be saved. The power of the mind over the body is unfathomable and deeply mysterious, often totally beyond the understanding even of one who has spent a life in research, but I do know that the greatest evil can sometimes come to terms with the purest form of good and then strange and unpredictable bargains are struck from which happiness can follow.'

It was a fitting observation and epitaph for John's deliverance from his addiction to causing hurt in the world. Happily, he was to enjoy the joys of that deliverance for the rest of his life.

❧ Sauce for the goose ❧

I like having neighbours and that's why I've always lived in flats I suppose. Last year I changed my flat and I eventually decided on buying rather than renting.
When I had the flat arranged as I wanted, I became curious as to what my neighbours were like. Since the door of my flat faced the door of the opposite flat it wasn't long before I met Jack and Barbara, He was about my age, that is fifty five, and his wife seemed a little younger.After a general chat about where the best local shops were,

where had I moved from, what did I do and so on, I was asked in for coffee a few days later.

Jack and Barbara were the senior residents; they'd bought their flat when the block was put up thirty years before. Two spinster Civil Servants shared the flat on my left but I never saw or heard any signs of life from the flat on my right and no one ever called. Flat 47 was empty, I concluded, and this was curious because good flats are pretty scarce in London.

One Easter weekend, when I had got to know my neighbours quite well, I had been invited to dinner by Jack opposite. His wife had gone to see her sister. Jack had to work on Saturday so he had to stay behind, but Barbara had cooked ample meals and left them in the deep freeze so Jack wasn't going to starve. Being very well catered for, Jack asked me to join him on Saturday night. I took two bottles of wine and we polished them off over an excellent steak and kidney pie with a strawberry vacherin to finish with. Jack put a bottle of port on the table when he brought coffee and I was relaxed and enjoying myself.

'What's the story of the flat on my right, Jack, and why does nobody live there? Is it haunted or something?' I asked.

'Haunted? Well, yes, I suppose you could say number 47 was haunted. It's been empty for two years now and likely to remain so', Jack replied.

'Sounds interesting,' I said. 'Tell me the whole story, if you know it.'

'The whole story!' said Jack, making *whole* sound ominous. And then began, 'I've pieced the story together from various bits that Randolph or Sylvia, who used to live there, told me,' Jack explained. Sylvia was much younger than Randolph. She was at drama school when she first met McGuire. 'Sylvia was in love with everything about the theatre and spent every penny she could afford on theatre going. About five years ago there was a spate of revivals, do you remember?' I had to admit that I was no theatregoer. Jack continued, 'That old warhorse, "Trilby" was being revived. It's the story of the power an older man has over a girl. He boasts that he can turn the most unmusical person in the world into a great singer.' I knew the story although I had never seen the play. 'The voice trainer was called Svengali and he makes Trilby, a very ordinary girl, into the greatest singer of her time. Randolph McGuire was perfect for the part of Svengali; Sylvia was mesmerised. She saw "Trilby" every night for two weeks, and on its closing night she splashed out on a seat in the front row of the stalls. Sylvia waited outside the stage door for McGuire to come out, and when he did, she was too overcome even to ask for an autograph. McGuire was wound up too; it was the last night of the run and the cast were holding a party. Actors live on their emotions and seeing Sylvia's tears, McGuire reacted; strangers one minute, the next, in each other's arms, crying their hearts out and then stopping and then shaking with laughter.

'The play. The play's the thing! McGuire shouted in the voice that had filled the theatre for the last three months. They went off together to the party and eventually back to McGuire's digs. Sylvia and Randolph were married two weeks later and came to live in Flat 47 which McGuire had bought. I got on well with them and was often invited for a chat and a drink. I liked them both and was sorry when I became aware that something was going very wrong with their marriage. One day I heard some shouting from number 47. I opened my door and saw Sylvia rushing down the stairs. Randolph was standing in the door of his flat; he looked so shaken that I asked him if there was anything I could do. He asked if I had any whisky. Barbara was out and I was alone. After the third whisky McGuire put down his glass and spoke

'Sylvia's left me and I don't think she will come back. I've got to talk to someone about it,' he said.' I've been married twice before, but each time it folded'. I refilled his glass and he continued. 'Being married's like acting; playing a part; sustaining a role. If I've had a few drinks, I can play my part; I can say all the right lines in the right voice. I'm good with voices; it's my biggest asset as an actor. With a bit of suitable make-up, I can be as dashing and romantic as you like, but I didn't want to go on playing a part in my marriage; this time I wanted to be myself. My normal voice, as you can hear, is nothing remarkable, and without my make-up I look more like sixty four than fifty four, which is what I am. 'I should have realized that Sylvia might be disappointed, but I never imagined just how much seeing me play Svengali for fourteen consecutive nights had affected her. The night of our marriage we came back to the flat. We'd had a good dinner and two bottles of champagne. She wanted to play acting games, I agreed, wanting to show off I suppose. Well, when we were in bed, just as a bit of fun, I thought, she wanted me to do my Svengali act, and in costume. I drew the line at making love in full tails – the top hat and the cloak will just have to do, I joked'.'Say it like Svengali', she insisted. To please her, and because it was all part of a drunken game, I agreed. I did *the voice, the eyes-* everything. She watched me like a child in a trance. We made love; me still wearing my cloak and topper and she, eyes half closed, making little moaning sounds. 'Svengali, Svengali, Svengali!' she kept whispering; I felt utterly ridiculous.Next day I told Sylvia I would never do it again; she must take me as I was or not at all.

I thought all was well until I came back to the flat early yesterday and found Sylvia holding an empty champagne bottle. She was in tears. Because of the drink, or because she just could not keep it to herself any longer, she told me all about her problem. She was very serious and quoted bits of psychology about marriage being the mutual sustaining of a role. She claimed that all great drama showed this and said that all Shakespeare's lovers insisted on role play. In "Winter's Tale", Florizel, a prince, falls in love with Perdita, a princess disguised as a shepherdess;

'Sure this robe of mine does change my disposition', Perdita says. Cleopatra was the same; in love with a fantasy, an Antony whose 'legs bestrid the ocean', whose 'reared arms crested the world', 'nature's piece gainst fancy', that's how Cleopatra saw Antony. She refused to see Antony as an old soldier, the weak fool who'd married his enemy's sister just to get the dangerous brother off his back. No, no, Cleopatra needed to love a demi-God, Sylvia claimed.

The noble Othello wasn't spared either. Othello, she said, knew his limitations – an aging black man who stood little chance with Desdemona against the young, white suitors. Othello had to set up another picture for her; himself as mighty warrior, a general whose life was full of 'moving accidents by flood and field; of hair breadth escapes i' the imminent deadly breach': an invincible and charismatic soldier. Othello knew the part he had to play if he was not to be a thing to "Fear to look upon" as her father says. But he can't maintain the image and Othello thinks Cassio, the handsome young white officer, has superceded him and he kills Desdemona. When he realizes what he's done, he takes his trusty sword and acts out the wonder warrior scene he thinks she wanted. You know – it's Othello's suicide speech:

'In Aleppo once, where a malignant and turban'd Turk beat a Venetian and traduced the state, I took by the throat the circumcised dog and smote him – thus!'
End of Othello; end of play. Sylvia was drunk with words and images; she went on to make all Shakespeare's lovers fit into her theory. She didn't want reality – there was no magic, no stimulus, no dream food in reality. Reality, she said, was the rank smell of sweat; reality was dirty finger nails, clumsy gropings, sour breath, snot on the cheek, thinning of hair, clouding of eyes and all the undisguisable marks of old age. McGuire realised that unless he acted Svengali, he would find no place as lover in the bed of the twenty year old Drama student he had so hastily married. Jack paused in his story to refill our glasses and to get my reaction to his compelling account of the drama of flat 47. 'And how did it all end? That's what you want to know, isn't it?' said Jack, pushing the bottle of port towards me. 'Well McGuire must have thought it all through when he'd sobered up, and rather than lose Sylvia, he decided to accept marriage on Sylvia's terms; he did love her very much you see. McGuire agreed to play Svengali in their bed as long as Sylvia wanted him to. The problem is seemed was whether Sylvia would agree to act out McGuire's fantasy in return. Freud says that all our sex drives and instincts are affected by something that happened in our youth, even in our infancy. What was the first play that you saw as a child? Jack asked. I was anxious for him to tell me how the story of flat number 47 ended so I said the first name that came into my head, "Wind in the Willows".

Jack continued, 'Well McGuire's first visit to a theatre was to see "Little Red Riding Hood". He was thirteen years old and he had his first sexual experience when in the dark the hand of the girl sitting next to him emphasized each exclamation Red Riding Hood made to the wolf on the size of his eyes, ears and teeth by squeezing the youthful McGuire on the thigh. Result? - A classis Freudian obsession with women in red riding clothes. Sylvia was very understanding about Randolph's fantasy and even bought a second hand Red Riding outfit.

The end of the story seemed in sight and Jack's voice was becoming suitably dramatic. 'McGuire had a heart condition. He had tried to look after it, but I have no doubt that one night, when his performance as Svengali was reaching its climax, he suffered a heart attack, and died in Sylvia's arms. The shock had such a traumatic effect on Sylvia that what had happened to Trilby in the play happened to her; she lost her identity and became permanently what McGuire had wanted her to dress up as – Red Riding Hood.

She still owns flat 47 but she lives in a nursing home in Eastbourne where they look after people who have to live in a world away from harsh reality'.

It was by then very late. I thanked Jack for a very enjoyable evening and returned to my flat. I the morning I thought over Jack's story and decided that he must have been pulling my leg. I felt sure that this was so when after dinner at Jack's some time later, the conversation got round to day dreams. I asked Jack if he had any secret fantasies. It was Barbara who replied. 'Fantasies! Jack's alive with them – mostly about thinking we can live within our income, but, you know, his dearest longing was to have been an actor.'

Later that year flat 47 was still up for sale. Following Jack's strange story I longed to see inside and pretending to be a buyer, I was shown over by the agent. Everything was just as it had been left by the last owners and the agent kept apologizing for the cobwebs. In the bedroom, on the bedside table, I saw a small book bound in red leather. I blew off the dust and read the title, "Trilby, by George Du Maurier." On the fly leaf there was a dedication in bold copperplate writing;

"For my Hooded Lady, the shadow of whose dreaming has become the substance of my life."

The flat has not yet found a buyer. 'Something about the atmosphere in there' each viewer complains and now I never doubt Jack's post-prandial stories, however incredible they might sound.

"We Said We'd Never Look Back"

What do you take a ninety nine year old when you visit him? My old teacher was a lifelong teetotaller and now had difficulty in reading anything, even books with large print. Books or a special bottle of wine were out then. A scarf? He never left the nursing home. A box of chocolates? They might well upset his rigid diet. A CD? He probably had nothing to play it on. What then? Well, chocolates or nothing, nothing., that is, but myself, myself and my memories, my memories of him, of days long gone, days when the world was a simpler, more honest, more enjoyable place.

I pushed open the door of the dayroom. It was very stuffy and far too hot inside. Six men and women in upright metal chairs were ranged in front of each other. A television set stood against the wall. Mercifully its screen was dark. The old people did not look up but either slept or stared vacantly ahead. On the bedside table in front of each of them was a cup, tea inevitably and inevitably it had been left to grow cold. Some had a biscuit beside the cup.

Mr Taylor had been in his prime, a large man, a dauntingly large man when one was a small boy of eleven. When I had last seen him, at prize-giving on the last day of term and my school life, his jet black hair had been plastered down, as always, and his creased tweed suit had been replaced by the dark grey one he kept for funerals and all other formal occasions. I can remember his shaking my hand far too many times and his deep and breathy voice when he haltingly congratulated me on gaining a Cambridge place.

'You'll do the school credit, and yourself, of course, my boy. How I wish I were going up to Trinity again. Things are very different now, in every way, I'm sure, but the important things; comradeship, joys of research, new horizons, they'll be the same.

Seize it all, it will pass so quickly, gone before you can turn round, before you can get the perspective right, but it will always stay with you.' His eyes met mine. Really for the first time he acknowledged me as an individual, not part of that corporate entity; a class. I blushed and could say nothing. I wanted to say how much I owed to him; to his inspiration, to his scholarly advice which had stood me in good stead in the scholarship papers, but above all, to what he stood for; a symbol of good sense and integrity to a boy whose father had died in the war before I was of an age even to miss someone I had never known.

All that was forty years ago. I had been married twice, had two children by each wife and five grandchildren. I had spent my working life abroad and had enjoyed the separation from England, which after so many years of being abroad, seemed an almost alien country to me on my return.

Mr Taylor had been pointed out to me by the young nursing assistant. 'He's over in the corner, doesn't like being too close to anyone else, likes to keep himself private. He's a very formal man, pity really because he has never joined in with the others in the social functions we lay on here. But he is our oldest inhabitant, patient, I should say. He's been here for the last ten years. He'd lived alone and after a small stroke, he found he could not cope on his own. Are you a relative? We've had no success in tracing any of his family and he never gets any visitors now, outlived them all, I suppose'. She laughed as though life were a game of hide and seek in which the oldest survived by hiding themselves more ingeniously.

'No, I'm not a relative. I was once one of his pupils, when I was at school. He played a very important part in my life when I was young. Is there a more private place where I could talk with him?'

'Well he is in a wheelchair so you could push him along that corridor to the little room at the end which we use when people want to be private. He is rather deaf, so you'll have to speak slowly and very clearly to get through. Don't tire him too much, he's taken a long time to get over a chill he had and much of his strength has gone.'

Time is such an elusive medium, like a river into which you plunge your hand and that impression is carried away, never to return? I kept seeing the image of Mr Taylor as he was when I had last seen him and when I was in front of this hunched sleeping old man. He was a total stranger; bald, sunken cheeked and so very much smaller than the burly rugby blue that I remembered.

'Mr Taylor', I said, self -conscious at the noise I made. He stirred a little. I repeated his name and then his eyes opened after several flickering attempts. 'It's Bartram, sir, you used to teach me Physics at King Henry the Sixth's School, a long time ago.' He frowned, shook his head a little then sat more upright, or tried to. I wondered why I had taken so much trouble to find the old man, track him down and now burst in upon his sheltered life just because I, selfishly, wanted to catch at the past, go back to another time and place.

'I 'm perfectly all right, I don't need the doctor. Just let me rest, ' he said slowly, in a weak high-pitched voice which made me think absurdly of old Gioppetto, the puppet maker in the film of Disney's "Pinocchio".

Reluctantly, I tried again. It would have been a long and pointless journey if I could not now make contact somehow with this figure from my past. 'I found where you were and I've come to see you, to talk with you, about, about old times, the days when you taught me Physics.' This was like one of those Plays of the Absurd which I found so tedious when I was a student and went to see such things put on by other students.

There was a long pause in which the old man's eyes focussed on me, with an intensity which recalled his manner in bygone days. 'Bartram? You went to Trinity. You'd lost your father, your father, in, in the war.' He gathered momentum as he dredged up the memories. 'Yes, yes, I remember you very well. I'm sorry about..' Here he waved his hand vaguely at the room and the other patients.

'I'll take you to another room where we can talk without disturbing the others,' I said and going behind his chair, I let off the brake and gently pushed him out and along the corridor to the private room.

This room was empty. Just a few chairs were placed near a radiator. There were large windows at each end. It was a soulless sort of place, but the windows made it very light and I thought it might suit him if his eyesight was failing.

'I'm sorry that you've not been too good recently, sir. I did write to the school to ask where you were living but they didn't seem to know. It was only by chance that I found out where you had got to. I just wanted to..' Well what had I "just wanted to"? The truth was that I had never understood how I had managed to get a place at Trinity College. I had been a poor student, usually well down the list when it came to examinations, yet Mt Taylor had insisted that I try for a place at Cambridge, and at one of the most selective colleges, Trinity. Much seemed to have depended in those days on the interview for my final exam results were nothing out of the ordinary.

I had gone up for interview and a day or so later, had received a letter offering me a place at Trinity.. I could not believe my luck; perhaps I was more able than I had thought? Perhaps I had impressed them at interview? It never struck me as more than a coincidence that the don who interviewed me was also called Taylor, Dr John Taylor. I told my Mr Taylor all about the interview and he nodded. I said what a coincidence it had been that the don's name was also Taylor. He had just smiled at me and wished me luck.

'Do you remember my going up to Cambridge for the interview? You insisted that I go. I owe all that I have done since to your encouragement, you know. I never stood a chance.'

He wiped his glasses and gave me a long look. 'You didn't have much of a chance, really. I wanted to do something for you; you having lost your father in the war and your mother having had such a hard time since. I never told why I suggested that you try for Trinity. The man you saw there was my cousin. We'd never been very close but I wrote to him about you, said I thought you were worth a place. I have to say that I did exaggerate your grades somewhat. I'm glad that it worked out, but I was in trouble with my Headmaster. He found out what I had done. He called it very unprofessional; a sort of cheating. I never did get the promotion to Head of Department that I particularly looked forward to. The man who did get that position was a tedious fool, but I had to put up with him until I retired. I'd blotted my copy book, you see. But that's all in the past; doesn't matter now, though it did at the time, very much so, I can tell you. I shouldn't have told you all this, but I'm afraid that old men do get silly with age. I never had a son of my own, never married, never found a woman who'd have me. But I don't in any way regret what I did for you, lad.'

We talked on for a while; about other boys from the school, the changes made since our time to the buildings and how everything was so different now in education, but I could see that he was in some pain. At last I said my farewells and wheeled him back to the general day room and left. My last image of him was his giving the box of chocolates I had brought him to the young assistant. Our relationship had always been like that, I thought; he giving and my not being able to give him back what he wanted. I was sorry that his action on my behalf had cost him dear at school. I should have liked him to have been recognised for the excellent teacher he had been and also for his being such a kindly and unselfish man. I wished now that I had not found out that my later success in life and in business had been built upon a lie and something underhand. I thought about the matter as I drove home; perhaps good in life is always related to sacrifice; without sacrifice, no feast, the ancient Greeks had said.

The title of one of my favourite songs from "Salad Days" came into my head. I hummed the tune as I drove, wondering if I agreed with the sentiments of the lyrics. "We said we'd never look back."

⇝ I Cried to Dream Again ⇝

"Once away from home, a good thrashing was accepted as an essential part of the process of turning out a gentleman. The champion flogger was the Reverend Dr John Keate, appointed headmaster of Eton in 1809 who beat an average of ten boys each day (excluding his day of rest, on Sundays) On 30th June 1832 came his greatest achievement, the thrashing of over eighty of his pupils. At the end of this marathon, the boys stood and cheered him. It says something about the spirit of these places that he was later able to tell some of the school's old boys of his regret that he had not flogged them more often. When the time came for him to retire the Eton boys subscribed large amounts of money for his testimonial"
Mentioned by Jeremy Paxman, "The English," Penguin, 1998.

Wednesday the 4th, the Founders' Day of the school, began with a thunderstorm. The flashes of lightning and the incessant rolling drums from the heavens did nothing to soothe the throbbing head of the headmaster, the Reverend Dr John Keate. He had attended the Founders' traditional feast on the previous night and had shown no moderation in enjoying the excellent wines and viands that the Lords and Governors of the ancient foundation had provided. The matron of the school, Miss Florence Hobbs, had knocked as usual on the Doctor's door at six in the morning to give the headmaster time to rise, wash and robe himself ready for matins in the chapel at seven. She had waited for his accustomed acknowledgement of her knocking, hearing nothing, she had entered his room.. She had found the venerable bearded figure of the headmaster lying wrapped in blankets on the floor. He was moaning quietly. The matron slapped him smartly on the cheek and shouted, 'It's Founders' day, Doctor, and you have a service, a dedication and the customary floggings to administer before the eleventh hour.'

The headmaster opened one eye slowly and considered the matron and her announcement..

'Florence, bring me my sal volatile and my clothes and robe. Be assured I shall not fail. The service is prepared, my Founders' Day oration already penned and I shall use the new hazel birch for the traditional floggings- six, is it not?'

'No, sir, it is not six, but fourteen miscreants who attend your good offices outside your study. Two of them, newcomers to our ways, no doubt, have seen fit to wail most objectionably, I commend a double measure of discipline on this occasion.'

'Florence, I can barely stand, let alone wield a birch yet you would have me administer ninety two strokes of the birch to the recalcitrant hides of the these wretched boys and before luncheon too, I should imagine.'

'No, Sir, your mathematics is in error- the customary six strokes per boy- fourteen of them-is eighty four plus a double measure, a further six strokes each for the wailers, makes twelve more bringing the grand total for this splendid Founders' Day to ninety six strokes- an auspicious total- with God's blessing. We might yet achieve a round hundred and so rival your illustrious predecessor , Dr Pagget, who managed ninety eight on Founders' Day morning in 1792 . Be of good cheer; there's hope!'

The doctor rose from the floor and splashed cold water from the ewer liberally on his face, dried it on the cloth that the matron held out, then proceeded to don his formal dark clothes and then his academic robe. He paused, looked at the matron with whose ample frame he was intimately acquainted, and then, gaining strength and confidence, he exclaimed, 'By God, you are in the right, Florence, I shall indeed exceed Pagget's performance this day or lose all credence in this ancient school. If any boy but coughs in chapel, I shall add him to the list of those to be flogged, no, if but one is tardy in falling to his knees at the Blessing, he will round out the figures. ' The Dr smiled, went over to his desk where a decanter of the college port stood, quaffed a tumbler of it in one gulp and was ready for any and all challenges that the day might hold for him.

That year exceptionally icy winds had piled the winter snow high in the playing fields and courtyards of the school. Boys whose parents had not felt inclined to provide their offspring with suitable clothing against the rigours of the season, shivered and coughed continuously. No blazing fire welcomed them in their restricted quarters and they had donned every item of clothing they possessed, but still the chill assaulted their meagre frames. One boy in particular, rejoicing in the name Benjamin Stoutly, attempted to pull his threadbare tunic closer to his emaciated shivering body, but was unable to stop alternately sneezing, coughing and then chattering with cold. His rheumy eyes had not discerned the ponderous figure of the headmaster before his collar was grasped and Dr Keate's booming voice declared that he intended to thrash him, within an inch of his wretched life, as soon as he had completed his thanksgiving to almighty God for the establishment of this noble school.

And so the day progressed. Archivists of the school in centuries to come would acknowledge that the year 1809 was remarkable in that fifty boys were given a suitable and satisfactory flogging on the morning of Founders' Day and that six of them had been honoured with an unprecedented treble measure- eighteen strokes from Dr Keate's new birch.

Oh if we could recapture those days and see for ourselves what such an achievement demanded of the protagonists, we should see the bent figure of Eton's headmaster, his trusty right arm twitching and flexing uncontrollably as at last he laid down his birch, stumbled towards his armchair and fell back, gasping and incoherent from his superhuman exertions.

Florence, the school's matron, placed a cold compress on his sweating brow, kissed both his closed eye lids and tiptoed from the room. Was there a tear in her eye? There should have been for she had witnessed the sight of a dedicated pedagogue broken on the altar of his idealism.

And so the seasons and the years came and went. At every following Founders' Day, the illustrious headmaster, Dr Keate, strove to outdo his performance on the remarkable day in 1809, but time, age and what we now know to have been severe arthritis with complications, excluded a repetition of his earlier triumph. It is true that he managed to maintain high daily averages in his dedication to the boys' welfare; he never dropped below ten floggings per day, but he was an ageing man who could not realistically hope again to reach such heights.

The upholding of a tradition sometimes constitutes a very mixed blessing and so it proved for the conscientious and idealistic Reverend gentleman who experienced every year a gradual and insidious diminution in his bodily strength and stamina. Matron Hobbs knew all too well the superhuman efforts that her master made to uphold the high standards of the school in all matters moral and scholastic. But the years will exact their homage and the gallant headmaster found the upholding of the school's highest ideals in corporal punishment made demands upon him that he could no longer meet.

The years leading up to the retirement of Dr Keate were particularly hard. He continued to conduct both full matins and evensong in the chapel and every Sunday would preach a sermon that rarely lasted for less than a full hour. These duties apart, he bore the sole responsibility for the financial well-being of the school, the appointment of staff, the overall direction of scholarly work and himself prepared boys in both Latin and Greek. Yet he increasingly felt that his appeals to the Almighty, both in his personal payers and in those he led for the whole school each day, seemed to have a hollow echo to them, as though he was knocking incessantly upon a locked door behind which the tenant had departed ,or worse had never ever been in residence, It began to prey upon him.

Matron Hobbs would still comfort his bed as she had always done, but for some time she was aware that the good Doctor acted out of habit or duty and not in response to the lusty appetite that had characterised their early relationship.

In 1832 the Doctor was to retire. Well-wishers, past pupils, former colleagues, fellow ecclesiastics, all the domestic staff from boot boy to butler viewed the approaching day with apprehension. The Doctor had been following a strict regimen of training and diet- two pounds of prime beef, lightly grilled each morning, followed by a bumper of old ale mixed with a generous measure of brandy. These he repeated for luncheon and dinner. He would swing a heavy exercise weight from hand to hand and then in circles above his head all the while chanting , "The Lord be with me. The Lord be with me." The aim was to strengthen his forearm and biceps in readiness for his last great service to the school he so loved and which he had served for almost twenty five years.

On the morning of the thirtieth of June in the year 1832, his last day as Headmaster of the ancient school, he rose early. Matron Hobbs was there to supervise the breaking of his morning fast and to rub soothing and sweet smelling unguents into his wasted arms. The tears were near for her, but she put on a steadfast expression and urged her master to even greater feats as he swung his new birch above his head and brought it down upon the cushion laid ready to receive the blow. For the first time in their long relationship she was forward enough to address him by his first name, ' John, dear, noble John. You go out this day to do battle for school and for tradition and for England. Wear this simple kerchief around your right arm so that I may see it when you go forth. It is but a simple thing I ask, but the significance for me is very great. You will be my champion.'

'Florence, I shall for your sake wear this .kerchief and with as much pride as any knight wore Lady's favour as he went out to the lists in times of old. And now I must eat and dress for I intend this day to do wondrous things.'

'Not the flogging of fifty boys, as was once your dream. It is not humanly possible. forebear.'

' I shall with God's good grace, this day take up my trusty birch and not put it down until I have administered just discipline to- not fifty, not sixty, not seventy but eighty! Eighty honest young souls who lives are trusted by their progenitors into my care.'

The Doctor's sermon that morning was to be always remembered as his best. He touched on duty, courage, self-sacrifice and honour. Then, with robe flowing out behind him, he came down from his pulpit and took up his position in the wide nave. The boys who were to receive his final flogging stood motionless in a long column. The college butler proffered on a gold and silver cushion, the new and freshly oiled birch. The last vibrant chords from the great organ hung in the air. And then there was silence. As each boy's name was called, he stepped forward and bent to receive the customary six strokes from the birch.

At first and until the fortieth name was called, the venerable figure of the old headmaster showed no sign of the pain he was experiencing in his arm and through his whole frame. He raised high the birch and it came snapping down with a satisfying swish familiar to all the boys. Matron Hobbs alone knew at what expense to self the old Doctor pursued his duty. She could not bear to see the line of moisture- honest perspiration- that clung about his temples. His knuckles now were livid white and the finger nails had flushed a deep and scarlet red.

The second master, one who was widely thought to be a worthy successor to the

Doctor, stepped forward after the seventy ninth boy had received the birch. He could sense and see what ghastly strain his old master was under.

'Sir, entrust the last to me. You have done mightily and no man could do more.'

The Doctor wiped his forehead with his gown and spoke with effort, ' God's peace. I would not lose so great an honour as one man more, methinks, would share with me. Now set my teeth and stretch my nostrils wide; Hold hard my breath and bend up every spirit to my full height! On, on you noblest English!' And at that signal the eightieth young man; the school captain and captain of sport stepped forward to receive the homage of his old master.

There was not a single soul in the hallowed precinct of the chapel who did not feel each sinew's struggle; each muscle's strain as the old man's arm was raised on high for what was the very last time. The brittle slap of wood on cloth was heard distinctly, even to the furthest corner of the noble chapel where all the domestic staff, from butler to kitchen skivvies, strained to feast their eyes upon this glorious sight. And when the last of the six strokes was done, there arose such a tide of cheering, such a joyous chorus of delight as made the vaulted ceiling ring and yet ring again.

Fancy and legend has it that Matron Hobbes heard her old lover and master sigh, 'Nunc dimittis' But who can tell? Sufficient to say that when the boys crowded round their old master with tears spurting from every eye, he was most clearly heard by all to gasp,' I did my best; I wish that I had been able to do more , but eighty is not without credit.' And then he broke his birch between his knotted fists and strode out slowly to thunderous cheers and cries of joy.

That very night the Reverend Doctor, John Keate,M.A., D.Phil., High Master of Eton College lay on his death bed. Matron Hobbs was by his side and heard most distinctly his closing words in this life,

' I had a dream . In that dream, it seemed to me, I gave a flogging to some eighty boys and I did not cease until all were most soundly and faithfully beaten as they should have been. And then I woke and cried to dream again."

≈ Miracle at Breakfast ≈

'Why do you always think you know better, Bill?'

'I suppose it's because I usually do. It's just the way I am.'

'Oh God. There are times when I really hate you, do you know that?'

"Of course, Myra. There's really not much I don't know, especially about you.'

They were sitting opposite each other , nicely chilled camparis in hand and two weeks of sunshine, idling, swimming and fine Italian food and drink to look forward to. They always came to the same little place by the sea. That way there were no surprises but no shocks or disappointments either- usually. This summer things were to turn out quite differently and in ways that neither of them could have predicted.

Bill's income as a gynaecologist made staying in the best hotels not only possible but a matter of course. The private patients ' consultations saw to that. They both loved ordering whatever they wanted and Ramon, the owner of the Hotel Bonadies, made sure that his wine list included some of the best vintages that sheer money could buy. The sun had been shining as it can do so wonderfully in Southern Italy in September and now in the magic hour before dinner it was just luxuriously balmy. They had spent some time peering at the extensive menu and wine list and the waiter had noted all down with appreciative nods and smiles as though they had just solved some intricate puzzle. The sea lapped the shore and the wooden pier which supported the decking where they sat. Myra had been about to say, as she always did, that this was definitely her idea of heaven, in fact what could a heaven provide to rival this? And in any case, if such an impossibly unlikely place as a heaven were to exist, how could one enjoy it if one had no body? Ridiculous! 'No, carpe diem whilst we still have bodies and health enough to do justice to all the luxuries which came our way, I say, was her view.

' If we did go to some other place next year, we'd have to start all over again; sussing out the right hotel, the right places to eat, the right beaches to snorkel in and, and... Well it's just not worth it; don't you see that, Bill? Things might go wrong and we don't want to waste one single wonderful September of our lives, do we?'

Her husband sipped his drink slowly, rattled the ice cubes in the tall glass, and sipped again, ' I was talking to Edgar last week and he said that he and Fiona had found a place which we would love, just love It's an island off South Carolina, can't remember the name, but I wrote it down in my diary. Apparently it was where the English who didn't want to be part of independence after the War of Independence settled after leaving the new World.'

'Sounds a bit tedious and political to me. Probably full of people who spend their wretched lives protesting. You know I can't stand that sort. No, No. NO!'

Bill would have lit a cigarette at this stage had he not given up a month before and was still firmly addicted, in his mind at any rate. 'What an old stick in the mud you are. Where's your sense of adventure, your hunger for fresh fields and pastures green, eh? Go on, give it a go,' said Bill

'I was thinking about Ramon, he'll be so hurt that we've abandoned him, and for what- an unknown political refuge off Florida, of all ghastly places. Emphatically no. And that's final'

Our scene moves to a year later and to the Island of Man of War, a thirty minute flight in a six seater plane from Miami. The sun is, of course, shining as hard as you'd expect it to on a Caribbean island. The coconuts cluster tantalisingly at the top of tall coconut trees. Bill and Myra are sitting on rickety bamboo chairs looking at the small crabs scuttling across the beach and the sparkling wavelets lapping the white sand and at a very overweight man trying to start an outboard engine on his inflatable boat.

'That's what I love to see; people working in the sun and failing in all they do. We didn't get this sort of floor, or rather beach show in curry combed Italy at the Bonadies, did we?' asked Bill.

'We didn't get giant bloody cockroaches in the bathroom, if you can call it that, or a total absence of anywhere you could possibly call a restaurant either. The ice maker is pathetic, the towels are worn out, the "included maid" is always in church and there is absolutely nothing to do. I suppose now you're satisfied and we can book up again with Ramon for next year, if we ever survive this sentence on Devil's Island.'

Bill pulled luxuriously on his cigar, 'Cigars aren't really smoking' he argued, and defended his choice of holiday resort. ' I like the little cafe, the cracked conch, the home made rolls, the simple salads and the fruit! That's to die for '

'And we may well die of something here' Myra snapped. 'You hadn't bothered to find out that they are all born again Puritans here so there's no alcohol. You shouldn't really smoke as they don't "hold" with smoking and other *depravities*. No two piece swimming costumes allowed for the ladies and no "overt signs of affection" in public places, particularly the beach. The television only picks up religious programmes from the Crystal Cathedral in L.A. and the only books on sale are moral tracts. Congratulations; you've ruined our whole, long awaited, richly deserved two weeks' holiday. Talk yourself out of that, you bastard!'

Bill stubbed out his cigar after savouring its last pungent inch of Havana leaf. He had learnt long ago that when his wife had changed up into *top gear* in her ranting, then she would run herself down and eventually become reasonable again. That's what usually happened and for a man who believed he always knew best, he saw no reason to think things would go differently this time. But he was wrong.

Myra refused to say anything at all to Bill for the rest of that holiday. He pleaded, he sulked, he raged; all to no avail; Myra remained silent. The two flights back to Heathrow and then the taxi back to Chiswick also passed in silence. Bill's confidence in his judgement was thoroughly shaken and it wasn't until the morning of his birthday that Myra gave up her campaign.

After opening the pile of cards he had from family or friends who knew him well enough to know the date of his birthday, Bill looked expectantly at his wife. This would be the time that she'd speak, surely, if only to wish him a happy birthday. She did, in fact, smile, a wan, superior, preoccupied sort of smile, but Bill took it as a hopeful sign.

' Penny for them', he said.

'They're worth a good deal more than that. Why don't you open your birthday present? It might be something nice', said Myra passing him the scissors to cut the string.

Now if there was one thing that Bill really enjoyed in life it was a surprise. As a child he often had to go off to bed when his parents or a friend had promised him a special present if he'd been very, very good. The sheer excitement of anticipation would bring on a dizzy spell, frequently followed by nausea and a blinding headache. The passing years had not entirely cured him off this embarrassing reaction and when Myra presented him suddenly with a quite unexpected birthday present in reconciliation, he began to feel his old problem coming on again.

Myra watched Bill as he unwrapped the brown paper parcel, his nervous fingers clumsy in his haste. Inside there was a cardboard box and inside that, a book. Bill took it out, puzzlement and pleasure on his face. "Life with Bill", was the title of a well presented hard-backed book He sat back, waves of tension making his body twitch in reaction. He turned to the opening page and read, "A frank account of the confusion, exasperation, surprises and shocks of being married to a self-opinionated megalomaniac. Myra Brown describes in intimate detail the tortured yet exuberant effects of being marred to an eminent consultant gynaecologist. Open and enjoy"

The first page was thick cardboard and in the space below was not the pages of a book but a flat bottle of Bill's favourite and now almost unobtainable fifty year old Calvados. He felt so many emotions at once, but the predominant one was love and delight.

'Point taken, my darling, but how extraordinarily clever of you to have had this amazing book made up! It's really a sort of miracle! I'd never have believed you could arrange such a thing.'

'Ah, now you will understand me a bit better; you certainly don't know all about your clever, resourceful wife, do you?' said Myra, giving him a birthday kiss.

'Enough to know that we'll always go back to dear old Ramon's for all our holidays from now on.'

⤝ All in the mind ⤜

Emily had always wanted to live on a pier but she did the next best thing, she worked on one. Her little booth was the very last before you came to the end where the anglers laid out their lines or cast their rods, summer or winter. She had never seen one actually catch a fish, but that wasn't why they were there, she suspected. They all seemed to know each other. When they had set up their lines, they would talk, Emily could just hear what they said if the wind wasn't howling under the planks of the pier and the jazzy loud music from the dodgem cars wasn't playing. She couldn't always see the person talking because he might be round the corner from where the one window of the booth gave a view, but she preferred this, just as she preferred listening to the radio rather than watching television, it gave her imagination something to do.

The end of the season was Emily's favourite time for the pier because the noisy young had left and the retired couples on cheap coach holidays made no noise and seemed to respect what the pier had to offer. They would sit for hours in the few deck chairs left out for hire, drink their tea from their flasks, open the lovingly prepared sandwich packets, then nod off, particularly if there was any sunshine. Not many of them came through her door to have their fortunes read; time had taught them to be wary of planning for the future, and also they had no money to spare for indulgences like listening to Emily's reading of their palms or the Tarot cards.

One Friday afternoon, when Emily was thinking about turning off her oil heater and closing up for the, the door was pushed open very hesitantly and a small man wearing a thick overcoat came in. The coat was a size too big for him and this made him look even smaller. 'You read fortunes,' the little man stated rather than asked.

'I can't tell you what your future holds if that's what you want, but I have some skills in telling you about yourself, things which I can read in your face and hands.' Emily had given that explanation thousands of times. It was her insurance against having to go through any mumbo jumbo or make a pretence of being able to know what the future might hold for any of the apprehensive and self-conscious people who came through her door prepared to part with five pounds to have Emily focus her eyes and attention on them for twenty minutes. It was as much an ego trip for the "clients", as she grandly called them, as an opportunity for Emily to practise her special skills.

The little man hesitated. Emily guessed he would be trying to decide whether it was worth five pounds to hear what an old woman might have to say about him. All depended on what he thought of himself. He was Emily's only customer that day and the five pounds would pay for her fish and chips supper and a seat in the cinema afterwards. Besides, she rather liked the look of him.

'What do you see in these?' said the man as he held out his hands, palms upwards to her.

'Take the seat in front of me first then put the money in that box. Good, now, close your eyes and just relax for a few minutes,' she said. He left his hands open on the table and she looked first at the small fingers then at the face. He appeared to be very peaceful, the breath coming and going gently, the mouth relaxed, the eyes moving slightly under the closed lids. She liked the face. She felt she had known it a long time ago. It was a face she would be happy to see first thing in the morning, bringing in a cup of tea to her in her bed. No one had ever done that for her. She touched the ends of his fingers with her fingers and felt a peace growing within her.

'Right, you may open your eyes now and let me look at you,' Emily instructed. Outside she could hear one of the anglers cursing, probably because the wind had knotted his lines. Inside through the one small window filtered just the sort of calm evening light suited to the unreal intimacy she found necessary if she was to be able to concentrate effectively and productively.

For all the years that Emily had plied her trade on the pier, she had relied on giving herself entirely over to her intuition, Yes it was true that one could tell quite a lot from the hands, but early on she had learnt that it was not so much what various whorls, lines and crosses on the palm might signify, but how her client reacted when she pretended to see in the hands the information that had suddenly come into her head; a sixth sense which seemed to tell her in her secret consciousness something about the client.

Sometimes she had had to wait quite a time and she would go through the motions of being intensely interested in what she saw in the palms, but it was her secret inner voice that gave her the message and this could never be hurried. If she heard nothing, she had her strategy; she would stand up dramatically, look the client in the eye and say. 'I'm sorry; I must return your fee. I see nothing in your hands that you would wish to know.' Human nature being the perverse beast that it is meant the clients would then become all the more eager to stay to hear something- anything at all- rather than be rejected. They would offer to double or quadruple the fee. Occasionally a woman, it was invariably a woman, would become angry or tearful, blurt something about being sorry for what she had done to someone, a deceased husband, Emily guessed, then she would leave, sometimes not bothering to take back her five pounds.

Emily looked at the hands and then at the face. The little man smiled, not nervously or foolishly, but as though he knew exactly what Emily was thinking and approved of it. The secret voice in Emily's head was at once very talkative and yet also silent. She was disconcerted. She waited patiently, she knew the matter could not be hurried. The lone fiver, her day's income, wasn't really that important; she could do without the chips or the cinema if she must.

'You've been here quite a time haven't you? I was here thirty years ago but I wasn't ready to come and see you then, but now it's time,' the man said softly, as though to a, well, to a lover, yes, that was it, as to a lover, Emily thought. Still she said nothing, waiting, waiting. She was certain that she would hear something soon and that it would be something she would never have predicted.

Then he spoke again,' You like to listen to the waves under the pier, to watch the water frothing against the iron supports when it's rough, that's what you like most, that I know. You like being on your own, but sometimes you like to talk, but there's no one to listen to you, no one who understands you, understands how important it is to get three, always three chapters of your book read before you go to sleep, put out the stale bread pieces, soaked in water first, of course, for the birds, not to watch them eating it, that wouldn't be polite. You need some new shoes, but you won't give in to buying them before the end of the month, You wonder about my hands, why they are so delicate, a gentleman's hands, yet my coat looks a though it came from a charity shop, which it will do, soon now. You don't need to wait for your *voice* to tell you what you already know; why I'm here.'

Emily smiled also, not wanting to wait, not needing to wait any longer for her .*voice* to tell her about her client. She knew everything about him already; his loneliness, his shyness and his consequent retreat from the world into the world of those who worked from home, not wanting to mingle, chat or have demands made of them. Cyril, for that must be his name, worked at proof reading. He was meticulous and worked fast with intense concentration. He read for pleasure only first thing in the morning, it prepared his eyes for the demands of the day. He never ate out, never went to the cinema, but he was thinking now of fish and chips, perhaps it was the men outside fishing that suggested this to him. Now they could both smell the hot oil, the salty tang of the batter on the cod fillet, could hear the chips being shovelled up hot, and wonderfully fat and soggy into the paper bag, then the wrapping paper, then the newspaper to keep it all warm until they could eat it sitting in the shelter on the esplanade.

'This will cover us both for the fish and chips', Cyril said, pulling the sole fiver from the box. 'And I'll stand us the cinema seats. Thank God you and I don't have to make small talk, at least not out loud,' said Cyril. Emily turned the wick down to extinguish the stove, flicked the card round on the door to read "closed" and took Cyril's outstretched hand as they walked back along the pier.

They missed the angler reeling in frantically for at last he had a fish, his fish, his unexpected great big fish, the only one he had ever caught. Now he could stay in on the cold winter nights and not have to dream impossible dreams ever again.

Mutatis Mutandis

HIM

'You're a fool. It never pays to go back,' Jane would have said. Jane, my dear sensible wife. But being a fool comes naturally to me in some things, things that don't really matter, that is, and seeing again the woman I once had wanted to marry was the act of a fool.

Carol had written that she'd seen my name on the Head Teachers' conference list. Her name was different, she'd married, twice, I think since our days together. She had only recently become a Head or otherwise our paths might have crossed earlier.

I wrote back to fix a meeting in the bar of the conference hotel. All the old excitement, then always sexual, came back as I thought about the meeting, How I had loved her hair, the sleek dark petals round her bright sad face. And her eyes; I had lived in their gaze. She had been so shy; difficult to imagine her now as a stern school boss.

I waited. She had never been punctual. I made myself remember how it had all been twenty five years ago. Her lips, slightly pouted, the hushed sibilant whisper of her, 'Kiss me Charles, I need you'. Oh Jane had been right – the past is a foreign country.

But no temptress from the past appeared. The big lounge with the bar along one side was almost empty. I looked around. A stout, grey-haired woman in the far corner was reading a file, her thick eyebrows were puckered and her half glasses seemed poised on the end of her nose; every inch a redoubtable Headmistress in her expensive looking executive suit.

Carol would never be seen dead in anything like that. Carol! As I spoke the words in my head, the old longing came back. I saw Carol so clearly. She was sitting by the river at Granchester, throwing sticks into the slow brown water, the old "Red Lion" in the distance, scene of those precious meetings.

She was ten minutes late and the plenary session would start in the hall in five minutes. Carol, my lost love. Where are you?

'It's Charles, isn't it? I thought it must be, but I wasn't sure. I've been sitting over there in the corner, reading some of the paperwork.'

'Carol? I'm sorry. I didn't see you over there. You look wonderful. You're just the same, a little fuller, perhaps, but that suits the role.'

How easily these lies came to me. I did not know this stranger, with her aggressive confidence, her strident voice, her probing eyes and tight unpleasant lips. Could this really be the woman who had torn my life apart when she had left me, left me to go away and marry another man, a man I never knew.

I could not fit this face over the face I remembered; that dear dream face from my past. This stranger talked about "Central funding, corporate insurance advantages, staffing problems" and I joined in as we walked towards the conference hall, two elderly and formal establishment figures not student lovers watching the waters flow past on a still and sultry evening spent beside the Cam a quarter of a century but a whole lifetime ago. "That was in a foreign country and besides the wench is dead."

HER

'Charles Mason, King Edward the Seventh School. Could it really be funny old Charles that I'm going to see again after all this time? Charles, the slow, Charles the slobbery, Charles of the wandering hands and sheep's eyes. What had I ever, ever seen in him? But here he is, back from the past of twenty five years ago, come to haunt me at my first Head Teachers' conference. What can he look like now as a Head and quite a respected one too from the name of his school. I'd better write to warn him that I'll be at his conference. He'll want to start it all over again unless I do something to keep him off.

Well this is the bar and there's no sign of lover boy. Oh God I remember those pleading eyes and the bleating voice. It just couldn't go on; Andrew Agueface had to be left, pity it was only for Billy, he was no knight in shining armour either. Why can't I ever get a *real* man, a man who knows how to wear a good suit, how to have his hair cut – cropped close even- if it is going grey? A man who looks like Sean Connery; tall, head held well, a man with a presence, like the man over there in the dark suit- Saville Row that if I know anything about it. I wonder whom he's waiting for; his sexy secretary I bet – fringe benefits and all that. He is rather dishy though. Meantime I wait here for the thing from the past, the creature from the black lagoon. Well where are you Mr Charles Manson, headmaster? Late as usual, as you always were, even for that dreadful night we spent in the "Red Lion"! The night of the limp hands everywhere, except in the right place at the right time. He'll probably still be wearing that awful duffel. What an escape.

Oh sod you, Charles, I'll go and chat up that distinguished type, Head of Marlborough or Eton perhaps. He seems to be waiting for someone. I'll take off my reading glasses then I might see him better. My God, it can't be, but it is – Charles, my droopy old Charles; wonderfully transformed; my Sean Connery man! He even stands differently, that old duffel and the sweaters did nothing for you, Charles. Now I could really go for you. If I play my hand right I could be in for an Indian Summer; a last fling.

'It's Charles, isn't it? I thought it must be, but I wasn't sure'

'Carol! I'm sorry I didn't see you sitting over there. You look – wonderful.'

Oh I love the way he uses his eyes, that slow commanding sweep, and the voice has changed – assured, the voice of authority – no paunch, no wrinkles, firm handshake, I expect he wants to touch me, but I'll play this carefully and just be very suave; the distant glamorous sexy Headmistress of St Anne's Girls High, 'I'll blind him with business talk, it will drive him mad when I know all he wants to do is talk about when we can get together, like old times. Why not a "Head teachers' Reunion" at the old "Red Lion", Grantchester,? And this time we'll play our song in tune, won't we boy? I can hardly wait. Wow! WOW! 'Got a new master, got a new man!'

❧ An ill wind ❧

Of course it might have been mere coincidence, but when the pattern of cause and effect became so firmly established that he began automatically to rely upon it , Dan knew that chance played no part in his sudden and unexpected success as a writer.

It was after one of his occasional family rows that Dan suddenly noticed that afterwards his writing style glowed and his creativity positively sparkled. Ruling out coincidence, Dan assumed that the result must be some sort of by-product of the desperate searching for telling and apt phrases which always characterized his verbal duels. At first he was reluctant to recognise and accept this unlooked for compensation for his Scorpio's splenetic disposition, but he had a very clear memory of the occasion when the strange connection had first struck him.

Following a particularly arid period in his writing when the blank page in his typewriter mocked him, he had sprung up from his comfortable writer's chair, plunged downstairs in his slippers, thrown open the kitchen door and enquired, of anyone who might be present, exactly how long he was going to have to continue to wait for his morning cup of coffee. His youngest and divorced daughter , who had returned to the family home after the collapse of her marriage, was leaning over the table reading the paper. She straightened up, looked at Dan over her glasses and took up the challenge, 'Since I didn't know that you wanted any coffee and in any case, I've never timed my coffee making, I've no idea how long you might wait. But even if I knew how long coffee takes to percolate or to make in the filter, how should I know which you wanted? You're always changing your mind about every damned thing. Remember that visit to the Chinese restaurant-half an hour deciding and then writing down the portions and half portions of this, that or the other whilst the waiter looked on and then you'd change your mind! Never again. I've never been so embarrassed! ' She laughed sarcastically and continued to read without turning to look at him again. Dan stood in the doorway, a hand on each doorpost. His stance fleetingly and incongruously suggesting to him the classic pose of Samson gathering his energies, his arms around the pillars of the temple before he brought all down, "post and massy bar" on the heads of the Philistines. The picture faded.

'If…. you were less sarcastic and more prepared to lend a hand to someone who has put a roof over your head, you might still have a husband', Dan spat out, but his sap had not risen sufficiently yet and Jean clipped the ball back effortlessly,

'If- as you suggest- I had been "lending a hand"- whatever that might mean- we're not on a ship, for Christ's sake, although, God knows, it feels like it sometimes- if I'd been here, "lending a hand," then according to marriage breakdown statistics, I would be putting attention to parents before my matrimonial obligations to husband. I'd be spending my time in the "old home" and so giving husband some grounds for complaint. Talk sense, Dad, for once.'

A quick change of tack was needed if Dan were not to lose the next set. ' On a ship the expression is , "Bear a hand ", "Lend a hand isn't exclusively nautical in usage; it simply means extending a hand to someone who's in trouble- drowning, perhaps,' he added enigmatically.'

That's "giving a hand up"- pulling one from danger. You'd better throw in your hand,' his daughter countered. Dan pressed the *Action Stations* button in his head but no fighting crew mustered to the assembly point. But he was not yet beaten.

'Your sarcasm ill suits both your face and your situation', he served defiantly.

' "Ill suits"! Is that what passes for writer's rhetoric now? Sounds more like the ranting of a drunken King Lear. Ok, I will een arise and een go and prepare your coffee, but don't blame me if it's not exactly as you like it. You like freshly ground coffee not the filter stuff, I remember that , and there's no beans left' Jean pushed the paper aside and left to make her father's coffee.

Dan turned over a few phrases from "Lear" on the subject of daughters, "Gods we adore, wherof comes this?" or more obviously, " How sharper than a serpent's tooth it is to have a thankless child." What he settled for and found himself saying aloud and overdramatically was, "Mend when thou canst; be better at your leisure." Returning to his room and the typewriter, suddenly ideas were coming easily to him and words were now flowing so well that he did not hear Jean calling up to him that coffee was ready and when she brought it to his room, even managing to knock first, he sent her away with a snarl that he was 'not to be disturbed now, for anything! .' She shrugged, took the coffee downstairs again and drank it herself whilst enjoying a cigarette, a habit to which her father objected, but she knew he would not be leaving his room for some time now as the rattle of the keys of the typewriter had fallen into a familiar mechanical rhythm.

Dan had wondered at the connection between having a row and overcoming a writer's block. He decided that it might have something to do with adrenalin flow, but however it affected him, a good row became after that the indispensable rocket fuel for launching each novel or story. Each of his three most successful novels bore the hallmark of a particular row; the more absurd the cause; the more effective the result. A two day row with his wife about whether a Yorkshire pudding should rise aesthetically and airily, as she maintained, or remain flat and absorbent to all the delicious juices of the meat under which it was to be placed, as he insisted, had sparked off "The Impasse" which ran into three editions.

Another memorably acrimonious exchange, again with his daughter, had been the means of salvaging a radio play which had become stillborn. Dan had laid down that if Jean did borrow the car, then appreciative courtesy dictated that it be returned with a full tank, regardless of the level when it had been taken. Jean condemned this as ungenerous profiteering on her lack of a car through unfortunates circumstances.

'Thank you for nothing. I drive twelve miles into town to sign on. The car's almost out of petrol and I'm supposed to spend thirty pounds of my dole money filling it up. You're doing yourself a favour by lending it to me at this rate. Ok, I'm grateful for the use of the bloody car, but not on those terms. I'll wait for the bus next time; it's cheaper,' she screamed as she slammed the kitchen door after her and went out into the garden to have a smoke. It was in vain that he pointed out to her the cost of getting the garage to come out with a can of petrol when he had run out on two occasions because Jean had failed to note that the needle was on empty. His mind had been on his book. He was a writer not a car rental service, for God's sake.. He expected the car to have petrol; he had left it with petrol in it. He had to maintain it, tax and insure it. Why could she not just be reasonable?

The connection between row and writing eventually was taken for granted by Dan, his family automatically adopting roles and preparing their *scripts*, as it were, in these ritualized word battles, without being aware of the vital part they played in making Dan's writing lively and saleable.

Dan had never mentioned the unlikely secret of his success to anyone. Superstitiously he sensed that to acknowledge it publicly might be a betrayal of trust; an outrage to that illusive deity, the Muse. However, after a memorable dinner in his favourite restaurant when his closest friend had insisted upon a second bottle of claret, he parted with his secret. The friend, Frank, also a writer and one who had known Dan since their schooldays, surprised Dan by his reaction.   ' Well old sport, and you've only just stumbled on this? There's no mystery; nothing magical ; it's all very logical, pretty obvious when you think about it. You could call it "The gold panning principle" He said, emptying the last of the wine into their two empty glasses with fairness and precision. Dan looked enquiringly and Frank continued.

'Gold comes to the top when you agitate the pan. It shakes the water, the dirt, the sediment out so the trace of gold comes clear of the dross and is left in the pan. It's an energetic business'

'But hardly the same as trying to stir up one's imagination to get a novel or story finished, 'Dan observed.

'Same principle, different technique,' Frank said, closing one eye and peering at the glass with the other as he turned the wine, holding it to the candle flickering in its holder on the table. ' Do you remember coming home after, shall we say a *romantic* evening; your head filled with thoughts, inspirations- words and words; wonderful words and phrases?' Indeed Dan recalled such moments and had written many poems and long love letters under the influence of that evening of *romance*.

'Are you telling me that any emotional agitation, "perturbation of the spirit" Shakespeare calls it somewhere, is going to have a direct effect on my writing?' He asked.

'Just think of the whole business of writing,' Frank explained. 'Look at what we know of the private lives of the great writers. They almost all had unhappy childhoods. They were disturbed people, often miserable. They went away to sublimate their despair; turn it into something they could respect, accept, cope with.
 Shakespeare's rows with wealthy old farmer Hathaway when he had got his daughter pregnant, *out of wedlock.?* You'll find it all in the plays. The death of his son, Hamnet, his misery then? All came out in the Last Plays. Dickens shouting at his family through the locked door of his study yet at the same time weeping as he wrote of love; love between father and child, even father and grandchild- "Old Curiosity Shop". Kenneth Graham hating his family for putting him in the bank, the rows with his wife, perhaps over their poor wretched son- you knew he threw himself under a train?'

'Not Graham, the son, of course,' Dan interposed..

'Yea, the son. But the result of all this emotional turmoil? A masterpiece- "Wind in the Willows.!" '

Van Gough, Hemingway, Somerset Maugham, Dylan Thomas, Swift and others were cited for the way deep disturbances had helped them to achieve greatness.

Dan accepted Frank's "Gold Panning Principle." It was ironic that his new understanding of the workings of the Muse brought peace of mind to Dan He no longer found himself having rows so frequently and as a result, he had to engineer a row or two, even just a disagreement, but something was lacking and his voice and attitude failed to carry conviction and get the adrenalin flowing as it had done before he had been *enlightened* about the Muse. He could no longer easily provoke the instant quarrels and exchanges of words. His work suffered. His forms of attack became increasingly predictable and easily repulsed.

'"Could not countenance!" You said that yesterday, Dad,' Jean , usually his most effective sparring partner, complained. 'Our rows don't seem to be what they used to be- no zing; no fireworks, just nonsense and archaic phrases.'

'So I'm burnt out, am I ? Only fit to sing seconds to your tunes? Dan tried, hoping that the old anger would rise and like a wave lifting a surfer, carry him forwards. But he was left paddling in shallow water; nothing had happened. The *rocket fuel* for completing his eighth and overdue novel was not forthcoming. He was too much in control of himself. He slammed the door- a time honoured move in keeping a good row on the boil- but ineffective now. He went off to the pub to loosen his reflexes and try to blow upon the embers of his almost extinguished creative sparks.

'Usual?' Jerry enquired, seeing Dan waiting at the bar.

'The usual. Yes, the mixture as before,' replied Dan. His reply was slow as he was wondering if he could start an argument with Jerry, there in the "George". He had tried picking an argument with strangers in the bar before without achieving the necessary effect. The nature of the disagreement and the high slang content had been far too humdrum to provoke him properly and Jerry had not been pleased that Dan was causing a scene in his pub. He had been warned. No, it would not be possible to use Jerry as a row stimulator. He returned to his house and his incomplete novel.

For a week he did nothing but type a few pages, read them, then tear them out of the machine and throw the paper in the bin in disgust. He decided to meet Frank again and see if he had any advice for him.

Frank, plausible and apparently knowledgeable as always, offered a solution very quickly, much to Dan's relief.

' Just what I would have thought, old sport,' he said over the dinner for which Dan had insisted upon paying. 'Yes, it's like taking drugs; you need increasingly bigger doses to get the same effect after a time.'

' So I must have more and bigger rows?' Dan concluded despondently. 'It's just not going to be easy or perhaps even possible; Jean's found her *ideal* man and she's left home to join him. Mary, bless her, has decided to do a, *I'm being a reasonable and understanding wife* thing and forgives me everything, everything!' he repeated. 'I suspect she's read about dealing with an impossible husband in one of her magazines

and is putting it into practice. 'I'm sure you're right, love,' she says. 'What can I do?'
He passed the expensive and glossy looking menu to Frank.

'Fancy anything on that, tonight?'
Frank gave his full attention to ordering before returning to Dan's problem.

'Start reading papers that you dislike, watch quiz games on the box, they're enough
to make Mother Teresa homicidal. Volunteer to help with any local activities, get onto
committees; be political and be difficult with everyone '

'Must I?' Dan asked hopelessly.

'You asked for my advice and I'm giving it to you. Show your gratitude and order
us a bottle of that special claret, there's a god chap.'

Dan could not bring himself to take any of the tabloids which he knew would
disgust him rather than sharpen his wits. After watching two quiz games, he became,
much to his surprise, quite interested in them and caused Mary to say, ' I think I'll join
a bridge club, Dan, if you're going spend your evenings watching that rubbish and not
talking to me. I'd rather have one of our rows than see you slipping into senile decay.'

It was acting on the last part of Frank's advice that finally changed Dan's fortunes.
He joined the local Conservative party and attended meetings, handed out pamphlets
and even acted as a subscription collector, much to the amazement of all who knew his
previous extreme left views. When, after two years of such industry, he was put up as a
prospective Tory Candidate, and was elected, no one was more surprised than Dan.
Frank's curiosity was so strong that he stood Dan a lavish dinner with two bottles of
the special claret to celebrate.

'But why a Tory, Dan, with the views you hold?'

'That's just it, with the views I hold I was much better at knowing what arguments
my opponents would use on me-I'd used them all myself in the past, and with effect! I
could anticipate their every move, their line of attack and prepare for the hecklers,
have my answers ready, even write them out beforehand and learn them by heart. I've
earned quite a reputation for keeping my cool, especially coping with aggressive media
interviewers, you know the ones I mean.'

Frank acknowledged the truth of all this and encouraged Dan to tell him more.

'It was so much easier than arranging domestic rows just so that I might get my
wretched novels finished. I just went along with events really , but-'and here he leaned
over the table to say softly to Frank,' but I've stumbled on the secret of how to succeed
in politics, it's this; always profess the exact opposite views to the ones you really hold.'

"Get thee glass eyes; and like a scurvy politician, seem to see the things thou dost
not, " quoted Frank

'Good old Will- Shakespeare knew it all. I wonder if the teachers realise what
they are instructing their pupils in. What made that rebel of a drunken prince- Hal-
the most respected and obeyed king of all time- the glorious Henry the Fifth? I'll tell
you- insight, insight! " I know you all and will a while uphold the unyoked humour of
your ways" Dan had had his share and perhaps more than his share of the excellent
claret and was in an expansive and happy mood.

'And shall we have an excellent port to follow this excellent claret? On me. I'll
tell you what I've called my discovery, the method for being a successful politician, it's

called" The Double Agent's Gambi;" Whatever you're against, you defend; whatever you condemn, you uphold. That's the way to beat them at their own game; better than your old " Gold panning" to get the novel finished any day.'

Dan never wrote or even tried to write another novel once he entered politics, but he did become one of the most famous and unchallenged Foreign Secretaries of our time.

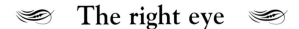 The right eye

Just a bit of fun, really…

It had rained softly and unceasingly on the day of Mrs Patterson's funeral. The Reverend Sidney Tomkins, who was conducting the service, was not displeased. 'Ashes to ashes; dust to dust. The Lord giveth and the Lord taketh away. How easy and helpful the old familiar words were. He was almost able to detach his thoughts from memories of Mrs Patterson, alive, noisy, and entirely hateful only two weeks ago.

It had been the second Wednesday in December and as cold as predicted. Much as the Reverend Tomkins detested the cold, he hated the second Wednesday in each month even more. On that day the Diocesan Church Council met. On the Tuesday nights before those meetings sleep had become impossible. He had even taken up smoking again after having abandoned the habit twelve years before.

Mrs Emilia Patterson, the village's wealthiest widow, had bullied her way into the little group of parishioners who liked feeling important. She became one of the seven members of the Diocesan Church Council. She owned several houses in the village and since two of the other members of the Council were her tenants, they felt obliged to second any motion proposed by their landlord. She particularly enjoyed making the vicar feel uncomfortable and she did this whenever possible, but she was at her best, or rather, worst, at the monthly meetings of the Diocesan Church Council. Ever since the vicar had dared to accuse her of snobbery and petty mindedness the previous year she had relentlessly pursued her revenge. Her grating contralto voice had reverberated round the cold vestry and the Reverend Tomkins screwed up his toes and struggled to keep his anger and dislike under control.

'And surely, Vicar, it's not too much to ask, is it, that people dress themselves suitably to take Holy Communion on Sunday in the House of the Lord? That new person, the one that bought Maciver's garage last year – I never go there now, I wouldn't trust him with my car anyway – he – well, you all saw, actually came to the alter rail dressed as a gym instructor – absurd baggy tunic and trousers and wearing running shoes! Gym shoes! I ask you, why do you put up with it, Vicar? Are you going to be happy to see every young person in the village taking communion dressed in sloppy fancy dress?'

The Reverend Tomkins itched to reply, 'You come each Sunday with that enormous mole on your nose for me to feed with the wine and the water, would you be happy to see all the parishioners bringing a mole like yours to the altar rail each Sunday?'

What he had said was, 'If all the parishioners, particularly our few young ones, actually came to church, I should rejoice, whether or not they wore jogging suits to take communion. Mr Lacy did apologise to me, in fact. He'd been jogging, missed his way, and there was no time for him to go home and change without being too late for the service. I reassured him that the Lord was only interested in our hearts, not our clothing.'

Major Cullinan, who never missed one of Mrs Patterson's Bridge evenings when she served such large drinks and such delightful Marks and Spencer's canapés, cleared his throat self importantly before springing to his patron's support.

'Damn fellow should never have gone jogging if he couldn't find his way about. And I think you're wrong, Vicar, about clothes, the proper dress shows a proper respect. A badly blancoed belt is an affront to the Colonel, to the Regiment and to the Queen.'

'But perhaps not to God. And I understood that the business of painting one's belt had been abolished in the modern Army,' Tomkins slipped in, and knew that he would have to pay for reminding Cullinan that his army service had been almost forty years ago. Since then he had worked for a soap manufacturer. He decided to revive his army rank when he retired and came to the village nine years ago. And so the awful charade was played out each month. Once, in the forlorn hope of miraculously defusing the tension, Tomkins had asked the Council to put their hands together,

'Let us close with a prayer. Oh Almighty God, our strength and our Redeemer, who sees into the hearts of each of us.' but the new schoolmistress, Marigold Prince, had cut him off in mid flow,

'Surely that should be "heart" not "hearts". We have only one heart each, Vicar,' she said, giggling at her joke and catching the wandering eye of the Colonel, as she often found herself doing.

'Or none', Tomkins was about to say, but he merely stalled, then apologised. Of late he seemed to have been apologising a great deal- 'I'm sorry the Church is rather cold this morning'. 'I'm sorry, but as the bridegroom has been divorced, I'm not permitted to marry you in church.' 'I'm sorry, doctor, to take up your valuable time, but I keep having these headaches and I just can't seem to get rid of them.' 'I'm sorry to put you to this trouble, Mrs Smart, but I feel that it's really time that my study was given a good hoovering and I don't drink coffee you know. Well, you'll remember the next time I expect, but do keep the rest of the packet for yourself.'

He always finished with a perfunctory little laugh; half cough, half gurgle. It was an absurd noise and he hated himself for making it. The meeting ended and the members of his council, his supporters and facilitators, left, chatting and laughing and, as usual, shutting out the Reverend Tomkins. He turned off the electric heaters in the vestry, extinguished the lights and locked the heavy oak doors of the church. The vicarage felt damp as well as cold when he returned, but for economy's sake he only had the heating on for two hours each evening and he would have to freeze for an hour before it came on at eight o'clock.

The small fan heater did little to warm him as he sat at his desk writing up his diary. It was a habit and a discipline which put the day's happenings into perspective. He released into that diary all his frustration and annoyance with his Diocesan Councillors. Of late he found that he was becoming increasingly vitriolic about the Diocesan Council and Mrs Patterson in particular.

To whom does one write a diary, or was it rather, *for* whom, he wondered. Maybe it was the only way that he could communicate with that other person, the boy become man inside him with his dear and familiar memories, his wretched self-consciousness, his need to rehearse everything in his mind before actually uttering any words. It was disconcerting that of late he found he had been writing up his diary in the third person.

'Dear Diary, today, had a genii granted Sidney a wish he would have seen the Patterson creature saddled and on all fours struggling through a foul pond crusted with ordure, spitting and retching, blinded by indescribable filth which hung from her and which she could not wipe from her face. Cullinan, with his apoplectic face terminally inflamed, would be in the saddle, grinding in his spurs and using his whip unceasingly on his mount whilst a mist of yellow horseflies stung and stung and closed up eyes, nose and mouth. One word from Sidney would have ended their misery but he was sucking a big, juicy peach.' Tomkins stopped, reread what he had written and cried out aloud, although only to himself, 'How much longer must I endure these creatures? I am consumed with loathing and rage every time I have to listen to their hateful bleating. I have still no answer from my letter to the Bishop requesting him to move me to another parish. He's too busy on committees, or having dinner with a millionaire or pop star to be concerned with one of the poor wretches whose fate he controls. If I could remember how to pray, if I believed it would not just be me talking to myself, as I now really think that I do, I should beg for patience, and even welcome this testing of my love for my fellow men. But Mrs Patterson!'

He entered those thoughts also in his diary, then put down his pen and rubbed his hands together for warmth before snapping the diary closed. Outside it had grown dark and the wind found every whistling entrance into the old stone vicarage. Perhaps there was some whisky left in the bottle in the dresser. He knew that he had drained it yesterday, but nevertheless he got up to look, then changed his mind and went to the kitchen to open a tin for his supper.

Mrs Patterson was walking primly back to her car. She stopped when she heard the Major puffing along behind her.

'I've written to the Bishop, George, that damned vicar must go, he gets worse. What on earth was last Sunday's sermon about might one ask? Just nonsense, showing off his bits of Latin.'

'Greek, I think, actually, but it's all the same,nobody knew what he was on about – the Mosaic Law;"If thy right eye offend thee, pluck it out lest it corrupt the whole body." Where's the application? Where's the relevance? If we all went about tearing out things that upset us, there'd be chaos.'

Mrs Patterson's two tenants fell into step together as they walked home from the diocesan meeting. Mrs Turnbull, the undertaker's wife, spoke first,

'Mr Hornby,'

You can call me Sam, you know, Mrs Turnbull. I think we've known each other long enough for that'

'Sam then, right. You can call me Ada. That Mrs Patterson gets right up my nose'

'Mine too, Ada, She's a cow, if you'll pardon my speaking the way I feel.'

'Go ahead, Sam I can think of some other names for her, not so polite, but you're always so generous. Has she put up your rent too and got her bloody solicitor to tell you that under the lease of the letting, you've got to repaint the exterior of the house this year, and to the colour she chooses?

'Has she! Double cow! Yes I had the same letter. And she sits there, in the vestry like she does, giving the old vicar the needle; it's wicked the way she treats him, and she expects us all to fall in with all she says! I hate her; everyone hates her, but what can we do?'

' Funny you should ask that, Sam, I've been thinking all evening how I might fix her and I've got an idea.'

'For God's sake, Ada, tell me; I'll do anything I can to help sort her out. You can rely on me.'

'I'm sure I can , Sam. Now you know how she likes to think she can organise the Church Bazaar, well how about this for an idea?' Their steps slowed and their heads came together as Mr Hornby listened to the scheme described by Mrs Turnbull.

The Church Bazaar was the one social event which most of the village attended. Everyone tried to make it a success, but as Oscar Wilde might have remarked, "It's with the best intentions that the worst work is done" There was no vicar's wife to oversee and organise the stalls and the events; the tea tent, the tombola, the croquet and bonny baby competition and all the other traditional goings on in any traditional English country village whose parishioners, out of duty or misplaced optimism that it might just be *a bit of fun*, turned out in the inevitable drizzling rain. The members of the Diocesan Council were in charge of the event. Mrs Patterson had appointed herself chief organiser and so therefore, did not feel herself called upon to do any of the actual physical work involved in the event. She stood aloof as Mr Hornby, Mrs Turnbull and two other helpers put up tables, set out stalls and rigged umbrellas and canopies, for it clearly looked as though the drizzle had set in for the afternoon..

Major Cullinan, being a military man, felt he should direct the action, which he did in his best parade ground voice, shouting orders which frequently countermanded Mrs Patterson's instructions. Miss Marigold Prince, the schoolmistress, had gone to London for the weekend because after the last bazaar she had rushed home in tears when Mrs Patterson had refused to put out the scones she had so painstakingly made. Mrs Patterson, seeing them, had declared 'I don't know who's responsible for these ghastly offerings, a child, a deranged child, by the looks of these abominations! Someone might think that I had something to do with them- the thought!'

The Reverend Sidney Tomkins had made his own preparations for the day, of which, by far the most important for him was the half bottle of whisky which he had purchased. He just did not think he could face Mrs Patterson and her inevitable attacks upon him without some sort of defence.

A modest public address system had been put together for the afternoon to lend an air of ceremonial to the announcements as to who had won the egg and spoon race, the knobbly knees competition and so on and also to jolly the villagers into buying tea and home-made cakes. Mrs Patterson had tried the device briefly and had rejected it as not being adequate for her demands and standards. She had taken it upon herself to make all the announcements that she considered were necessary. Mrs Turnbull had tried to point out that if she did not use the loudspeaker system, she would certainly offend the old shopkeeper, Mr Ottery, who rarely came to church, but this year, for the first time, had shown some interest and had even offered to mow the grass in the churchyard. He had devised and made up the public address system and had spent the whole morning setting it up. All Mrs Patterson said to this was, 'I'm afraid it just won't do.' She in fact had hired a powerful and expensive amplifier and enormous loudspeakers, the wires, of which equipment trailed all over the ground and were hung from trees, here and there, to the inconvenience and nuisance of all.

The Reverend Tomkins maintained a fixed and benign set smile as he went from stall to stall; here feigning amazement at the children's skill in throwing a wet sponge at a volunteer exposing his head above a screen and there congratulating members of the Council on the amount of money taken by each stall. He turned, and there was Mrs Patterson confronting him from the announcer's table she had had set up.

'Vicar, I think it's time our guests were welcomed. I would have done it, but really I think it's something you could do; we're all very busy, you know; no time for just wandering about enjoying ourselves. I had to get in a proper public address system; I wasn't going to use that wretched bag of tricks that Ottery knocked up- ridiculous!'

The Reverend Tomkins stopped, braced himself and would have taken another discreet swig from his trusty bottle, but this was not the time, and, anyway, he had now finished the contents of the bottled. Then with his face still in its set smile like a mask, he advised, ' Mrs Patterson, you must, of course, do as you think fit. By all means speak to everyone, if that's what you think is called for. I think, though, that many of us were enjoying the delightful informality of our little social occasion.' Here he made a hand sweeping gesture towards the microphone on the table. The text of his sermon of last Sunday came into his mind, " If thy right eye offend thee, cast it from thee." If only the Lord, he thought, saw things as he saw them, but he felt a sudden sense of guilt at the unchristian nature of his musing.

It was when Mrs Patterson had taken up the microphone, blown noisily into it, by way of testing it, then begun the speech she had prepared for the occasion that the lightning struck her. In the event all she had had time to say before being silenced was, 'I'm sure that you all don't want to hear me, but...' The Reverend Tomkins opened his eyes, he had closed them as though to blot out Mrs Patterson when she started to speak The scene faded for him and he seemed to be back in yesterday's funeral service saying the usual words of comfort to the bereaved,' The wind bloweth where it listeth. The Lord giveth and the Lord taketh away and the ways of the Lord are hidden from us."

The funeral of the late Mrs Patterson was on a Tuesday, two weeks after the events of the Church bazaar and the lightning strike. Mrs Turnbull and Mr Hornby were standing beside the open grave, prepared to throw the customary handful of earth onto the lowered coffin. Mr Turnbull, in his function of undertaker, had been in charge of the matter. The Reverend Tomkins had officiated. He came over to the only two of his parishioners who had found time to attend the funeral of their late fellow member of the Diocesan Church Council and in a hushed voice observed, ' The wind bloweth where it listeth. The Lord giveth and the Lord Taketh away and the ways of the Lord are hidden from us.' The little procession wound its way out of the cemetery. Mrs Turnbull felt into step with Mr Hornby,

'You don't think that what we did to the wiring might have had anything to do with the lightning striking, do you, Ada?'

No, of course not, Sam; we just unplugged the electricity when she was making her speech, nothing to do with that. I just couldn't bear to hear that woman enjoying the sound of her own voice bellowing all over the churchyard and the village. That didn't stop the lightning though, did it?'

Mr Hornby could not help himself; he gave a little titter and remarked, No, Ada, 'twas nothing we did, it was like the vicar said, " If thy right eye offend thee, pluck it out".'

'You mean, God's doing, Sam?'

'Yes I do. What's the good of being God if you have to listen to that woman nagging everyone everyday?

Shame on you, Sam Hornby, shame on you.' But neither of them could keep back their laughter any longer and let it out. 'We can paint our houses whatever colour we please, now, can't us?' The Reverend Tomkins wished he could share the joke as well as he made he returned to his vicarage, little realising that, of course, he had.

❧ Let nothing you dismay ❧

Why must you always have to be different, for God's sake! David wondered just how many times he had heard Molly's complaint, always delivered in the same petulant tone, during the eighteen years of their marriage. There had been times when he had been tempted to reply to this rhetorical question and after appearing to be calculating, he might reply.' Seven times,' or or even, 'Seven hundred and seventeen!' But he had long ago decided never to make any answer- what answer was possible? It didn't matter; very little indeed did seem to matter between himself and Molly now.

On this particular occasion Molly had been making her arrangements, the same every year, for celebrating Christmas. The programme for the three days of holiday had never varied; a walk in the morning followed by a pub lunch. The afternoons were spent reading, watching television or visiting friends. In the evening various exotic dishes that Molly had prepared in the weeks before Christmas were taken from the deep freeze and heated up. David would open two bottles of wine, one red for himself and one white for Molly, who disapproved of the profligacy which red wine symbolised for her.

The events had become a ritual; predictable and undeviating, but this year David wanted to be different for once, just once. The idea had come to him of spending Christmas Eve and Christmas Day in a hotel. They had no children so all the business of the stockings, Father Christmas and so on didn't involve them; they could do as they liked. David had imagined them spending Christmas being waited on, eating food that Molly had not prepared and meeting new and perhaps more interesting people than those they met each year, on Boxing Day, in the local pub.

'You've always enjoyed my cooking before. I've done some different things this year, things I've never made before. The drinks are so expensive in a hotel and you can't do what you like. Why do you suddenly want to change everything? I just don't understand you at all.'

Still David said nothing, not just because he knew that his silence would infuriate Molly, but an answer, any of the myriad answers that he might have given, would have precipitated a bigger row. It was all trivial; but then the whole subject seemed trivial. Why did they bother to mark, if not celebrate, the birth of the son of a Jewish carpenter in the Middle East two thousand years before? David understood that the actual date of the birth of the thirteenth Christos was in January, probably the 4th.

The 25th of December had been settled upon by the church in the Middle Ages as a counter to the Pagan feast normally celebrated on that day. This was the speech David made, to Molly's annoyance, every year , when the shops started to put up their decorations.

From past experience David had learnt that voicing his atheistic views, particularly at Christmas, would bring down cries of, 'May God forgive you for such blasphemy! Jesus Christ died for you and this is the way you show your gratitude. God hears what you say and he will take a dreadful vengeance on you.' So much for an all forgiving father, thought David. This time he. kept silent, but he continued to think.

' I was thinking of you, Molly. It's such a lot of work, all the Christmas business. Let's spoil ourselves, we can afford it this year, with my bonus. You can relax for a change, take it easy, let other people do all the work. You'd enjoy it, I know you would'

This is what he felt he should say or he might say; what he actually did say was quite different and came out as much of a surprise to him as it did to Molly.

'We would have such a load of fun- we'd complain about everything-the service is never very good, I understand, in hotels at Christmas. Just think of all the simple pleasure we can squeeze from just making people feel self-conscious, inferior or just boring. I could get really nastily drunk, abusive and seriously unpleasant- plenty of bad taste jokes to embarrass all the quiet little ladies - might even vomit when the Christmas pud. comes round. You could be spiteful to the poor old chambermaid, trying to earn a bit extra to send to her crippled blind mother, get her in tears; she'd answer back; no need to tip then, eh? There's absolutely no end to the general beastliness we can wallow in if we spend the season of good cheer in a hotel. What do you say. Eh? Give it a go, Eh? I can hardly wait!'

Molly blinked, took a step backwards and then rushed out of the room. David soon heard the tears. Was this what he wanted? Why else would he have said what he had?

The idea of Christmas in a hotel in fact still seemed a good idea to David, but after his last outburst to Molly, it was no longer a possibility. There must be some other wild change he could ring out to break up the monotony of the impending "Christmas at Home". So far nothing had occurred to him.

It was just as the office party was breaking up on the afternoon of the twenty second of December that inspiration came to David. George, One of the oldest, if not the very oldest employee of the company, was looking for a bottle which still had some wine in it. He was picking out the last crumbs from the crisp bowl, he popped an olive into his mouth and then stood swaying a little when David came over to him.

'George, old chap. I've hardly had a chance to have a Christmas glass with you. Great old custom the office party, eh?' George's department had very little to do with David's but it was the department in which David had started with the company over twenty years ago.

'Oh, hullo, David. Do you like these things? Personally I hate them- so hypocritical; pretending to like people you've had rows with most of the year. I'd rather we went home early.'

'Much to do by way of getting ready for Christmas, George?'

'Nothing at all. I live alone, I go nowhere at Christmas, just watch the tele, eat my piece of turkey and bits and pieces that comes ready for the oven from the supermarket. I do treat myself to a really good bottle of malt though. Not one of those over advertised bits of nonsense, but one you can only get direct from the distillery in Scotland- individually signed bottles; cost a bob or two, but what a difference! Nectar!'

David nodded in conspiratorial agreement, then said. 'Molly and I were only talking about you this morning, George. Molly was saying, "I wonder how old George is getting on, he'll be all alone. Wouldn't it be nice to have George over for Christmas He could come on Christmas Eve and spend Christmas day with us. I should really like that. Good old George, such a good friend to you, David, when you first joined the company."'

George put his empty glass down and gave David a good stare. 'Did Molly really say that, David?'

'Cross my heart and hope to die, George. She's very fond of you, you know. Do you remember that evening at the Chairman's house, when he retired and we were all invited to his farewell party? Well you certainly made a hit with Molly. She was hanging on your every word when you told us about your trip to Florida. You made it sound so exciting. She was on to me for ages to take her there for a holiday. We'd have gone too, if I didn't get ill on planes.'

'Well if Molly really meant it, I should very much like to come to you for Christmas. I'll bring some wine and some nuts'.

'And a bottle of that special malt, eh? So we can all have a taste, eh, George?'

George just gave his dead cod fish stare.

On Christmas Eve, Molly had laid the table and was polishing the glasses when David came into the dining room wearing his new quilted smoking jacket. Not that he smoked, but he liked the idea of wearing something specially intended for relaxing in.

The door bell chimed.

'Who the hell can that be? It's not carol singers; those little so and so's get so much pocket money they can't be bothered to go out in the evening, even to collect for themselves, let alone a charity, as we used to do. See who it is, David, and get rid of them.'

'I know who it is, Molly. It's our special Christmas guest that I've invited because he's alone. I kept it as a surprise for you.'

'Stop fooling about, you idiot and get rid of whoever it is. Fancy calling on Christmas Eve. Bloody inconsiderate bastard!'

'That's what I like about Christmas, Molly, it seems to bring out the best in you,' David said.

Molly did deign to laugh. 'God, I've had a most awful thought- nightmare really. Just imagine if that old bore, George, from the contracts department had somehow thought that we'd invited him for dinner. Ah!'

'Not just for dinner, Molly, but to stay the night and then spend Christmas Day with us. Where's all that Christian charity you're always saying I haven't got.'

The door bell chimed again, plaintively this time, it seemed. 'Coming, George, coming.'

When George finally left on Boxing Day morning, Molly could not get out of bed to say goodbye. The thought of having to listen again to his account of how he knew this special distillery where he got his malt would have been too much. And then to have the temerity to say that he'd forgotten to bring his malt. Lying, hypocrite. She told David to say that she had one of her "heads".

Molly heard voices below, a laugh, David's, then the sound of the door closing. At last, at long bloody last he had gone. She heard David's footstep on the stairs.

'Well that was nice of us, wasn't it? Good old George. Gives you a warm feeling to do someone a kindness, I always feel. He certainly enjoyed your cooking, Molly, pity that he's allergic to fish otherwise he might have liked that salmon dish you did. And wasn't it nice to hear his story of his trip to Florida again? There were one or two bits that I thought he'd changed since I'd last heard it- had to tell him, ha, ha, had to! He said he was grateful as he'd forgotten some bits himself and was glad that I had remembered it, must have showed I'd found it interesting.'

Molly's face remained entirely passive. She was not going to give David his satisfaction , the violent reaction that she knew he expected." I 've been thinking how right you were to invite poor old George. I'm glad that he's much the same size as you so I could give him the cashmere sweater I'd bought for you, pity, but I knew you'd understand and there just wasn't time to get him anything else, was there?"

David almost smiled but instead, he said, " Quite right, I wouldn't have worn such a poofter's outfit anyway. Oh, and you'll be glad to know that I managed to get him to take that box of Belgian chocolates that I'd originally bought for you- never knew mere chocolates could be so expensive. You're putting on too much weight anyway, doesn't suit you so you're better off without them. I said that you wanted him to have them, one each night, after his supper, just to remind him how much we enjoyed his sharing his Christmas with us."

There was nothing worth watching on the television. David had his usual moan about the putting on of past programmes of the same pair of so called comics that he had never found funny when they had been alive. So they set off for the pub.

David said for at least the tenth time and after ordering a third bottle of the most expensive red wine to go with his overcooked and gristly roast beef. "Don't moan about my drinking- if we'd gone to a hotel. as I suggested, you'd still have your chocolates and I could drink as much as I liked without your saying how the Police had tightened up on drinking and driving at this festive season.

It was when they had turned into their road that David skidded. Perhaps it was a bit icy or else he had lost concentration for a second but the result was that they slammed head on into the new sports car parked outside their neighbour's house. He had called the police at once when he saw that it was David who had wrecked his daughter's new car They had never got on together and it seemed a good time to have his own back on the snobbish neighbour who had dared to complain about what David had called the " Borstal Blue" that he had just had his house painted.

After that Molly and David became statistics; a three hour wait to have Molly's bruises attended to by the sarcastic duty doctor in casualty, about the same time for David in the local police station where his blood count showed that he was three times over the legal limit, and days later, when the offices were open again, a refusal to insure David in the future after his second conviction, within a month, for drinking and driving.

Molly refused to say anything at all to David except that she was leaving him. Then she sniffed, in the special way that he found irritating, and she knew it.

" Caught a cold for the New Year, have we, that's nice. Well that's another Yuletide romp behind us for a year. Perhaps we should invite old George, the mean old bastard, over again next Christmas to give us another of his celebrated travelogues and help us enjoy ourselves as much again at next year's Season Of Goodwill."

Molly put on her coat and went out for a walk in the sleet despite her incipient cold.

❧ Exiles ❧

'I can give you an address' I was leaving, but stopped in the doorway, turned my head and looked back at him.

'Well, you never know,' he said. I'd no wish to be indebted to him or to anyone, but he went on;

'62 Darley Street. It's near the harbour, You'll be made welcome. Bryan's one of your sort, oh yes, he'll make you welcome alright. And Tessa will too, that is, if she's around. Now are you ok for cash?'

'I've enough I believe and there's always ways of getting more,' I said. Perhaps he knew about those ways. I'd never made a secret of the knack I had of making the money machines in bars work in my favour. Some of them I'd worked with gave more thought to that than they did to the job in hand. That's why a partner was no use to me. Once they know I "had the touch" as they called it, they'd not stop pushing me to fund their drinking till they dropped down or started a fight or both. Being alone you move faster, quieter, get the job done and get to get away when the time comes.

'I'll maybe look it up. Bryan Doyle knows me.'

'I thought he might. Weren't the pair of you together on the Brighton job?'If he know about that, it was a pity. If he didn't, I was not the man to keep his file up to date.

'I'll let Lanaghan know when I'm ready. He'll need to send the stuff better packed this time – a chocolate box is not the thing, there's no strength there. Hardback books; centre pages cut out; there's plenty of protection in the cover,' I said by way of farewell. Kelly laughed at that, 'Send it book post! Top of the best sellers, eh? That's why you need a good address, a house that's not watched. Tessa's got everything in her name and Bryan's no record over here.'

'Yet, ' I snapped and left.

There are some places you can feel easy in the moment your feet touch the ground of the railway platform. Liverpool was not one of them. A smell that seemed familiar but which I couldn't just place hung in the air. It had been raining ever since I had left London and the roads had an oily shine to them. I picked up my light holdall and tried to remember the road plan I'd studied in the train. Darley Street should be in walking distance, just. It was Shamus McAnn that had taught me about "being invisible", as he called it . 'Rule one; never ask the way; it shows you're a stranger and someone will remember your voice. The accent is such a tracer. Rule two; never get a taxi if you can walk. A man walking knows where he's going, he doesn't look a stranger. And thirdly; don't look about you too much; the police would pick that up at once if they're watching and if you don't know the area you don't know where the plainclothes men watch.'

The holdall had doubled in weight in the forty minutes' walk it took me to find Darley Street. The dirty red brick houses had once been the homes of wealthy ship owners and men who made a good living from the dock and shipbuilding business when it was thriving, maybe fifty years ago. Number 62 was about the only one that hadn't been turned into a warren of bedsitters where every room had its TV to keep the inmates entertained as they ate their takeaways and listened to hear when the one bathroom or toilet was free. I'd had a deal and enough of that in my time.

A house, a whole house with a woman who cooked and wasn't on the game would be the right place to lie up for the week or so that lay ahead before I could expect to get the signal and the "Book of the Month" parcel.

There was no answer when I pressed the bell, probably broken like everything else about. I rapped on the glass. I could hear something, then the door opened a little; enough for me to see Bryan Doyle. He looked older than when I'd last seen him, but then he would; the Brighton job was eight years ago now.

'It's Michael O'Leary. Will you be letting me in now?' I asked.

Bryan said nothing. He opened the door very slowly. When I was standing in the hall, he looked outside, up and down the road, like a ferret smelling the air, then he shut the door. I followed him down the bare stairs to a large room with a table that filled it.

'Billiard table, full size; it's covered with sheets of shuttering, that's why she always leaves the cloth on,' Bryan said as though he were expecting a question about the table. He patted it affectionately

'Headquarters said you'd be likely to find a place for me, for a week, perhaps two,' I explained. Bryan stared at the table, then without turning, he replied, 'It's Tessa you'll be wanting to see. I don't exist in this country- no papers, no job no existence.'

He had changed. I could see at once that something had gone out of him, like stuffing out of a rag doll. His gaze kept shifting from place to place but his eyes always avoided mine.

'It's been a time, Bryan. How have things been since Brighton?'

'There's not much now I can do in that line; a marked man, you see. Someone spoke out about me. I can't get home without them knowing, the police, that is, they'd nail me. Tessa's my eyes and ears out there now. Shall I make us a brew of tea?'

'Or something else, for old times' sake,' I suggested and I put a litre bottle of Paddy's on the table. He took it up again, at once and gave it back into my hand.

'I can't be doing with the stuff now,' here he tapped his stomach as though this explained all.

'Well then I'll take the tea, 'I said

The kitchen had only a small window at head height. The pavement was just outside and you could see feet passing, ' Can be useful; you can see if it's a pair of size ten, government issue, outside,' he said as he filled the kettle in the sink

Well later, about six, when I'd put my things in one of the spare rooms, I heard the front door opening downstairs and had a look over the banister to the hall below. There was a big, red-haired woman taking off her coat and kicking of her shoes. She gave a great sigh as she did so. I went down.

'O'Leary; it would be you they sent me. You'll not be wanting to do any of your special jobs from here, I hope.' She didn't smile, hardly looked at me, except for a quick glance as though checking something. ' They said you had this house and could maybe take me in, just for the time. A room in a boarding house wouldn't do; this is better.'

'Better for you, yes. Well you're here now. Come down and I'll get something cooked.' I followed her down to the kitchen.

'Can I be doing anything? I can pay, you know, if you're short, that is,'
'You can open that tin,' she said, passing me a large tin of baked beans. Later we had the meal. It wasn't a social occasion. Tessa looked exhausted. She ate her beans and fried egg and mopped up the with a slice of bread. Bryan cleared the table, careful to sweep all the crumbs from the dirty tablecloth which had been spread over the billiard table. You could have seated twenty people round that table had you a mind to and had the chairs. Tessa lit a cigarette, blew out the match wearily, then spoke,

'So, now that I'm settled a bit and the heat's off Bryan, they want to start again? What is it this time; Buckingham Palace, Westminster? Any place where a nice fat bomb would leave a mark, take a few lives? How can you still be doing with all that stuff? My mother left me this place; it was all she had and it's all I have now. You maybe heard that Tyrone died last year, of the cancer and my son, Michael, has four years to run in Strangeways- armed robbery. Sure it was a put up job; they pinned it on him because he was on their list and he had no alibi- bastards! I couldn't sell this place if I tried and I'd have no place to go if I did and they'd pick up Bryan in a moment.'

' You knew I'd married Mary Sullivan; Jim Sullivan's widow?' I asked her.

'I never took to Mary, but Jim could have done better for himself, I always thought, he being a graduate of Trinity and all. Should never have left County Antrim; only got himself into trouble coming here' said Tessa, and she pulled angrily on her cigarette.

'I can get out a bit, if I have my uniform on, that is. Do quite well on Saturday afternoons in the shopping centre,' Bryan observed.

'You're not wearing the uniform in this country and in this place?' I asked him, amazed.

'Not that sort of uniform,' Tessa snapped irritably.

I found out what uniform Bryan wore two days later. I'd been in my room, lying on the bed. It had rained ever since I'd arrived. It was the same pattern every day. After the baked beans, I'd go up to my room, Tessa went to bed and Bryan would take the cover off the billiard table and spend hours putting the balls down the pockets, on his own. A silly game, I'd always thought, billiards, and I'd refused to learn when Bryan wanted to teach me to play. It was Saturday afternoon, a half day for Tessa, but she went to bed just the same, when she got back from work.

I heard the door slam downstairs. Tessa was already in her room so I went down. A strange figure was standing in the hall with the rain dripping from him onto the floor. It was wearing a baggy suit, a bowler hat, white gloves and when it turned to me, I saw that it was a clown with a white face, big red mouth and a black cross on each eye. It must be Bryan. He shook a tin at me and in a voice that quavered from drink or emotion, began his chant,

'There's a gentleman with a kind face, yes you sir. Will you spare something for "Aid to Romania" now?' It was grotesque. I laughed at the absurd figure and said, 'What's this Bryan? Have you gone in for the charity work or what?' He unscrewed the bottom of the collecting tin and started counting the coins in it.

'Will you look at these bleeding one p's! Bastards! Can't they give like Christians to help their fellow men? There's no bloody Christians round here – Sikhs, Muslims, West Indians, Christ knows what! You'd think that even they might take pity on a fellow exile, a man shut out from his own home. Bastards! Look at this – three pounds thirty seven p, and a washer! And I have wept blood for that. Told them about the little Romanian kids starving in the streets, dying in their own blood, shot down in the gutters like dogs, tanks driving over their little bodies and, and...'

Here Bryan swayed, reached out a white gloved hand for the wall and then slowly slid to the floor. His head fell forwards onto his chest and he started to snore. When I looked up, Tessa was leaning over the banister. She must have been asleep and had not bothered to tie the string round her dressing gown, it trailed behind her like a sort of mangy dog's tail.

'He's been on the booze again. Were you fool enough to leave out that bottle of Paddy's? He'll have drunk that if you have and he'll spend what he's got in that collecting box on more drink tomorrow.'

'What about his stomach condition and what about the starving Romanian kids?' I asked.

'They're both in about the same condition and with about as much hope,' Tessa spat out and went upstairs again, her dressing gown "tail" following her up each step.

Two weeks slipped by with no delivery of Book Post for me. I needed to raise the matter with Bryan and Tessa over the baked beans to get their reaction. Bryan reacted first,

'I'm not the man to be getting worried about the next bit of destruction. It's not me that will be going back to Belfast now or anywhere else in Ireland, if all the truth's told. Sure now wasn't I once upon a time the very man for supporting the cause and I believed in it, then; I was *their* man; did all they told me to; wreck this; bomb that; burn this; blow that place to kingdom come. All that's in the past; I've me billiards now, Tessa to cook my baked beans and there's my collections for charity to pay for a drop of the hard stuff when I'm feeling up to it, that is.' And he winked at me.

Tessa wiped up the last of the baked bean sauce with her bread before adding her views,

'I work at the checkout at the supermarket in the mornings, afternoons I sometimes clean offices. The both of them's badly paid but there's always what they call "fringe benefits" – small change and packets of cigarettes left in drawers in the offices and baked beans past their sell by date; anything that's not going to be missed. Doesn't cost me much to live and sometimes Bryan gives me some of his "charity" money if he's had a good day. Kids' charities are best; "Save the Children", Prevent Cruelty and all that , then after comes the "Save the" lot; "Save the Ethiopians, the Rumanians, the Kosovians. the blind, the spastics and the disabled are good too sometimes, he says, specially if he shakes his tin very hard under their noses and gives *the eye* like. Me and Bryan have nine hundred pound in the Building Society. When it's a thousand we're going to Miami and we'll spend, spend, spend. Your bloody "Cause" was never going to do that for us, was it?' Bryan nodded and added,

' If you'll take a bit of advice, you'll forget about waiting for that Book Post parcel; forget about waiting here to do their bloody work for them. Get yourself an accordion, an old broken one for preference, learn to play about three chords and sing to them-badly mind. Sing outside the pubs and in the underpasses and outside the cinemas; anywhere there's a lot of people. You could stay here a while, put your takings in our kitty, look after the place and then we could all three go to Disney land, lie soaking up the sun and drinking the bourbon. Ah!'

As it turned out, a parcel did come the next morning. I took it in, it was Book Post. This is it, I thought; I'll be moving this week for certain; Lenaghan will have sent the stuff for certain.'

Taking the paper off took time, I had to be careful. It was well wrapped and I didn't want to damage what I thought was in the centre of the book. There were two layers of wrapping. When the last was off, the book was in my hands. I opened it slowly; the pages were all real; there was nothing hidden in a hiding place cut out of the centre. It was just an ordinary book. I looked at the title , "Working from Home. A Thousand ways to turn your spare time into spare cash". Then I saw that it was addressed to Tessa.

I waited two more days and there was no more Book Post. I went out and looked for an old accordion to buy.

Terminological

When Humphry had come across an article headed, "Getting it off your chest"in his Sunday paper, he felt it might have been written specially for him. He had been suffering since Christmas with a nasty cold on the chest. He looked at the bottle in the medicine cupboard. This was the third bottle he had swallowed optimistically. The words on the bottle read, "An effective expectorant" Indeed, as expectorants go it had lived up to the claims on the bottle- his expectorations had indeed been great- Dickens would have approved, he joked to himself, but as he read the article, he realised that words had again played him false. The article in fact was about breakdowns; in communications and in the nervous system, the two, it was argued, were related.

Humphry was always interested when he came across a word used in a new context He worked for a publishing firm which produced dictionaries and it was his job to check on changes in meaning and to add new words as they came into general use. The article began, "Catharsis; getting it off your chest, is the best way to come to terms with depression from which we all suffer for some of the time, at least." He read on with interest. " A course on co- counselling where two or more people take turns at being the counsellor or the client has become increasingly popular recently and has helped many people to free themselves from feelings of guilt which can destroy the psychic balance. The focus is not so much on problem solving but on CATHARSIS or getting rid of bad feelings when life gets on top of us. Emotional repression leads us to compulsive, maladaptive and and rigid behaviour patterns."

A few days later and when his chest was feeling definitely improved, he saw in the local paper that a group of *Co-counsellors* met not very far from his home. He decided to attend if only to discover whether the course would prove as effective in *getting things off the chest* as his expectorant linctus had proved to be.

Feeling somewhat foolish as well as apprehensive, a week later he rang the door bell of the house where the local group of co-counsellors met. A large woman whom Humphry's etymologicall bent immediately labelled as ,"blousy," opened the door to him and he was ushered into a fairly small room where a semi-circle of chairs were drawn up in front of a small electric fire. The eyes of five people were trained on him at once. The blousy lady, whose house this was, introduced herself as Gladys and then went on to introduce the other four women and one man who each gave a sort of world weary nod of acknowledgement as Gladys called their names.

'We don't stand on any ceremony here, Gladys announced in the tones of a seaside landlady reciting the house rules. Humphry tried to smile reassuringly and said, 'I'm hoping to get it all off my chest and find personal equilibrium like it said in the paper.' Their faces did not change. They had either not read the article or just did not want to unbend in any way in front of a stranger.

Mercifully Gladys at any rate understood what he was saying, ' We all know exactly what you mean and we are all dedicated to helping each other with our little problems as far as we are able.' Humphry sat down on the chair which had been added to the semi-circle for him. There was a silence until Gladys spoke again, 'Billy was just telling us about his schooldays and the way that things had gone wrong for him.' Billy, a podgy looking man of about Humphry's age, cleared his throat and continued with what he had been saying before Humphry had entered.

'Well when this master took to coming round each night after lights out to *tuck us in,* I began to look forward to his visits because I had no friends in the dormitory. I didn't say anything at all, even when he did some unexpected things to me under the bedclothes. 'Just checking things for you,' he used to say but I didn't know what he meant. Do you think that what he did has stopped me getting promotion at the library? I've been there eighteen years and everyone's moved on but me. I feel such a failure.'

Clearly Billy's predicament appealed to the mother in the ladies who all looked sympathetic and knowledgeable. They muttered reassurances, 'That's what goes on at all boys' boarding schools and they don't lower the fees at all.' Another added, 'Ought to be special terms if things like that go on, stands to reason. They can't expect something for nothing all the time, can they?' Billy basked in the attention and in their smiles and nods.' I feel better already. You are all so understanding. I'm glad that I've got that off my chest.'

Then a little old lady sitting on Humphry's right was called upon by Gladys to talk about things that she'd kept bottled up all her life until now. 'I always wanted to be a dancer, you know, but I never had the chance. I used to play ballet music on the wind-up gramophone in my room and dance about there. I used to tell my mother that I had to study the music for my lessons, but that was a lie. She used to ask why I had to make so much noise in my room and I said that I was doing my gymnastic exercises to be ready for Sports day. But that was a lie. I spent all my childhood lying to my parents and now I find it difficult to tell the truth, as I said last time.' Again there was a gush of sympathetic noises from the others and the little lady bowed her head and smiled.

Humphry felt disappointed; he'd been expecting to hear some really disgusting secrets that had been kept in for a long time and were now going to be aired. He tried hard to think of something to say to the group but nothing came into his mind. Fortunately he was not called upon to say anything. Gladys seized the opportunity herself to say her piece and *get it off her chest.* 'As you may know, I'm a manageress of an up-town department store. I've worked my way up over twenty five years. I've had to put up with some awful manageresses in my time, particularly the last one. I hated her more than I've ever hated anyone in my whole life. I got rid of her in my own way, though.'. Here Gladys paused for effect and was not disappointed,' Tell us what you did,' they cried.

'Well,' said Gladys, breaking into a breathy whisper, 'I got her the sack; I sent in wrong orders in her name and I wrote letters of complaint about her to the company complaining, you know -discourteous service, inefficiency and so on. The best bit was when I put some expensive underwear in her shopping bag and the security man spotted it. Out she went the next day, you should have heard her screaming and her tears when they took her away. Then I got her job and I've been miserable ever since.'

Humphry didn't know how to react to this, but the others did,' Serve her right, she brought it on herself,' If she hadn't been so beastly, it wouldn't have happened. I'd have done the same myself', and so on, they reassured her. After that the other ladies had their turns at catharsis. One told how she had stolen from her younger sister, another confessed to having gone to school without wearing knickers for a dare. Another told how she had sprinkled weed killer on her neighbour's lawn because he'd shouted at her dog. Humphry had still thought of nothing and was getting anxious. He wondered what he might find himself saying under the pressure of all this soul searching and chest clearing but he was spared that week. Gladys said as they were drawing to a conclusion, 'We have a rule that no one confesses anything at their first meeting, Humphry. We shall expect you to declare yourself at the next meeting in a fortnight's time.' Then they all had some dreadful coffee and went to their homes, no doubt, much liberated..

In the two weeks before the next meeting Humphry wondered whether to go or not, and if he did go, what was he going to say? He really had no childhood revelations to confess nor had he ruined anyone's lawn nor gone to school without his underpants nor got anyone the sack. Something will come to me when the time comes, I'll just wait and see, he thought hopefully.

At the end of the fortnight he was sitting in his chair in the circle again. All eyes were on him. Gladys looked at him expectantly, Well, Humphry, it's your turn now.' Humphry closed his eyes and began. He was astonished at what he heard himself pouring out in a great breathless gush,

' I've never quite believed that I was a man. I used to put on my mother's clothes when I was a boy and go out into the street, into shops, into ladies' lavatories. Sometimes I'd ring up total strangers, the first names at the top of the page in the telephone directory. I'd say that I was going to come round and beat the living daylights out of them. Then I'd leave parcels of rubbish at the station and ring up the police and get the station closed down in case there was a bomb.. I'd drop eggs onto people's heads from the top windows of buildings and I'd wear dark glasses and carry a white stick and go about knocking into people on purpose. I put "Ex-lax" chocolate through the door of houses where there was a dog left on its own. I'd make tape recordings of amazing farting noises and hide a speaker in the toilet and the tape played when anyone went to the toilet and those waiting outside wouldn't know where to look and I'd', but Humphry sensed a definite change in the atmosphere and stumbled to a halt.

Gladys gave him a long stare and then said, 'Goodness me, you've given us enough material there for several sessions. We like to ration ourselves, as it were, otherwise we'd soon run out of things to confess.' One of the other ladies, the knickerless wonder, muttered,' Bit selfish, if you ask me. Showing off, I'd call it and I don't like people doing things to dogs.'

The confessions of the others came as an anti–climax after Humphry's mammoth clearout. Bill tried to get their attention, with a complicated account of how he'd put salt into sugar bowls in a hotel he once stayed in when he was young. The others had obviously shot their bolts in Humphry's honour on his first visit and were clearly scratching about to find anything even a tiny bit unpleasant which they could offer up for general comment and absolution.. Finally Gladys, as a point of honour, decided to share with the group how she had cheated in the Bible Study group and had wound up winning the prize. 'Trouble was, it wasn't a trip to the seaside that time but an enormous new Bible, one of the modern sort not the proper Authorised version and I couldn't even sell it and I'm too superstitious to just throw it out, so I've been stuck with it filling up the bookshelf ever since.'

Humphry decided against going to the group again, Whilst he had been inventing all his *confessions*, the others, he felt had actually been spilling beans of truth.

Well that would have been that as far as co-counselling groups were concerned for Humphry. He'd learnt something about human nature and had had a certain amount of fun. It was to be a year later that Humphry heard about his old counselling group again. He'd given Gladys' group's address to a journalist friend who was looking for material for an occasional article.

'Most interesting,' said the journalist, 'I went to that group whose address you gave me, Extraordinary; they all seemed intent on confessing the same things and they got very annoyed when someone got in ahead of them with their story.'

'What sort of things?' I asked.

'Odd- grotesque accounts of playing tape recordings of farts, dropping eggs out of windows onto people's heads, making phone calls about bombs which weren't there, feeding dogs with laxatives and even cross dressing! I'd never have believed such things of such a mousy lot.'

'They must have been short of things to confess if they all tried to confess the same things. Wouldn't be any good for one of your Writers' Groups. Perhaps they should all take up Bridge or Yoga,' Humphry suggested.

All that was last winter and ever since there had been a discernible spring in Humphry's step when he thought about how he'd livened up Gladys's co-counselling group.

❧ Two lives ❧

There were fewer guests at Mr Throgmorton's farewell than anyone might have anticipated when a surgeon of his eminence retires . His senior colleagues, of course, were well represented, but it might have been expected that very many of his patients would not have wished to miss the chance to say thank you and to wish long retirement to a man to whom they all owed their very lives.

'Yes, you're right,' the .surgeon replied to the reporter who was covering the occasion. 'I suppose I am responsible for giving a great number of unfortunate people a second chance in life. There is always an element of risk in all surgery; minor as much as much major. I ask my patients to make their decision; assured death or a reasonable chance of continued life, albeit on a different basis from that which they had known before.'

'Your specialism, if I've got it right, was to take on brain cases that had been otherwise declared inoperable', said the reporter.

'No case is "inoperable"; some present with very slight chances indeed of any success whatsoever, but if there is any chance at all, it is surely better than the alternative,' the surgeon replied. 'I see' said the reporter. But he, like all the others there, did not and could not comprehend the full implications of the surgeon's claim.

One patient in particular had every reason not to miss the occasion and his absence did not pass unremarked, 'I haven't seen .Thomas Dreiser; I'm sure he, of all people, must be here,' said the eminent neuro surgeon, Edward Tarbutt, to his old colleague ,but Throgmorton merely shrugged his shoulders. 'He is a very busy man as you can appreciate; a financial empire cannot be abandoned just for the opportunity of raising a glass of champagne to one's medic, you understand.'

'You're always too, er, too, accommodating, yes, accommodating, John. Damn it, the man would never have had any chance whatsoever of a new life, but for your skills and, and courage. Has he no sense of gratitude at all?'

The surgeon took his colleague's arm and led him a little apart from the throng. 'Edward, at this late stage in my career, I am still learning, and one of the greatest things I have learnt is that sometimes nature itself has its own reasons for allowing a life to come to an end; to prolong it unnaturally, as I did with Dreiser, is to play God, or worse, his opposite.'

'My dear chap, you're not telling me that Dreiser might have reason to regret what you did for him- gave him his life back, for ,God's sake'

'That's just the point, Edward; was it for "God's sake?" '

The man they spoke of had not forgotten the occasion of John Throgmorton's retirement, far from it. He had lain awake all the previous night turning over in his tormented consciousness his feelings about what Throgmorton's miraculous surgery had meant to him. Before the operation he knew that he was inevitably going to die, and that his death would be very soon. After the operation, when he at last recovered himself enough to resume possession of his body and his life, he knew that he was not the same man that he had been before the operation which had given him back a future. His life before had been utterly happy and utterly unremarkable. He had been a parish priest in a little village in Somerset, nestling under the Quantock hills. He had been married to Molly, his boyhood sweetheart, and he had three delightful children, Ben, George and Sally and they,with Molly, had circumscribed his whole existence.

His daily round of visiting the lonely, sick and despondent had brought its special rewards; he was valued; appreciated and, he liked to think, loved. What else could a man wish for or deserve? Then had come the illness and the shattering news that he was going to die of an inoperable brain tumour. His dear family had shared his anguish as had all his little flock of churchgoers.

One Wednesday, when he was supposed to be attending the hospital, his appointment had been postponed and he returned to his village and had walked to the church. When he looked in, as he always felt a compulsion to do when passing, he was reduced to tears to see that the whole church was full and that his church warden, old Major Plumley, was leading them in prayers for their "beloved vicar who was facing a dreadful illness and that without divine help, he would be lost to them". Then they prayed and he had felt a physical change or impact within himself, the result of that corporate act of prayer, he was certain.

He remained hidden from them as he stood at the door, but he longed to speak and to tell them that he was quite prepared to face his fate and that the words, "Thy will be done" were always in his mind and had brought him a wonderful sense of peace. He wanted to say that death is the lot of all mankind and it did not really signify whether the end came early or late. As Hamlet had said, "If it is now, then it is not to come: the readiness is all." What did matter was the use one had made of the time one had been allotted- had it been for good ?

He said nothing about his awareness of the special intercession made for him by his parishioners. He continued to set his domestic life in order and to arrange things to the best of his ability so that his family would not be faced with unnecessary problems if he could avoid them by action before his death.

Then out of the blue, came John Throgmorton who had asked to see Thomas. Thomas had tried to explain, very simply, that he was expecting nothing, resenting nothing and was quite prepared to allow "God's will to be done"

'But what, Mr Dreiser, if it is God's will that I attempt to save your life? I can only say that the chances of success are infinitesimal; yours is a very extreme case, but there is a very remote chance, I repeat, a very remote chance indeed that surgery might possibly give you back your life.'

When charged finally with ingratitude and even callousness in depriving his wife, his family and his church of the only hope of having him restored to them, he had reluctantly, very reluctantly, agreed to the operation.

That had all been fifteen years ago. Thomas Dreiser had made a slow but complete recovery after the amazing operation But when he was capable of taking up again the reins of his life, a change had come over him; he felt himself to be indeed, a different man. He had stared unfeelingly at his wife, at his children and all the others who had hitherto been central to his life. He had become totally obsessed with financial matters, with stocks and shares, investments developments and everything which hitherto, in another life, he would have called, "The world of Mammon."

And he had prospered. It was as though he had acquired some strange and secret knowledge of what would be successful financially and he had managed to get loans, cash in insurance policies and everything in which he invested blossomed in an extraordinary and utterly spectacular fashion. He had left his little vicarage and lived in an opulent apartment in Park Lane. He had expanded his empire and opened offices in all the great cities of the world.

There must have been times when he thought back on the life he had led before and of his wife and children and his little church in the Quantock hills, but then, as though a shutter had come down, he would blink and resume his study of the international financial scene and of his large part in its fortunes.

After enjoying the leisure of his retirement for several months, John Throgmorton decided to visit to visit an old friend in Somerset and since this would involve his driving near to the Quantock village where Dreiser's family still lived, he made a diversion to call upon them. The non appearance of his star patient at his retirement party had puzzled him. Dreiser owed him his life and what an amazing new life it was. The Dreiser Corporation owned many of the vast new office blocks in London and elsewhere, a Dreiser Mercantile bank had just been launched and Dreiser seemed to be behind almost every big insurance and investment project. How had it been possible for a country vicar, with no previous business or banking experience, to have achieved this amazing eminence, he wondered.

Mrs Dreiser was hanging out the washing in the orchard when Throgmorton drove up to the cottage and despite the surgeon's apprehension, she did look pleased to see him.

Over tea and home made cake, the surgeon watched her and then chose his moment to ask his question. ' Do you ever regret what has happened to your husband?'

Her reply was slow in coming, as though she had been preparing a considered answer for a long time. 'Thomas was utterly resigned to his fate, you know and had not pressure been put on him; hurtful charges of ingratitude and so on, he would never have submitted to your knife. But he did. I wonder how he stands now towards his conscience.'

The surgeon put his cup down, then spoke, 'I have to tell you, Mrs Dreiser,that it is rather a matter of consciousness than conscience that has puzzled me. There is a brief moment, just a nano second, when the brain is utterly vulnerable; poised between annihilation and life . And in that fleeting moment the brain- the consciousness- is in a sort of limbo without direction or control, then some changes can occur. It is very rare indeed, but it can occur and I think that it did occur in your husband's case.'

'You mean that in that strange non time something *entered* him?' she asked.

'I cannot say exactly what did happen; I don't understand it; I'm a surgeon not a metaphysician, but it has preoccupied me not a little since that time.'

'Thomas has not abandoned us, you know. His accountants place a large sum at my disposal, but he entirely refuses to see the children or me. I never want to touch the money. The children feel the same. We get by. The new vicar and the village look after us very well.'

'You are a remarkable woman, Mrs Dreiser. Not many others would have been so, so forgiving, or so unmercenary,' the surgeon observed. 'But he never once expressed to me any gratitude for what I had done for him.' And then he added as an afterthought, ' I have to admit, on my retirement, I had thought that he might have perhaps have sent me a card.'

'You asked me a question earlier and I shall do my best to answer it,' she said, looking the surgeon full in the face. 'I can answer by telling you by telling you Thomas's last words to me before he was wheeled into the operating theatre. He took my hand and in a strange whisper he said, 'What shall it profit a man to gain the whole world and lose his immortal soul, Molly? My soul is in this life; it's the other life for which they want me, that I fear.'

On the drive onwards to see his old friend, John Throgmorton for the first time was pleased that he was retired and no longer would he now be called upon to exercise his awesome powers over life and death. He tried to dismiss the memory of what he had heard from Mrs Dreiser. He tried to whistle to himself, from childhood a way to get himself into a good mood, but he stopped when he found that he was whistling the theme from Lizst's macabre, "Mephisto Watz."

≋ Nil Desperandum ≋

I like a man who stammers; a man who can hold the world and his listeners up to ransom, machine-gunning them as they wait, patiently, even patronizingly, for the fit to pass.

Bertie Davenport had perfected such a stammer. At prep school, where we spent two happy, undemanding years together, at the same double desk, there had been no sign of the mannerism which he was to use to devastating effect in later life. It was at senior school that he evolved and perfected his protective weapon.

'Why weren't you at the cross-country, Davenport? It isn't the first time I've had to reprimand you for absenting yourself from games afternoon. What have you to say for yourself. eh? Speak up. Boy.'
Standing just behind Bertie, I saw him tilt his head forward, very slightly, like a bull focusing on an intruder crossing his field.Bertie's hands clenched into fists at his side. The loathed Games Master drummed his fingers on his attendance sheet. He waited, sure of himself, but unprepared for Bertie's counter-attack:
'Die,die, die,die,die,die!', snapped Bertie's sub machine gun. The master frowned, his eyes narrowed- did he detect mockery? Bertie was learning timing, but even then, on that preliminary sortie. he achieved his effect. Before the master could speak, Bertie twitched his head twice, blinked and then answered, quite calmly, as though nothing before had taken place,
'Diarrhoea, diarrhoea, sir I had diarrhoea; the prunes last night's supper. You see cunt,cunt,cunt,cunt- can't take them, sir.
Oh joy! Oh wonder! Inside and silently I exploded in laughter. A hit, a palpable hit. The master was at a loss; outwitted ,insulted and out manoeuvred, and he knew it.
'I see, Davenport, but you should have reported it',
'The di,di, di, di di di diarrhoea, sir or the pru, pru, pru, pru prunes?'
The master could not trust himself to answer and walked away.

I wanted to hug Bertie, but we had been told by the Headmaster for some reason recently, that 'Displays of physical affection between boys were emphatically banned.'

And so Bertie's secret weapon was launched. After we left school, I lost track of Bertie until, one night, many years later, I was watching the "Ten O'Clock News" and the Minister for Defence was being interviewed. There had been some scandal involving the sale of arms to a Foreign Power and Bertie was the Government's spokesman on the matter.

'The re, re, re reason that the opposition has seen fit to fabricate this li,li,li - lie is that they don't want you to know that it wa, wa wa, wa, was their idea originally. Just do your homework and look it up in Han, Han, Han Hansard before wasting any more of my time.'

Now for a stammer to be effective, certain rules must be obeyed. First, and above all, decide exactly what you want to say beforehand. The professional stammerer can use far more pauses than the ordinary speaker can. He must decide which words he will repeat and on which syllable the stammer must fall. A loud voice with a stage colonel's accent is particularly effective. It can demolish the opposition, however intimidating, like grapeshot demolishing a line of attacking soldiers.

I learnt that you should fix your eye on the victim whilst "Pressing the trigger." Words with a glottal stop-"Clo".as in "clodhopper" are excellent in a stammer, as are sibilants, particularly followed by a vowel which has the effect of stretching the mouth into a teeth -baring snarl, as in -"Si,si.si,si- siphylitic!" This can be particularly intimidating and is ideal for use against the timid or socially disadvantaged.
Gladiatorial contests between seasoned stammerers could become popular events on television were it not that the fullest impact of the combat relies in an important way upon the deployment, en passant, as it were, of the full weaponry of which the mouth is capable- spitting and frothing of saliva.

I saw a good example recently. I was waiting in line at Heathrow airport to check in for a flight to New York. The man in front of me, an insignificant enough short fat man, held the queue up to ransom whilst he exploded over the girl at the counter, managing to spit extensively in her face every time he repeated his demands. The unfortunate girl was too occupied with wiping her face with her handkerchief to defend herself. He continued; " I want the bis, bis, bis, bis, bis-business class seat that I reserved. I don't want a cla-cla- cla-cla, club class seat, you ef,ef, ef, ef-foolish woman." It was masterly and brought back vivid memories of dear old Bertie.

Then, as I was savouring the impact of a well modulated stammer, in the queue at London Airport I felt a sudden and great call to join the ranks of the "Warrior Stammerers",the "Royal Multi-articulators" as I called them.
All art is built on sacrifice; on pain, hard work and opportunism. My first attempts at multi-articulation involved some pain, some work but no sense of timing. They were abject failures; I hadn't bothered to consider the centrality of timing in these delicate exchanges.

I have always had a deep-rooted hatred of the unannounced visitor, whether the visitor be a friend, relative or door to door salesman, my reaction is the same- intense irritation. Why should I be looked upon as fair game simply because I was at home? Friends and relatives had accepted my feelings in this and always wrote or rang to say that they were going to call and at what time.

The Mormons who called on a Saturday when I was not working were to be my guinea pigs for the "Fighting Stammer I had been practising. The two young men were incredibly neat and clean looking and spoke with clipped mid-west American accents

The dialogue went as follows:

Mormon 1:   'Good morning, good morning. I hope that this is not an inconvenient time to call, sir?'

I said nothing, merely opening and shutting my mouth.

Mormon 2:   'I wonder if you have a few minutes to spare just to think with us about what life means and what death means, sir?'

I maintained my silence. The Mormons continued.

Mormon 1:   'You see, we are told by God , in this book, that death is not the end but the beginning of life. Does that not seem good to you?'

The two men, smiled patiently and waited. I set the timer in my head and started the count down..

Mormon 2:   'Do you understand what I am offering you, sir?'

I kept on counting-Seven, eight, nine ten. Then I attacked:

Me: 'Go-go-go-go-go-go-go- God,God,God, God,God God,God, God,' and so on, endlessly, with much eye rolling, twitching and uncertain movements of the arms. Nothing was under control. I went with the stream, increasing the volume of the stammer, frothing, shaking my fists and then, at last, collapsing in a heap on the floor at the door, concluding the show with a last, magnificent, total body convulsion, involving jack-knifing backwards and then rolling into a ball and lying quite still. The two young men stood there, said nothing, then left hurriedly on tip toes, I had the impression.

Mormons nil. Me Ten I decided. It was an honourable score for a first trial of my powers.

Encouraged, I did some research on stammering but could find little information. Perhaps out of deference to the afflicted or else because of typical English good manners, stammering was not a subject upon which anything definitive had been written.

The effect of a stammer upon the hearer is to force him into maintaining a neutral expression. The victim would listen carefully without reaction but should never under any circumstances, commit the unforgivable sin of supplying the word which was giving the stammerer so much trouble.

An acquaintance of mine, knowing my interest in public speaking, had put my name forward as one who might be prepared to fill the gap when their after-dinner speaker at the local Rotary Dinner was indisposed. I decided to accept and said that I would speak on the subject of ,"Communication." I expect they imagined that I would talk about the place of computers since, at the time, I was working for a company that sold them.

Now the members of the Rotary Club took themselves and their dinner nights very seriously indeed. This involved them in wearing formal and over-tight dinner jackets and consuming a good deal of alcohol before, during and after the dinner. I, uncharacteristically, drank nothing alcoholic whatsoever before my speech .I disguised this fact by getting a waiter to fill my glass with red grape juice. I did not wish to upset my hosts who traditionally prided themselves on the excellence of the wines served.

The moment came for my speech. The flattering introduction had been made, faces turned expectantly to me, and the animated talking stopped. I rose, put what appeared to be my notes in front of me, and began.

'I am going to speak to you on a very important su-su-su-su-su-su-su, sar-sar-sar-sur-sur-sur-sur,sa-sa-sa-sa. Sa-sa-sa-saaaaaaa-aaaaaa-sub,sub-sub-sub-sub-sub- sar-sub-sub-sar,sar, subbub-ub-ub- bah baa-baa,baa baa,baa,baa..' Someone would surely break soon, I hoped. I continued, tempted to throw in also a sample of the head twitching and eye-rolling so successful with the Mormons. But it was not necessary.'Baa,baa,baa,' I stammered on insanely, Then it came-

'Baa ,baa, baa. Baa. baa black sheep, have you any wool?' The chorus came from one then immediately and full-throatedly from every member there. Inhibitions loosened by all the drink, were cast aside and they all joined in, making incoherent animal noises, gargling, baaing, croaking and some just banging the table and crowing like cocks. I sat down and enjoyed the schoolboy fun. When it at last stopped, there was a self-conscious silence. I stood again and continued.

'Gentlemen, I congratulate you on your initial forbearance and then on your understandable and justified reactions. When we are faced with the unacceptable, we English, tend to imagine it isn't there; that that there has been some mistake, and if we maintain our cool and calm behaviour, the outrage will go away. In politics we like to give the other side the benefit of the doubt as far as that is possible, although standards in that direction vary, as the televising of the House shows. But there is a finite limit to what we will endure; I exceeded that limit and you acted accordingly. It was totally natural. We are not prepared to suffer fools indefinitely. Just now I wondered how long you would keep down your natural reflexes when subjected to the stupid noises I was making. My timer tells me fifty eight seconds. I congratulate you'

And I went on to give more examples of how we can take liberties with our hearers, not just through aggressive interruptions, increasingly the technique of certain "tough" radio interviewers, but by manic facial expressions, ambiguous throat clearings-is he actually going to be sick?- and idiosyncratic emphasis of unlikely and unimportant words. But the king of all these devices remains the "Warrior Stammer". There was no other weapon in its league. I got my formal and serious audience to practise a few stammers with their neighbours, suggesting that they concentrate upon expletives, sibilants and rapid glottal stops. The noise was deafening, but they were enjoying themselves. My task was over and I signaled the waiter to bring me a glass of the excellent wine that the others had been enjoying.

The members of that Rotary Club must have had considerable influence in the worlds of business, education politics and the media because in the months that followed my talk I became aware, slowly then increasingly that more and more people were stammering. Politicians as a matter of course, if not privilege had used the stammer frequently when asked for a straight answer. They had never provided such a thing, but now that stammering was universal, even obligatory, they had a licence to delay and confuse. They accepted it with open arms.

Every one, everywhere, was stammering. Once this had become the norm in television "Soaps" as well as on the radio, it was rampant and even took a hold in "The Archers", the long-running serial about simple country folk One after another the rustic characters the would dissolve as they were seized by the convulsive spasm and the action would grind to a halt.

No one was exempt from the dreaded scourge. I had started this revolution, I was all too aware, and now found that I could not break myself of the habit; my "Warrior Stammer" would leap in unsummoned and uncontrollable into my every speech. Everywhere civilized discussion and basic communication became impossible. Lovers would blot out their tender protestations to the beloved so that those, most egocentric of all statements, "I love you" was reduced to an incoherent babble of noises; ' I,I,I,I, Lah-lah-lah-lah-lah-lah lah-larver,larvehr-larvah you '

Clearly stammering was more infectious than the common cold and far more deadly. I looked for a cure- for myself as much as for humanity as a whole. One ancient medical book found in the Cambridge University Library suggested that, "Chronic cases of uncontrollable stammering are sometimes cured by a loud noise, such a gun shot or a heavy ruler brought down on a flat surface such as a desk". I bought a starting pistol and a supply of blank cartridges. Attempting to buy some sausages in my local organic butcher's shop, I only managed, 'Sauce,-sauce,-sauce.-sawwse.' before being stricken. I drew my starting pistol and fired a salvo. The shop cleared, the other customers imagining this to be a daring daylight robbery, but I was able to complete my request for two pounds of sausages without any more trouble. The old remedy had worked; I was cured.

After that most people took to carrying some means to make a loud noise- a rattle, a starting pistol or cap gun, two rulers to clash together, and so on. "Today in Parliament" took on a new dimension when the efficacy of a loud noise in quelling a recalcitrant stammer was appreciated. The "Speaker" in the House soon became the "Slammer" as she excelled in producing the loud noise necessary to stilling the stammering gibberish which had become the norm in the House.

Slowly the tide subsided and sanity returned. People went about their business without fear that they would be reduced to incoherency and verbal fit by the dreaded stammer. Sadly, the Mormons returned and this time they found me weaponless and powerless. Powerless, that is, until inadvertently I farted in the silence whilst they waited for my reactions to their proposals for salvaging my spirit from eternal damnation. The effect was, if anything, more dramatic and instant than the stammer had been. They left instantly, without attempting to say another word.

Now, I wondered, if this, my latest contribution to human communication catches on as universally as did the Warrior Stammer" then we might all, one day, witness a new era in the Houses of Parliament, the theatres, the schools, universities, law courts, opera houses, and everywhere that civilized men and women meet. I might earn a small note in history as the originator of rhetorical flatulence.

The Facts of Life

Jeswold, the 13th Earl of Drumcadre, paced the library uneasily in his new slippers. It was his birthday and the Earl had decided to tell his son, Lord Randle, the *Facts of Life*. The birthday of the Earl's fourteen year old son fell on the same day as that of his father and they both knew and dreaded the formalities which had to be got through on that day.

There was a discreet tap on the library door and the heir to the earldom was invited to enter. Randle was the first to speak,' Sorry the slippers were such an awful red, father, but nanny thought you might welcome a change from the blues ones I always give you on your birthday.'

'They are refreshingly bright. Old chap. Thank you for your card as well. Painted it yourself, I take it.' The boy immediately became embarrassed at the mention of his artistic interests, such skills were, of course, irrelevant to a young man who would one day lead hounds, shoot birds, preside on the local magistrates' bench and have sole control of the considerable income from land, cottages and farms which made up the Earl's estate.

'I was just messing about with some paints before I threw them out so I did you a picture of Chancellor.' Chancellor was a large and extremely evil smelling Great Dane to which the Earl was totally devoted.

'Just so, old chap. Just so, but it doesn't do to get into the habit, what?' And here Jeswold gave one of his characteristic guffaws to emphasize his contempt for all things he considered to be not egregiously masculine. Randle's eyes searched for and found with relief a particular red pattern in the corner of the immense turkey carpet and felt as uncomfortable as he invariably did in the presence of his progenitor. His father completed the last of the deep throated bellows that revealed his massive molars and made the red bristles of his moustache stand out flamboyantly.

'Right, now we have to get down to brass tacks- *Facts of Life* – just as your grandfather did for me on my fourteenth birthday. Dashed odd thing, you and I having the same birthday, what? Well, here goes then.' Randle pressed his knees together until his muscles hurt and then plunged head first into the dark vermillion pool in the carpet.

'Short of some sort of act of God; falling on my head at the hunt, my old Purdey taking me with him on double choke, or floating away on a monstrous wash of Dow's 34- good way to go that, ha! ha! I intend to be around for a year or so more. The familiar guffaw was just a little too pat Randle felt and kept his eyes fixed on the edge of the red pool. Sensing his son's impatience with his preamble, Jeswold took a closer cut at his target.

'Well, short of my unforeseen and untimely demise, you will inherit the title, the estates, the income and, of course, all the responsibilities' Here he appeared to lose the thread of his uncomfortable speech and had to force himself to continue, 'Ah, the responsibilities.' The unnecessary sibilance on the last word grated on Randle. ' Responsibilities, yes responsibilities, yes, when I'm dead' The red slippers flashed at the edge of Randle's vision. 'But before that you will need the wherewithal to be your own man. And now I feel you may well be old enough to face the, what shall we say- *Facts of Life,* right? Your mother's decision to divorce me costs me thirty five thousand in alimony each year. The interest on your great grandfather's death duties unpaid by my father is a further charge upon me, this year amounting to one hundred and thirty two thousand pounds. To comply with the Ministry of Agriculture's asinine and quite unnecessary regulations will cost a further twenty eight thousand pounds. Even your fees at Harrow have to figure in my accounting nowadays since they are exactly eleven times greater than in my days there. In short, old chap, you will have a very reduced sum to get by on as your allowance from your eighteenth birthday. I have done my best, but the fact is'- the red slippers flashed at Randle again-' the best you can hope for me to give you as an allowance will be in the region of twelve thousand a year and no more. Sorry about that, old chap.'

Randle said nothing; the edges of the red pool became unattainable shores. It was only when the father put his hand on his son's shoulder that Randle came back from his carmine retreat in the carpet. He looked up and gave his father the same slow smile that lit up his face and made his eyes twinkle in the way that had brought Jeswold into hopeless servitude to the rare beauty of Randle's now departed mother, years ago. The Earl looked away and through the tall windows to the lake and the parkland beyond.

In the next four years Randle often thought about that confrontation in the library when the *Facts of Life* had been spelled out so bluntly by his father. By his eighteenth birthday, Randle's circumstances had changed greatly and he was about to leave school. He had been moved out of the nursery wing of his father's castle on his sixteenth birthday. Randle had looked round that room which had become so dear to him since his childhood days when his kind old nanny had done her best to make up for the absence of a mother's presence in the boy's life. There on the mantelpiece stood the tin soldiers, in their alert and shining ranks . The antique pistols in their cases had played their part in bringing him to an acceptance of life as being always a form of warfare, armed or unarmed.

It was in that room, on his fourteenth birthday that Taylor, the youngest and most attractive of the chambermaids, had so gently bewitched him and brought him to a full and at last direct knowledge of the nature of those other and most unmercenary *Facts of Life.* Oh how totally different he had found them from the grotesque and smutty distortions that constituted the average public schoolboy's speculations on matters carnal and forbidden.

On leaving the nursery room had he imagined it or had his old nanny- she had been his father's nanny too- spoken to him with a deference he had never before heard in her familiar voice? Nothing was moved or changed in that room, cradle of his boyish idealism. The transition had to be total and only in that way could he cast off the shards of his early life.

Randle's rooms in the west wing were fully prepared to complete the process of transition from boy to man; even the wardrobes and chests of drawers were filled with new sets of clothes; the formal and ritual vestments of an earl in the making. There was a dinner jacket, a tail suit, a morning suit and other costumes appropriate for the various roles Randle must now play; huntsman, Master of the Hounds, country gentleman.. The books on the shelves were uncompromisingly concerned with serious and relevant matters; good husbandry, land management, legal and fiscal considerations and , of course, the proper care and selection of fine wines. Randle could see how the coming years would unfold for him and the fuller part he must now play in them now that his father's health had become less certain.

His schooldays over, there would be Oxford, but only for the two years that the aristocracy could spare for making useful contacts, gaining a smattering of culture and generally enjoying wining, dining and wenching. He would be assigned his forebears' rooms at Christchurch and begin the process of being introduced to the clubs to which, in the fullness of time, he would inevitably be elected. It was tacitly assumed that he would marry, at a convenient time, the unimaginative and entirely decent Lady Felicity Fitzroy-Cunningham whose father was an old friend of his father's and whose lands adjoined the Earl's. It was the sensible thing to do, after all, as his father had so many times intimated.

Dinner on his eighteenth birthday was a solemn and formal affair. Stiff in his new tails, Randle had sat on the right of his father at the great table capable of accommodating thirty guests on ceremonial occasions. Morton, the butler, had come out of retirement to preside over the wines at dinner and had earlier taken Randle round the cellars outlining the provenance and character of each of the noble wines stored there and listing the vintages and saying how many of each had been laid down.. He was nervous when it came to the ports, stocks of which had been seriously depleted to satisfy the Earl's addiction to that superb postscript to any dinner worth the eating.

'There remains barely half a pipe of the Dow's 34', Morton remarked dolefully, as the torch lit the distant corner of the cellar.

After dinner the Earl and his son had adjourned to the smoking room where Randle was given one of his father's prized "Romeo and Juliet" cigars to savour and to mark the occasion of their birthdays. The practice of giving presents had been abandoned some years ago now, along with all other juvenile customs of behaviour.

That morning Randle had been in the village and had caught sight of Taylor, the young chambermaid, who had initiated him into the *Facts of Life* so delightfully on his sixteenth birthday . He had looked for her again, hoping she might make another visit to his room the following night, but she seemed to have vanished from the castle. When he had brought himself to ask, as casually as he could, why he no longer saw the girl, Taylor, cleaning his room, he was told, perfunctorily that she had, "moved on".

In the small hours between three and four in the morning, Randle would lie awake and remember and long for the warm closeness of that pretty village girl with her soft smile, her hair smelling of lavender and her hands, so strong yet so sensitive, timorously awakening his manhood and summoning him gently to the delicious offices of lovemaking. When Randle had seen the girl again that morning, she had been walking hand in hand with one of the farm lads. His eyes were only for her and their happiness was evident in the way they moved together in concert as they walked .

Randle's heart had cried out. He had wanted to attract her attention and longed to be able to stroll openly and proudly with her on his arm and lead the simple life of a country boy, entirely free from all the expectations, demands and formalities of his rank and position which made impossible all such natural and uninhibited actions. But yet she must have felt some attraction that night when she had come to his bed. He had that at least to hold on to. Might it, he dared to wonder, have been more than simply attraction and curiosity? Might it even have been-*love*? If he could believe that, then he would be able to face the years ahead; years dedicated to the duties of his inheritance and meek and seemly conformity to the vows of marriage which would bind him and the Lady Felicity.

The girl had come to him of her own volition and had left because she knew the impossibility of continuing that relationship; how solicitous. His heart had gone out to her. Seeing her, his secret lover, again that morning brought back a rush of memories and desire, but no one must ever know of that hidden fire, fire kindled on the night of his sixteenth birthday .

Logs were spitting brightly on the massive fireplace when Randle went to join his father in the smoking room. The Earl stood with a poker in his hand subduing the leaping flames. The main lights were unlit as father and son both preferred to sit in their armchairs on either side of the fire, sipping their ports, pulling on their cigars and watching the flickering magic of the firelight. Neither of them spoke, At last, as though he had been winding himself up to the matter, the Earl put down his glass, took a mighty pull on his glowing cigar, exhaled an expensive cloud of aromatic smoke and said,' Do you remember my telling you on your fourteenth birthday what we might call *The Facts of life?* Well, as it turns out, things are not so bad as I had then feared they might be; the interest on the death duties has been paid off , the Home Farm has done really quite splendidly this year and some shares I'd lost hope of, have miraculously blossomed, and indeed are a little gold mine. Fact is, old chap, you can count on at least twenty nine thousand as an allowance next year. That's good, isn't it? Oh, and by the way, man to man and all that, now I have something I feel bound to confess. Those other *Facts of Life-* you see, when it came to it, I found that I just couldn't go through with telling you myself, did what my father did, got Morton to slip fifty pounds to one of the youngest chambermaids in return for her going up to your room on your fourteenth birthday and, er. She jumped at it, Morton said, wanted the money to get married to some farm lad it seemed. Well, there we are. Hope it all went off satisfactorily and you were filled in on that side of life's facts. Meant to tell you before, but you know how it is.'

'Yes, father, I know how it is. And thank you for *The Facts of Life* and the doubling of my allowance; dashed considerate. It's good to know how things stand; I might have gone on thinking that some things were quite different from what they are. It's best to stick to facts, however cold and disappointing they seem. Happy Birthday, father.'
'Happy Birthday, my boy.'

Davy Jones's Locker

Written after attending an ARVON course.

In my life I have met only two people who were committed, heart and soul, to serving an ideal. For the sake of that ideal all consideration for personal comfort, convenience and family ties had been ruthlessly set aside; even being in their presence made me uncomfortable. My friend, Willoughby Carter, was no such martyr, but he did have one ideal and had dedicated himself to its service in a way that inspired amazement rather than simple admiration.

Suffering is said to ennoble, but there were definite limits to the rigours that Willoughby was prepared to undergo in the cause of upholding his particular resolution. I can see him now, smiling enigmatically at a private joke or suddenly narrowing his eyes to fix you in a stare of such intensity that your every hidden shortcoming seemed laid bare whilst he remained detached and coolly aloof. I had discovered that in his youth Willoughby had once sworn a great and inviolable oath that never in his life would he ever give way to writing a novel. It was not that he considered such an action beyond his abilities, quite the reverse, but that he believed that everyone should have some standards of behaviour and try their hardest to uphold them.

Those who hold strong convictions are normally quite prepared to have those convictions put to the test and even to do battle in their defence when necessary. It came then as no surprise to find numbered amongst those enrolled for a week's course on Creative Writing, the illustrious name of my friend, Willoughby Carter, the committed non novel writer. The course was held in rural Devonshire, in a large thatched mansion, once the solid home to generations of English yeomen. The initiates on this course were to spend a week together talking about and listening to every kind of story; accounts of doughty deeds; parables of an inscrutably psychological nature and some totally incomprehensible tales without vestige of any apparent meaning or purpose whatsoever. After exposure to these, the course members were directed to embark upon some form of literary creativity themselves. These perpetrations they would variously scribble on scribbling pads, tap into sophisticated laptop word processors or grind out on ancient typewriters.

On the occasion of which I write, the course was in the charge of a poet and novelist from Cornwall. After a preliminary exhortation to the members to at once lay in necessary and adequate supplies of alcohol, if they had not come suitably prepared for the rigours of the trial, the Cornish writer made his opening move. The nature of that move requires a little explanation for those fortunate to have been spared the ravenings of the creative psyche in a state of bestial arousal.

The leader, let us call him Jones, read a short story to the group. His technique was all the more effective for being unobtrusive. He made no comment on the style or the content of the story, he merely gave an ambiguous glance around, then with a warm and avuncular smile he said, ' That little tale is considered by many, including, of course, its publisher, to be a work of manifest genius' Over coffee the course members in ones and twos compared notes; each reluctant to say aloud what they all secretly felt. But eventually, with a dramatic lowering of voice, one of them came out with it;

' That story; the one he's just read us, well I didn't think it was all that good, did any of you, honestly? I mean, unless I missed something. I reckon that each of us here could do just as well, don't you, eh?'

Another instantly chimed in, 'Bloody sight better, I should think. I've go a story of my own which I've brought and it's on much the same subject-I'd be happy to let any of you read it if you're interested'

And so it continued; each one agreeing in turn that they thought nothing of the story of *manifest genius* and then adding in mock modest tones, that something he or she had written was more worthy, *really*, of being published than the wretched- it had now become *wretched*, story that they had just had read to them. Meanwhile, like a Machiavellian villain or an inciter to riot in a Medieval bedlam, Jones called them together again for a few thoughts before they broke to prepare for dinner.

He spoke slowly and deliberately, 'I was once on a course, not unlike this one, in fact, when one of the group, after hearing the wonderful story I have just read to you, said that he considered himself to be quite capable, unpublished and unknown, as he was as a writer, of producing a better story. He spent all that night and most of the next two days attempting to compose that *better* story. When he had finished, he gave it to me and I have to say, I was amazed; amazed and impressed. Not only did he handle the same material with a flexibility and panache which made the first story seem positively fumbling, but he had a far more assured feeling for a telling image or the way that an apparent digression can subtly enhance an effect; masterly. I insisted that he allow me to send a copy of his story to my own publisher for inclusion in an anthology which he was getting together called, "The Century's Greatest Stories." You may well have read it yourselves and if so, you will be familiar with the now famous writer of the story written on the course and which began his career as a novelist and master of the art of the short story.

He stopped. Glances were exchanged. Then he continued as though at their unstated but urgent request,' Yes, have a go. Who knows? There might well be another William Trevor, Graham Greene or Somerset Maugham amongst you!'

They were gone at once and several failed to reappear for the communal dinner such was the overwhelming power of the creative urge sparked off by Jones in throwing down his challenge.

But my story concerns Willoughby Carter; that indefatigable champion of that noble ideal; that magnificent obsession; that never, never, in all his life, however sorely tempted, would he give way to writing a work of creative literature. I shall not suggest to you that it was at all easy for him to withstand the siren calls which had so completely overpowered his fellows on the course. For at least two long minutes he stood motionless, fists tightly clenched, eyes staring unblinkingly ahead whilst wave after mighty wave of scintillating ideas, plots; openings, epiphanic conclusions and resonating imagery broke over him and sought to bear him quite away. His eyes closed as a violent spasm seized him that he should at once find a word processor or a typewriter not being used, or even a simple jotting pad in order that he could give himself over utterly and at once to the craven desire which had overtaken him. Then it was that he remembered the words of the spiritual father of all truly avowed non prose writers, the Stratford Bard himself;

    "Expense of spirit in a waste of shame is lust in action;

And till action, lust is perjured, murderous, bloody, full of blame,

Savage, cruel, not to trust"

And, like the bard before him, Willoughby Carter struggled to,

"Shun the heaven that leads men to this hell."

These timely words, mouthed soundlessly beneath his breath, brought Willoughby back slowly from the brink and gave him the courage and the power to fight off the insistent assaults on the calm and blessed mundanity of spirit that had up to then been his salvation in the tempest of life's many challenges. He knew that he must hold out against the depraved longings and urges that Jones's Satanic words had called up in him. He made his way to the kitchen where the group's cache of helpful bottles was stored. Here, not pausing to try to identify the bottle which he had brought- a complimentary Liebfraumilch given away with purchases over five pounds at his local supermarket – he seized, by chance, a bottle of Gevrey-Chambertin, 1985, Grand Classe that one of the more discerning and affluent of the group had brought for his personal consumption.

By assiduous commitment to the Gevrey-Chambertin and then, two Lynch-Bages, non-vintage admittedly, that fell to his urgent questing hands, Willoughby managed to meet and overcome the urges which remorselessly drew him towards composition. He sat, then sprawled on the upswept floor of the kitchen and, at last, was gathered into the healing and restorative arms of the goddess sleep, his *trammelled sleeves knit up* once more to face the cold world of the morrow's challenges.

In the morning, Willoughby having slept long and deeply, such is the bonus of drinking wines of surpassing excellence, was the first down to breakfast. Having piled his plate high with crisp bacon, plump field mushrooms, sausages, scrambled eggs, baked beans and, for good measure, a poached kipper, he felt ready to face whatever trials the day might have in store for him

Slowly, in ones and twos, bleary eyed and listless, the other members of the course tottered into the communal kitchen. Willoughby sat aloof, smiling as he listened to accounts of sleep sacrificed solely in the cause of writing some wretched story all night. The more fools them, he thought. He also had to listen to little whimpering cries of despair and shock when members discovered that their personal provisions for breakfast had been severely depleted. Breakfast was a do-it -yourself affair, and they regarded Willoughby's piled plate with open hostility and pointed remarks about, "Certain people's greed". It was, Willoughby concluded, part of the cross that he had to bear that he must listen to such trivia by way of conversation at this early hour. He rose above it.

It was on the third day that Willoughby's convictions were put to their supreme test. Jones had led a discussion on what constituted a *Great* novel. Readings were given from Joyce, Jane Austen, Dickens, Lawrence and their like, and finally from the work of a gentleman with an unpronounceable name who had recently won the Booker Prize through the judges' inability to agree on any alternative contender.

Jones, seated facing them, was like a zoo keeper throwing fish to hungry seals, had them all watching his every hand gesture and hanging on his gnomic utterances. His voice rose dramatically as he approached his concluding words. 'I want each of you to go to some quite place and write the first chapter of the undoubtedly great novel which each of you, assuredly, is capable and which, even now, is relentlessly gestating in your fecund imaginations; pressing to be given to a waiting world.'

At once, like flea infested cats, the members of the Creative Writing Course skipped and twitched to their respective quiet places in order to begin on the novel which would, infallibly, make their name a household word whenever lovers of great literature were gathered together. Willoughby began also to twitch, and recognising the early and unmistakeable symptoms of an impending attack of creativity, he rushed from the room to where the members had stored their wine; an antidote was essential before it was too late and he, Hyde-like, had become a helpless slave to his base literary cravings.

When he burst through the door, already mouthing a variety of stunning *opening lines*, he saw at once that all was lost; the cupboard was bare of any wine, with the exception of one bottle, his own undistinguished, undrinkable and gratuitous supermarket Liebfraumilch. This pathetic apology for an antidote was now all that stood between him and the extreme rigours of a full blown attack of literary creativity. The inadequacy of that antidote is largely to blame for the unfortunate events that followed.

In great breathless gulps Willoughby forced down the unprepossessing liquor, but to no avail; the first stages of his Hyde like transformation had begun and his imagination was awhirl with such dangerous matters as the importance of prose rhythm, the effective use of terse, incisive sentences at pivotal moments in the action, settings, snatches of coruscating dialogue and whole flights of telling images. When a plot also erupted; clear, utterly original and complete, Willoughby knew that a dedicated and determined non-writer of narrative fiction was very near to breaking point.

There had, of course, been earlier trials of his resolve. Several years before he had found himself making jottings for possible stories first thing in the morning, before he had even left his bed. He had been offered even urged to make free use of a writer friend's villa in Cap d'Antibes; home to Somerset Maugham at his most productive era. He had not succumbed but had rigorously devoted every moment of his spare time to watching television, particularly the so called, "Soaps" in order to purge his system of the poisonous craving to write; to give birth to an original and living story. In the past he had come through triumphantly and had gone on his way unsullied and innocent, but this time he was going to fail; his strength had deserted him in his hour of greatest need. He was an enervated St George confronting an implacable and all powerful dragon.

I suppose in retrospect, it must have been the challenge of the title which finally toppled Willoughby's resolution. Jones had suggested flippantly that they should all attempt an opening to a novel with the title , "Davy Jones's Locker". It was an uninspiring enough theme you might have thought, but not for Willoughby. His teeming imagination was at once at work on the novel which was rapidly gestating in his consciousness

What in fact saved Willoughby at the very last moment, before he was irrevocably lost, was one of those chance happenings, the timing of which can so often radically affect one's life.

A distant relative of Willoughby had unexpectedly added to his will a codicil to the effect that he wanted his yacht, a cruising vessel of seductive lines and proven sea-keeping qualities, to go to Willoughby. The relative had then promptly died By this time the course was over and Willoughby was well into the twelfth chapter of the "Davy Jones's Locker novel. Locked in his room at all available moments, he was oblivious of holidays, weekends, summons to dinner parties, celebrations of birthdays and national events and even of the need to launder and change his clothes. The tap, tapping on the word processor was unceasing. He was a recluse living only on snacks, coffee and good wine.

When he learnt that he had inherited a fine yacht, he was unmoved, and even reluctant to view it. The marina, where it was lying, then informed him that unless he was to be liable for a year's berthing fees, a surprisingly large sum, he must at once move the boat. He had been neglecting his office and had also fallen behind in his rent. Perhaps the peace of a yacht's cabin would solve both his need for privacy and provide a place where he could economically carry on with his novel. He left for the marina and his yacht at once.

To the dedicated non-writing fraternity, Willoughby's story and its outcome is well known. When he saw the fine lines of his new yacht, ran his hands over the gleaming brightwork, admired the tall mast, sat back comfortably in his snug saloon and inhaled the irresistible smell of polished wood, glinting oil lamps, ropes and all manner of nautical fixtures, he let the manuscript of his incomplete novel fall from his hand.

He set off at once to put the yacht through its paces and on a bright Spring day , with the wind plump in the sails,, the water curling away from the prow and the wake straight as a die behind him as the log registered seven knots, he sat tearing up the manuscript of his now never to be finished novel. His back began to recover from crouching over his word processor and his thoughts reverted to simple, unambiguous matters that before had been his solace and entertainment. He was free; cured of his unhealthy addiction and preoccupation. I'm happy to relate that since that day, never once has Willoughby swerved from his resolve nor his courage failed him to remain constant to his bright ideal and never, ever, whatever the provocation, however bubbling the imagination, would he be reduced to being a slave to his despicable vice.

Now his example stands to give hope and courage to all those who seek to end their days quietly without giving into that dehumanising craving; that despicable longing to write a novel, our very own novel, one of which lurks dormant in each of us, straining to be born.

A Fit for a Queen

'And don't bother to come back. Do you hear?

Sidney blanched at the insistent and rasping cadence; the voice rising in note and volume and emphasis. He dreaded those Sunday mornings when his neighbour, Mrs Talbot, would open the back door, throw out her husband's battered suitcase into which she had hurled an assortment of clothes, then a pair of shoes and a carrier bag which might have contained anything. You might have taken Mr Talbot for a rent collector, an unpromotable bank clerk or an undertaker. Indeed, at various times in his life he had played all three of these roles. Now he was usually unemployed. The only regular work and income he still had was entirely due to his being tall and incredibly thin and having a face which looked as though he had seen or experienced every conceivable misery to which mankind is heir.

The proprietor, or as he preferred to be called, "The Director" of the large funeral business in town had often been told how moved his clients' families had been by Mr Talbot's long melancholy face and dignified presence. 'It's as though he really knew my husband', widows would say when settling their accounts. 'Do you think that's possible?'

'Mr Talbot is a man upon whom the weight of human tribulation sits heavily. I have never known him to smile or laugh. It's as though he was just waiting for death, his own, ideally, and the deaths of other people act as forerunners to that event.' The Funeral Director would reply, always using the same form of words.

Sidney wondered idly what those bereaved ladies would have made of the undignified exit from his house of the man whose serious and dignified expression of sympathy they had found so strangely comforting at the funeral of their husbands. The ritual he had observed from his bedroom window never varied; Mr Talbot would slowly gather up his belongings , put on his shoes and overcoat, pause whilst he shook his fist at the now locked back door of his sometime home and totter to the back gate of the garden and then out into the back lane beyond.

Quite where he went and what he did Sidney could only guess at. He must have returned at some stage because a day or so later the tall figure of his neighbour could be seen lying in a deckchair, a newspaper over his face.

Mrs Talbot was the breadwinner Sidney discovered when he went to visit the tax office. His annual tax return had been queried and he had been called into the office to explain himself. Sidney found all confrontations intimidating; he would lose all his confidence, stammer and make absurd statements which he immediately contradicted and generally he behaved in a manner likely to present him as guilty of whatever charge had been made against him. At school he had been so in awe of the Headmaster that he would be quite incapable of meeting his eye, would blush and as likely as not, admit to something of which he was quite innocent.

On the occasion of his visit to the tax office, Sidney was asked to give his explanation to the supervisor. He was shown into a small office and on the opposite side of the table was Mrs Talbot. If she recognised him, she gave no indication. Her pedantic phrasing of her enquiries, her over loud enunciation, as though to a deaf or half-witted person, robbed him of all confidence and he was quite prepared to be told that he deserved a heavy fine or a spell in prison. He was, in fact, quite innocent of any transgression, he had merely failed to read his form carefully and had entered his occasional income from marking examination papers as income from rented property. An easy mistake, he would normally have been quite able to argue, but he felt intimidated by the daunting Mrs Talbot and even he would have to admit that his behaviour in front of the redoubtable neighbour would have branded him as guilty in anyone's book.

'Under the circumstances, Mr Harvey, I am minded to give you a warning and ask that in future you give the Revenue's lawful enquiries into your personal finances the proper attention that it deserves. That will be all.'

From that time on Sidney felt an affinity with the unfortunate Mr Talbot and tried to engineer an opportunity when he might, on neutral ground, such as in a pub, discus with him how "Medusa" might be tamed or out manoeuvred. He was uncertain whether he would actually refer to Mrs Talbot as Medusa, but he rather imagined that her downtrodden husband would not have been outraged had he done so.

The opportunity came sooner than expected. Sidney had a free day from his duties in the translating syndicate where he worked and he had decided to take a walk by the river. He was about equidistant from the town and the docks when he saw a tumbledown sort of shelter on the riverbank. It was like those on the promenade where the elderly sat and watched for hours on end the comings and goings of the tides and the seagulls. When he got nearer, he saw that there was someone sitting inside the shelter. It was Mr Talbot, his neighbour and Medusa's husband.

'You're Mr Talbot, my neighbour. We've never met. How do you do.' Mr Talbot turned his face to Sidney at this and fixed him with one of his best "Funeral" gazes.

'I have seen you. Your name is Sidney Harvey. One of your letters got wrongly delivered to my house once, that's how I know who you are. What brings you to this particular neck of the woods? I reckon to spend a day here without seeing anyone normally.'

'But this isn't a normal day, Mr Talbot. Fate has ordained that we meet in this very private and quiet place for a special reason, which, if we're patient, we shall find out,' Sidney responded.

Mr Talbot took this in carefully and then slowly nodded.

'We live in confusing worlds- you in yours and me in mine. Every day I begin by wondering what's in store for me; another experience of unalloyed irritation or possibly, one of jubilation. That last has never happened. I like doing my bit at the funerals, I like the atmosphere- so, so.' He struggled for the apt word, and then resumed,' so, parenthetical, yes, that's it, parenthetical. I think that would be the word to sum up what I feel about funeral work- outside the main dialogue; an aside really.' He nodded slowly in agreement with his own diagnosis.

Outside the little wooden shelter it had begun to rain; the sound of the sporadic dripping on the roof seemed, somehow, to bring the two men together as though they had both been given the same sentence or were waiting to begin a demanding musical duet.

Sidney, of course, wanted to raise the subject of Medusa. He wanted to ask why his companion in the shelter was periodically thrown out of his own home. He could hardly have asked if Mr Talbot was a man who drank heavily and in his cups would become violent, throwing around the living room all the tasteless ornaments given to them as wedding presents by his wife's relatives and which now only served to remind Mr Talbot of his past folly in binding himself legally to a monster. Mr Talbot was not uncomfortable in the silence. He enjoyed the commentary of the raindrops. He was relieved that his neighbour could and did manage to sit without asking him the questions that he must be wanting to ask and to which, sadly, he had no answer to give.

' Have you ever owned a dog, Mr Harvey?' Mr Talbot eventually asked, breaking a ten minute silence.

' Not *owned* , no. I was once asked to look after a neighbour's dachshund. He went away to bury his aunt and he was to come back in a week's time. But he never returned. I didn't like the dog, I hated it, so I took it to a park, tied it to a bench and just left it to fend for itself. If the owner had ever come back, I should have said that the dog had simply gone off, for whatever reason.'

' But, of course, he never came back. Perhaps it was his way to get rid of it by making you responsible for it, shirking his own responsibility.'

There was another long silence. The rain gradually stopped. Mr Talbot suddenly turned to Sidney and as though he could have read his mind, he said, ' Since you've been good enough not to ask, I will tell you. My wife is a collector. I wish I could say that she collected sensible, worthwhile things; coins, china figurines, musical toilet rolls and such, but no; she's only interested in collecting invitations.'

'Well they could be interesting, surely?' Sidney said.

'Indeed they could, but you see she's very selective; only invitations to private functions, closed exhibitions, prison burials, coroner's inquests, royal investitures-events like that not open to the public at large. And more than that, they have to be in their original envelopes. From time to time, when it all gets to much for me, I manufacture one myself- I'm very good at things like that. I take infinite trouble over the details; right paper, correct type set, dates and supporting information. Then there's the ageing, that's my forte. I say that I picked up the invitation on a stall in Leather Lane or the Portobello Market. To begin with she was always taken in, but then one day she came home early with a headache and found me writing an invitation from the Maquis de Sade to a lady inviting her to come to witness with him a ritual flogging. She wasn't to know that it was to be her own. Nice touch, that, I thought- drop of the macabre.' And he actually laughed a very little quiet and contained laugh. 'Anyway, my wife found me in delectu, so to speak. Well she went mad; threw all my bits and pieces out of the door and told me to leave and never come back. I knew she could never manage without me- I do all the cooking, you see. So, after a day or so, here, in this little resort, so to speak, I would go back, cook her a cassoulet or a bourguignon, her favourites, and things would go on just as before the row. But, you know, I still couldn't resist the temptation and the challenge of sending her a concocted invitation-to come and help judge the Chelsea Flower Show or write and tell her that she'd been selected on a random draw to spend a weekend with some pop star at his private resort in the Virgin Islands. That was safe as she absolutely loathes anything connected with pop music or pop stars.'

Sidney listened with growing disbelief; was he being subjected to a hoax? Mr Talbot's deadly serious expression could surely not be the mask for a practical joker's devious machination, could it? Sidney knew it was now time to ask, 'When you had to leave last week, was it because of another of your invitations?'

'Ah, I rather imagined that I saw the curtains move in your house when I was cast out. Yes, since you ask. It was as a result of an uncontrollable urge to concoct an invitation to the Palace. My wife is absolutely obsessed with the Royal Family. Knowing that thousands of people were being selected at random to attend a concert in the grounds of Buckingham Palace, I gave my best attention to this one, but ruined everything by being too ambitious. She'd accepted as genuine the invitation to attend the first night of the Jubilee celebrations- a Prom-serious music, not the pop people who did their worst on the second day. It was wonderful. I had won hands down on this one, I thought; she'd been tricked entirely by a forgery. Well it helped that she had, in fact, actually written to the powers that be who handle these things for the Palace but it appeared that she had not been lucky, so far, no ticket, then, suddenly, my special invitation arrived through the letterbox; I had made her dream come true and for a while she was blissfully happy. She even showed her joy in a most intimate way-something she hadn't offered me for many years. It was a pleasant surprise. Why, oh why could I not leave it at that? I 've heard that gamblers always suffer their biggest losses after making their greatest gain. So it was with me.

'What did you do this time?' Sidney had to ask.

'Yes, what did I do indeed but go out, get a little drunk, come home and set about concocting the "Addendum" to the first "Royal " invitation to the Prom. I sweated over the wording and presentation; did a lot of research. All must appear absolutely authentic if it were to stand a chance of fooling her. Then something came over me and I went over the top. Look, I'll show you. I kept the first draft.'

Like a writer who cannot bring himself to tear up the opening chapter of his first attempt at a novel, my neighbour had hung on to his chef d'oeuvre. Sidney took the piece of paper, put on his glasses and read. The paper was of very high quality, there was a royal crest at the top. The wording at first rang absolutely true. Where was the flaw?

....."whereas Her Majesty, after giving careful consideration to the unique nature of the event, wishes to let it be known that, as a special mark of their appreciation of what she has done over the fifty years of her reign, all those who received the invitation to the promenade concert shall attempt if at all possible, to be accompanied by a corgi dog and that dog should be of a colour as near as possible to the colour code on the reverse side of this addendum. It is further suggested that the colour coding of the dog should also be the same colour as that worn by the lady attending, that is; the hat, preferably large, the scarf, gloves, dress, shoes and accessories should be of the same colour as the dog. The reason for this will become apparent on the day of the concert. Should the exact colour be difficult to obtain, then Her Majesty has commissioned that that a special dog-friendly and harmless dye be available in larger pet shops. To obviate the likelihood of the colours of the dog not being fast by the day of the concert, it is suggested that the dog be immersed in the dye at least two days prior to attendance at the Palace.. You will note that your seat is numbered and you, together with your corgi, if brought, will make up part of the RED area, other areas being white or blue which together shall make up the pattern of the UNION JACK when filmed for television from above."

It was marvellous. Mr Talbot and Sidney burst into a giggle and then gave way to paroxysms of laughter so that they could barely remain on the narrow seat of the shelter. When, at last, they had recovered, Sidney asked what had gone wrong.

' Well I had noticed certain furtive signs in my wife's behaviour. She hates dogs of any sort, yet I discovered a book on Dog Management behind one of the cushions. It seemed that she had asked in the pet shop nearest her office for the special red dog dye that the Queen had ordered as she was going to take a dog to the Palace. The shop proprietor had become suspicious- he'd heard that an attempt might be made to sabotage the Jubilee celebrations and he had therefore informed the police. The police had visited my wife's office, seen her Head of Department on the grounds that they had good reason to believe on information received, that my wife was a terrorist who intended harm to the Queen. She had been sent home pending a full investigation and also a psychiatric report on her sanity after she had protested that she'd been specially requested by the Palace to get a corgi, if she had not already possessed one, have the dog dyed red and take it to the Palace to figure centrally in the Jubilee celebrations.

As a penance, Mr Talbot told me, when the whole embarrassing business had been cleared up with the police and put down as one of her eccentric friend's eccentric jokes, she was then prepared to allow me to return to their joint home with the proviso that Mr Talbot learn how to cook Chinese food as she was thinking of requesting a transfer to the Oriental branch of the Inland Revenue.

⤳ **The Hamlet Syndrome** ⤳

A sort of fairy tale of our times

And if he went out, there would still be the decisions; inevitably, the hated decisions. It was essential to the maintenance of his tender equilibrium that he should avoid all decisions. He wanted to go out, out of the restriction and refuge of his little house, perhaps to visit a restaurant - he loved the atmosphere, the attention, the change from his unvarying diet, but restaurants meant menus, decisions; fish , which fish? Or meat; what meat? Or pasta or ..? There were so many ways to prepare everything ; even the humble potato could spell disaster. Should they be mashed, roasted, croquettes, duchesse, boulanger, sautéed, fried or just simply and boringly boiled? Their versatility was devious and unsettling. Puddings, however, for Max, could sometimes pose a worse threat as they were trundled in; three tiers, each described in confectioner's precise detail by the waiter who looked enquiringly after each announcement and then again, with sharper gaze when the catalogue was done. Max had to fight down the growing, uncontrollable hysteria which threatened to overwhelm him and shame him in the public dining room. Mercifully, someone else normally decided on the wine for otherwise he would most assuredly be lost.

It was fortunate for Max that he could work from home and that is where he stayed as far as possible; safe inside; safe from the multifarious snares of choice; the sloughs of vacillation. He found comfort in sympathetic poetry; Eliott had known his anguish too as Prufrock showed; "Time for you and time for me and time for a thousand decisions and revisions". Perhaps he was not entirely alone in his plight.

At eleven precisely he made his coffee and took one biscuit from the box of unassorted, plain biscuits. They were predictable, known entities; sure and certain stepping stones to the ordered and regimented world into which he craved admission.

Last week's expedition into the wide world outside had cost him dear; he had not learnt his lesson. The day had looked inviting. He would take a walk. No stressful decision here you might imagine. He had spun his "Choices" coin – heads left, tails right. Then at the door, he hesitated; it might rain. Should he take his umbrella and be inconvenienced if it did not rain or should he stride out unencumbered and risk a soaking? He looked up at the inscrutable sky. He should take his umbrella, but there was no umbrella in its accustomed place in the stand. Then he remembered, he had left his umbrella in the library when he went to collect the single book he had ordered after reading an enthusiastic revue in the paper,

Library visits never entailed aimless browsing for Max; far too much choice, He always ordered his books beforehand. His umbrella was not by the door of the library when he came to leave. Someone had taken it as it was now raining. Now he must make a decision about its replacement. Should he buy a cheap one, the loss of which would matter less, but it would be sure to fail in a downpour or an expensive one; reliable but more attractive to the callous umbrella thief? Had he agonised like this when he bought the last umbrella? No, he remembered that he had found it in the library. It had been in the same place for some weeks so the owner was either indifferent to its fate or, perhaps, dead. He had noticed the high average age of most of the library frequenters. He had held out the hand of friendship to the abandoned appendage and had put it through its paces that day as it had started to drizzle when he finally left the library. The absence of the umbrella had taken its toll of him and after he felt quite unfit for a walk. He had taken three aspirins before lying down until the trembling stopped.

He sometimes wished that he believed in some strong and supportive religion so that he might kneel and seek for guidance. The words would bring him great comfort he had no doubt. "Compassed about, as we are, by a manifold and intrusive variety of every sort, give us, O Lord. To see our course clearly, our duty plainly, so that we, being delivered from the assaults and afflictions of cursed decision; the raging seas of manifold alternatives, might pass our days untroubled and at peace until our busy lives are silent and we are ,at last, at rest.."

Was there never to be a remission for him from the need for decisions? It was the day for his visit to the local shop to purchase some basic essentials for his uncomplicated life. He would buy milk, butter, eggs and bread; surely a straightforward business, you might imagine. He never went near supermarkets with their serried rank upon rank of alternatives to every single commodity. The dreadful memory of his one visit to such a place would sometimes wake him screaming from his sleep. He had succumbed to curiosity about the vast windowless building that had mushroomed up in the town. He had been, in fact, amongst the first to enter through the wide, revolving doors. Inside he had been passed a trolley and he had set off along the maze of aisles piled high with an unimaginable selection of tins, boxes cartons, packets, jars, heaps of vegetables and fruit, counters crammed with dozens of cheeses, prepared meals, cold meats, fish of all sorts; an endless and utterly alarming cornucopia. He had clenched his fists and tried to resist the siren calls from every direction and that imperious voice thumping in his head;DECIDE.

He had escaped from the frozen food section only lightly scathed; a packet of frozen lobster tails, but then he had been caught up in the whirlpool of the biscuit section. He knew of old his weakness for nibbles and to some extent had come to terms with their narcotic compulsions over the years. But the sheer dimensions of the section devoted to such things made him gasp. He tried to push on with his trolley, like Scott floundering through the driving snow behind his sledge, but then he stopped and began to fill it with one of each of the farinaceous creations in their seductive boxes. He had sunk at last to the floor, one hand still clinging to the overfilled trolley. He had given out a series of foghorn exhalations; his prolonged and awesome wails of despair until he lost consciousness.

The management had been as understanding as it could. It had been unfortunate that there had been so many people there, drawn by the attraction of the pop star who was to open the store officially at midday. The ambulance men, the two young policemen and a lady vicar had all wished to be seen doing their duty, for the television cameras might be recording the events for the regional news programme that evening.

On his release from hospital two days later he found a bill at home from the supermarket for two packets of frozen lobster tails which, becoming unfrozen, could not be returned to the shelves as the eighty seven boxes of biscuits and nibbles had been.

All that had been two years ago. Now he knew his limitations and had avoided all supermarkets and large stores since that day. The sole village shop looked after his food purchases well enough. It was run by an elderly widow who, out of whim or idleness, had made no changes in the shop for thirty years.

Max reached the shop without incident. The bell above the door clattered as he entered and the shambling figure of the old shopkeeper appeared behind the counter. In that time he might have snatched up a handful of the chocolate bars from the top of the glass display case on the counter. Instead he merely observed the tins of cat food, the one packet of tea and the box of simple biscuits on the shelf.

'Yes?' the shopkeeper enquired at last.

'Just a packet of the biscuits and half a dozen eggs please', he said.

What a relief it was to say "the" biscuits- only one type being stocked.

As he was leaving the shop with his simple purchases, a stunningly beautiful woman pushed open the door and waited beside him for the shopkeeper to return, but, her sales complete, the widow had returned to the dim backroom to be with her cats.

'Is there anyone there do you think?' the lady asked.

'Is there anyone there?' Max repeated then added, 'But no one descended to the traveller.'

The beautiful lady continued the well-known lines, 'No head from the leaf-fringed sill leaned over and looked into his grey eyes, where he stood perplexed and still.'

'Well your eyes are certainly not grey', Max said, as he took in the wonder of her perfect face. 'They are a most interesting blue-green.' The lady moved closer to Max and looked at his eyes now.

'Brown for faithfulness, and devotion too, I seem to remember', she said. From somewhere Max found the strength to meet and return the lady's intoxicating gaze. He wanted to put out his hands to her, to touch that gentle face and run his fingers through her hair. Auburn hair had always had an infinite effect upon him. He was lost; sinking under her spell and longing for nothing in the world but to be able to go on feeding his eyes upon this vision.

The spell was suddenly broken by the interrogatory croak of the shopkeeper who had appeared from the back room. Max heard the magical lady ask if skimmed milk was available, only to be told, in a tone which showed her contempt for all things in any way "fancy," that only ordinary plain milk was kept in a tone which showed her contempt for all things in any way, "fancy". And there was none left now as it was afternoon.

Max held the door for her and they left together. How natural it suddenly seemed to be talking to the lady. Max felt more at ease and relaxed than he could remember being at any time in his life. They walked slowly, side by side, along the tree-edged pavement.

'I suppose everybody has asked the same question about De La Mere's dear old poem,' Max suggested.

'And they'd want to know what was the word he kept,' the lady added, smiling at Max.

'He was probably bringing a late delivery of skimmed milk, smoked oysters, scouring cloths, large rodent traps and pumpernickel, whatever that is, to the little shop we've just left. It would have been kept, a century ago, by the old woman's great great grandmother and she didn't have time for any commercial travellers knocking so late at her door.'

'Of course, "The Traveller". The lady took up Max's fantasy much to his delight.

'My aunt kept a shop on the corner once and she'd embarrass me as a girl, by shooing out the "commercials", as she called them. 'I've no time for them; stopping me serving.' She'd say. I always felt so sorry for them having to trudge round with a box of samples of new products and having to wait at the door and be so nice to the shopkeeper just to get an order for some washing powder or tinned food or something."

They walked on, Max wondering madly if he dare take the hand that swung so close to him, but she might feel offended at his temerity and hurry away.

Then she spoke again, 'In the shop just now, I liked your sense of humour, it reminded me so much of my brother; he had the same zany imagination; it sparks me off into fantasies as well, as you can see.'

Max managed, 'Oh, I see.'

Suddenly the lady stopped and turned to him.

'Look, why don't we go and have a cup of coffee or tea, or something – perhaps a beer, it's lunchtime after all. I know the man is supposed to ask and to make that first move or whatever, but I have a sort of feeling that you'd prefer it this way. Am I right?' Her eyebrows rose in question above those spell-binding eyes.

'Don't ask me to decide, please,' he said.

Were there always to be decisions? In everything, everywhere? What if he had one of his turns like in the supermarket?

'I'd like to do that. You decide; I hate having to make up my mind, about anything, anything at all, you see. It's very difficult.' There, he'd said it; his nasty little secret was out and he felt suddenly free and at peace.

'I would like to talk with you some more; to see more of you,' he stammered out, blushing a little at the implications of that phrase. She obviously read his thoughts and smiled,

'I think it would be good for us to', she paused for emphasis, 'to see more of each other. I think we could have much to share. You don't have to decide anything at all if you don't want to. I like making decisions; it's my job, I do it every day and I like doing it. We'll go and have a cup of coffee; I know a place where they do really good espresso. There's nothing for you to decide; let's just go.'

Max's thoughts went wild; a future of no decision making ever again! Such things only seemed possible in his wildest daydreams, right outside the harsh world of cold reality. And yet perhaps sometimes wildest dreams did come true. He took her hand at last. He did not tell her what had just come into his head; he didn't really feel that he would have any problems in deciding, "For richer, for poorer, for better or worse, in sickness and in health". He would be very glad to be quite unambiguous and merely say, if it ever came to that moment, "With all my worldly goods I thee endow."

And he did, two months later and there were no two ways about it; they lived happily ever after.

The Last Meeting

Gerald propped the invitation to his old school's annual reunion against the coffee jug and peered at it again. This year it would be twenty five years since he had left the school- perhaps an auspicious anniversary? So this time, being free on the date appointed, he decided to go. The names of those who had already agreed to go were printed inside and and he ran his eye over them; A.D. Brown, G.S. Brown, G.J.

Coulter, D.R Denby, T. Elsworthy, M. Elton, F.F. Fotheringay. Gerald stopped at the last name, smiled, then said the name aloud, "F.F. Fotheringay." He pronounced the name slowly, almost in a whisper, savouring the sound and with the same formality as one might intone, " Abracadabra" and then wait expectantly. Suddenly a very clear picture flashed across his mind's eye. He shook his head, smiled again and .repeated loudly and forthrightly, "F.F. Fotheringay." And then added, "Good God, F.F. Fotheringay". The picture which had come back to him. still remained, the details standing out in a striking way; he was back in the assembly hall of his old school over thirty years before.

Dr Benthal, the Headmaster, was standing in the centre of the stage, his long academic gown accentuating his height. He was at the dramatic zenith of one of his notorious tirades which he so much enjoyed conducting.

'Unless the boy, or boys responsible for this outrage comes forward and confesses to his crime, you will all, ALL, stay here. There will be no half term leave and no boy will be allowed to return to his home for any reason whatsoever. Saturday's match against Radleigh will be cancelled and the prefects will supervise an hour's detention every day after school for every boy. I do not intend to stand for this sort of behaviour, is that quite understood? Wilful and mindless destruction of school property is a very serious offence indeed and one which affects us all.'

Gerald remembered so very clearly now how much he had hated and feared that voice; its deep tones, its sarcastic relish and the way that it always ended on a minor key. The silence after the outburst was total and electric. No boy dared move or even clear his throat. Gerald had felt the sweat oozing in his palms and under his arms. He must not move a muscle nor take his eyes from the gowned figure on the stage.

'I'm waiting! The boy or boys WILL come forward. You others, who know who is responsible, WILL force him to come forward, now, NOW!'

The last words hung echoing in the large hall. The tension was tangible, visible almost. Gerald felt that at any moment he would have to scream or faint or open his bowels. Something must happen. And it did.

From the back of the hall, surfing the silence and splitting it apart came a great and wonderful rolling peal of manic laughter, deep, yet rising to a crescendo and ending in a demented vibrant gurgle. It was marvellous: a joyous bubbling hypnotic outburst which instantly snapped the intolerable tension. A second, more emphatic, more outrageous peal followed.. Gerald felt the muscles in his face relaxing. He shifted his numbed feet as did all the boys about him. And then a third great roll of laughter blossomed upwards. Other laughs from all parts of the hall joined in to create a mighty and awesome paean. Some merely squeaked in an insane wail, others roared out exuberantly in triumphant and utter dismissal of the previously intolerable strain. Finally every boy in the school, juniors as well as seniors, prefects in their red gowns, every member of staff present, even Edwards, the living dead, who presumed to teach History, was caught up and swept along in the tide. . The trickles became streams, the streams, rivers, the rivers a flood and then the flood merged into one enormous and enveloping tidal wave, breaking and breaking, again and again. Mingled in the torrential chorus of freedom there could be heard voices singing and piercing screams and then finally, the stamping of feet; five hundred feet, a thousand feet. Emotions, pent up for so long, rioted; hands clapped and the roof of the great hall reverberated. The Headmaster, a lone figure on the stage, had become an absurd diminutive puppet, shaking his fists and shouting soundlessly, his face aflame with rage, but all his words were lost, he was totally powerless against the living wall of laughter. He gave up shouting and waving his arms about and stamped from the stage, his gown billowing bathetically after him.

And with his departure, his routing, the sun burst out after a sky blackening storm, after a wild clashing of thunder in a night of driving rain and howling winds.. Gerald danced with joy. All those around him danced with joy as well. A single boy's infectious laugh had done it; had destroyed the spell forever and brought them forth out of captivity. Now they were free; the future was theirs and they would never again allow themselves to be held in such bondage. Those who had been standing near the saviour might have be aware of who it was that had conjured up that laugh, but they said nothing. In the days that followed there was great speculation, but no certainty. The Headmaster never alluded to the subject, nor felt equal to investigating the matter in any way lest he should once again be destroyed by that strange inhuman force; the power, the overwhelming power of a single laugh used as an invincible weapon of war.

At the time of that apocalypse Gerald had been only a first former. As he progressed through the classes until his final year in the Upper Sixth, he heard one name frequently mentioned, that name was F.F. Fotheringay. An unspoken taboo prevented anyone from actually stating that he knew that it was F.F. Fothergay who had been responsible for that laugh and the overthrowing of a tyrant, but somehow the legend became firmly established; F.F. Fotheringay was their saviour. The name was always pronounced in a reverential whisper. It was an incantation. Gerald himself was too young to have come into contact with the senior, for it must have been a senior, who bore that illustrious name. Perhaps that senior had left school in the very year of his deification, known personally only to his immediate contemporaries

And now, after all these years, after so many chances and changes in his life, Gerald was going to attend a dinner at which the legendary figure from his far away schooldays was to be present. At last he would be able to look that god in the face, maybe even shake his hand, raise his glass in a loyal toast to F.F. Fotheringay's glorious past and his victory over a dragon.

Two weeks later Gerald was unpacking his dinner jacket in one of the rooms in the Cambridge college where his old school reunions were held. He picked up the formal menu and looked at the names printed on the back on the seating plan.. His own was there-G.D.P. Grant. It would be near the F's and , of course, F.F. Fotheringay as the plan was arranged alphabetically rather than in order of seniority. He felt an almost sexual tangle of excitement at the idea of being, at last actually in the same room and close enough to touch the man he had worshipped for so long. What glorious career must inevitably been F.F. Fotheringay's right, his birthright, a right won for him in his schooldays by a laugh, a laugh which had set the downtrodden and despondent gloriously and permanently free.

Sherry was being served in the common room before dinner and men were gathered in year groups. Here was the usual back slapping, joking and laughter. Gerald sidestepped the stewards when the sherry was being handed out and headed for the hall as though on an urgent mission to check a last minute detail and so be certain that all was well and entirely as it should be for such an important dinner to be graced by such an illustrious guest. He found his row; the name cards were indeed in alphabetical order and F. F. Fotheringay's name place was immediately opposite to the one that marked Gerald's own place.

The two sherries that Gerald drank when he returned to the common room were not the cause of his excitement, although they might have increased it . His tension was born entirely out of an unrestrainable joy of anticipation.

A gong sounded hollowly. They left their empty sherry glasses and in groups or singly made their way through the high double doors into the dining hall of the noble and ancient college. As they neared the white table clothed refectory tables on which fine silver gleamed, flower decorations adorned and college crested plates twinkled between stiffly starched napkins and patient, helpful glasses, each man peered about to find his name card and his place.. Gerald deliberately delayed the moment of looking about him. He sat and stared directly downwards at the cutlery and other tools for dining. He was intent only on the details of his own place. Then when he considered that all the guests would by now have found their appointed places, he looked up so that he might have his long awaited first view of F.F. Fotheringay, in his place opposite to him. The place was empty; no one was seated facing the name card of F.F. Fotheringay. Gerald's heart seemed to stop. Something had gone terribly wrong; a train was late, trains were frequently late; a car had broken down; places to park near Cambridge colleges were scarce and hard to find for a late comer struggling not to miss an important engagement.

The gong sounded for grace. The dinner had begun. They all stood and they muttered the suddenly remembered Latin grace from their schooldays. They say down again and the buzz of conversation resumed. Gerald's neighbour on his left nudged him and spoke,

'I say, my dear chap, are you all right? You look as though you'd seen a ghost.'

'I'm all right, thanks,'Gerald managed to reply.

'Haven't seen you at one of these do's before,' the man continued.

'That's because I've never been to one before; lost track of the school, only recently joined the Old Boys' Club and sent them my address. It's all new to me.' The neighbour nodded in understanding.

'I thought as much. Just now you were staring at F.F. Fothergay's place as though you thought he might be here.'

' Yes, I did. I do.' Gerald defended.

'I've been coming to every reunion diner for the last twenty five years and F.F. Fotheringay has never once appeared. Of course a place is always laid for him, it's tradition, but he never comes.'

'Not surprising, is it?' said the man on Gerald's other side. 'I understand he was one of the first commissioned young officers to fall leading his men over the top at the Somme.' Another further down the table leant forward and joined in,

' He was never there. He went into politics. With that laugh of his he was directly responsible for the sudden resignation of two Prime Ministers and caused several others to leave politics early and disillusioned.'

'I'd heard he made a pretty good thing out of being paid handsomely not to attend first nights of new plays at the West End.-that laugh of his- no play, or actor either- could survive a F.F. Fothergay "Special" '

An older man who had been listening put down his soup spoon and asserted, ' I taught at the school for ten years , It would have been after your time, of course, but I heard all about the story of the laugh and the man credited with it. I looked up the school records. No such person as F.F. Fotheringay has ever attended Bartlett's. That is a fact.'

The soup bowls were cleared, the glasses recharged and the dinner progressed in the ordered and formal manner that all such dinners in the older universities progress; with decorum, taste, good humour and much reminiscence and laughter over the port and cigars. An ancient gentleman was helped to his feet to round off the evening with the traditional and totally inaudible after dinner speech. The party was over.

As Gerald was putting on his coat in the lobby, he met his dinner partner from the left side again.

'Coming next year, old Chap, now that you've finally found us?'

'Can't say at this stage,' Gerald replied. But he was quite certain that he would never again attend another of the reunion dinners of the old school and from the bottom of his heart, he wished that he had not attended this one.

 It had begun to rain outside, lightly at first and then with increasing force and penetration as he walked back to his college room for the night, but Gerald was unconcerned. He left the college early next morning and without bothering to wait for his breakfast or to bid farewell to any of his now forgotten schoolmates.

In good hands

Most of young Frobisher's early days had been spent at boarding schools so women had figured very little in his life except, that is, for the school matron, who was the constant preoccupation of his waking and also his dreaming hours. His parents lived and worked abroad in a remote and inhospitable part of the world, so lacking grandparents, aunts or uncles or even friends with families in England, he often had to stay at school in the holidays as well as during term and this may well explain the events I shall now relate.

'I don't like the sound of that cough, Young Frobisher,' his housemaster had stated on hearing Frobisher's carefully rehearsed graveyard cough. He had copied the opening wheezing from his memories of his late grandfather, a very heavy smoker. That alarming overture was immediately followed by the main theme stated in two shrill staccato notes on a falling minor key. The cough was one of Frobisher's best impressions and perfecting it had occupied his creative energies far more exhaustively that the essay on "Patriotism not being enough" that old Morrison had set his History class for their weekend homework.

Young Frobisher gave a reprise of his first and inspired effort, but although the connoisseur might have considered the second cough lacked something of the original's militant tristesse, yet its more assured timbre had an epiphanic resolution to it reminiscent of the "Fate" theme in Berlioz's Symphony Phantastique. The finer points of the creation were not lost on Mr Carter who at once dismissed Young Frobisher to the school's sick bay.

Young Frobisher mentally rubbed his hands. He was in the habit of doing a great number of unlikely things mentally and that was as well since he could count on a flogging, at least if his schoolmasters were ever to learn the nature of his many depraved fantasies. On this occasion he was rubbing his hands at the thought of being sent to the sick bay there to be entrusted to the firm and competent hands of Miss Sweet, the school matron.

Miss Emily Sweet had joined the school as Matron at the same time as Young Frobisher had become a "Junior Bug" and one of the boarders in Scott House. That was two years ago now. Since that time our hero had matured fast and was now dangerously susceptible to the siren calls that Matron beamed out to all those watching and thinking fifteen year olds whenever they found themselves in the same room as that buxom young lady.

Young Frobisher had been the first to prefix the adjective, "buxom" to the youthful matron. He had looked it up in the dictionary when he had encountered it in "Tom Jones", Fielding's mind opening novel. "Buxom wenches" seemed to crop up with considerable frequency in the pages of that remarkable account of youthful dalliance. The definition given for buxom was, "Plump, comely, willing, espec. of women." It might have been coined for the generous and lascivious moulding of the delightful Miss Sweet, the school's new Matron.

Young Frobisher protested that his cough was 'really nothing at all, sir,' then, as though powerless in its malign grasp, he gave another, and definitive chesty roar and gurgle, doubling over in terminal agonies until his hair brushed the floor. There was no further argument; to the matron he must report without delay.

The sick room was not normally heated unless one of the three beds was occupied by a patient. Young Frobisher waited in the little dispensary after having rung Matron's bell. He heard her approaching; her crisply starched uniform's silken sibilance subtly heralding the blessed presence. Young Frobisher trembled with inner surges of electricity.

'Let's see, it's Young Frobisher, isn't it?' matron stated as she saw the boy standing patiently, waiting in her little room.

'Fraid so, Matron. Mr Carter said he didn't like the sound of my cough.'

'Are there coughs which your Mr Carter does like the sound of, I wonder,' quipped Miss Sweet. Young Frobisher laughed and felt warmly conspiratorial at sharing a joke at a Master's expense.

'I'll put a hot water bottle in your bed and turn on the heating. You can undress and get into bed in a few minutes when the room and the bed have had a chance to warm up a bit,' matron promised and smiled at the boy.

'What about pyjamas?' Young Frobisher asked modestly.

Matron turned at the door and said, 'We'll see about them in good time. There's always a pair kept in that drawer for emergencies, but they may not fit you.'

When matron had swept out, Frobisher opened the drawer and tried the pyjamas. They were absurdly small. Matron returned with the hot water bottle and told Frobisher to get into bed in his underwear since the pyjamas wouldn't fit. She said she would be back shortly, when he was in bed.

The sheets were cold and smelt of starch. He pushed the hot water bottle round the bed to spread its warmth, then tucked it under his toes and waited for Miss Sweet's return. Outside he could hear the distant sounds of the school's busy life; running feet, a boy shouting, 'Blake, you crud, I'll get you for that', a bell, then more running. A door slammed somewhere.

Young Frobisher lay back on his pillow and smiled to think how clever he had been to get away from all that, but he particularly thought about matron; her enveloping, containing, enfolding uniform; her long dark hair so strictly, so sleekly forced into neat coils round her head, her tapering fingers and carefully curved fingernails, her eyes, her dear warm soft calming eyes. He closed his own and let the picture of matron fill his mind and draw him into the fantasy that had dominated his very being and had made his body tingle in an exciting frightening yet delicious way. He felt his manhood strongly, insistently stirred and gave himself over to his favourite day dream and the magic of the tantalizing images which surged before his inner eye, the bliss of solitude.

He heard steps outside the door; Miss Sweet was returning to see if he was alright. Then she was beside him, her cool hand stretched across his forehead. He opened his eyes and put his hands out to touch those wondrous rings of shining, silken hair.

' You feel quite hot; I hope you haven't got a fever?' she gently enquired.

'Only when I look at you, Miss Sweet, then I feel very hot and excited. I keep wanting to touch you, and to loosen the tightness of your blouse. I think you would be more comfortable without it and I would so like to help you to be more comfortable because you're a very special person to me, dear, dear, Miss Sweet.'

The young matron blushed , saying nothing but taking the boy's warm hand , she held it between her cool slender fingers, then moved his hand to the top of her taut, crisp blouse and undid that button, then the next, the next, and so on, in a dream, until she wriggled out of the blouse and let his hand then both his hands reach out to hold, pluck and stroke the white silk of her swelling cups. Then his golden lady put both hands behind her and with a quick forward thrusting, she undid the clasp so her firm young breasts were gloriously free and released, swelling into the boy's searching , stroking, working hands.

They were so soft yet so jutting, the delicate pink nipples standing out firmly from their darker, circling rings and the perfume of her sweet body rose to his senses. He could feel tears forming behind his eyes; the joy was too great; he knew he could be, could do; anything, anything at all that he liked to her; her eyes gave him that permission. Then he felt her hands sliding across the bedclothes, under the bedclothes, over his chest, downwards, downwards and then, then she was pulling down his underpants to free the pulsing young organ of his manhood. If her hands should touch him- there; circle his hidden throbbing hero with her cool, soft, long fingers. If….

In that intense moment, young Frobisher forgot every other thought; of being just a schoolboy in a sick dormitory; of being lonely, uncertain, worried about his end of term report, his low marks, his father's inevitable nagging questioning, the unceasing troubles that he seemed always to be bringing down upon himself in every lesson and with every master. He was aware only of her hand, her gentle, helping hand, moving across his thigh; a deep longing ache grew between his legs. He reached out his a hand and drew Miss Sweet's skirt up to her thighs, over the proud buttons of her suspender belt, over her shining black stockings. She sensed his intention and moved accommodatingly so that he could ease down her lace edged panties, black and stark against her generous and so incredibly white thighs. In a minute he would be able to cup his hand over her warm, hidden mount of Venus; all things were possible. He closed his eyes and trembling, gave himself up to the ecstatic anticipation of wonders to come.

Ten minutes later, when Miss Sweet opened the door of the sick dorm, she saw her young charge, seemingly fast asleep. She went over to the bed and tucked the blanket closer under his chin, for the room was still cold, the heating being slow to take its effect in the large empty room.

She knew some of the boys quite well, particularly, if, like Young Frobisher, they often came up to her little room along the corridor which she called her dispensary. It was rare that any of them had any real ailment- cuts and bruises, perhaps from the Rugby field which needed a dressing perhaps, but mostly it was for coughs and the hope of a day in bed, particularly if a Maths test was imminent. They're just children, she thought; they're missing their mother's love and attention. A sudden pang of longing seized her; she wanted to have a child of her own to love; a clear-eyed, curly headed little darling boy, perhaps as Young Frobisher must have been, and despite his broken voice and downed upper lip, he still seemed that lost little boy as he lay there so peacefully asleep . The patient gave a soft murmur and moved in the bed; he looked so unspoilt, so very innocent of all the world's corrupting forces marshalled in waiting for him all too soon, but now, he was just a dreaming, vulnerable child. She bent and brushed a gentle kiss onto his forehead before tiptoeing softly from the room.

The insistent clanging of the prep bell and the shouts from the quadrangle below woke Young Frobisher an hour later. He blinked his eyes open slowly, reluctant to return to reality from his blissful dreaming. Perhaps, perhaps if he could tell his dear, young matron about his dream, then…?

The door opened and Miss Sweet entered the room with a steaming cup on a tray.

'I've something here to make a boy with a nasty cough feel wonderful,' she said. Young Frobisher needed no convincing of the truth of her words, so tenderly spoken, but he wished with all his heart that they had not been merely applied to a steaming cup of cocoa which the lady of his dream handed him with a smile.

The Reckoning

'Spirituality, Miss James, spirituality, it's what is at the very core of this work. I do hope that you have registered that.. '

'I've read the book three times, Dr Todd. I just didn't find any of your spirituality. To be honest, I can't say that I found any sense or plot or order in it; things just seem to happen; you don't find out why or how; it's just a lot of confusion.. Is it too late for me to choose one of the other options from the book list?'

He closed his eyes very deliberately then slowly opened them again She was still there. He picked up a pencil and then stared out of the window. The plump, dark clouds had no message for him. He looked down at his desk; his notepad had only one line of writing-"Miss James, 11o'clock. Dear God!" The Almighty had not intervened. Miss James had arrived exactly on time. Now she was blinking rapidly , head slightly tilted back, biro poised. She was desperate to know if there was any escape for her from the death sentence to which that the prescribed text for study had consigned her in the Modern European Novels paper.

'But, Miss James, you rejected all the other English or American authors, even Fitgerald, surely so accessible? But Lawrence, Lawrence! Almost "Women's Own "stuff by now but you even rejected Powys! Surely the most ordered and sensible of the truly English moderns; dear wholesome Powys'. She gave a sort of grunt. ' and the Europeans; Borges, Eco, spicy old Genet'. His student snorted her disgust at the last name.

'Why can't they put on people like Margaret Drabble, Catherine Cookson, Ruth Rendall; stuff you can understand; stuff that's got a plot and ordinary human beings in it, doing ordinary human things.'

'Like kissing and killing, cuddling and cooking!' He suggested. 'If we must have the Virago press mob, why not Virginia Woolf, Isabel Allende,Joanna Trollop, Delia Smith as well, God knows, she's best selling even if she doesn't write novels?'

'You don't like me, do you, Dr Todd? You think I shouldn't be here, don't you? You always use words I don't understand, you do it on purpose to make me feel silly, don't you? Well I'm going to write in a complaint about you-you're prejudiced against women, that's what it is, might be you're queer and don't want women in your university. You just want men; big rugby players with lots of muscle, musicians with long fingers , droopy looks, and sad, little boy eyes. I know your sort. You've never tried to look at my legs or my breasts, that shows you're one of them, and you're always looking out of the window, thinking about your boy friends, wishing I was one of your male students that you could lean over as they're reading their essay, play squash or whatever with them to get a bit of "bonding", I've read about that. I put on my new perfume, " Crime Passionelle", and I spent all the morning blow waving my hair for you,' and you don't even give me a look, I bet you didn't even notice my false eyelashes today- just for you, and you don't bloody care!"

Tears were just round the corner; tears of rage not disappointment.

Dr Todd breathed very slowly; IN, two three, four, five six, seven; OUT; two, three, four, five, six ,seven.

He felt in the pocket of his jacket for the pills he had been prescribed for such moments as this. The packet felt flaccid and emphatically empty; stress that week had depleted his emergency reserves.

'Miss James', he pronounced.

'Trace. Can't you call me? Trace, that's what my friends call me.' He stared at his desk.

'I see from your details in my register that your forenames are; "Prudence, Cheryl ", Tracy or even ',he closed his eyes again to blot it out; "Trace" just doesn't figure on the list. It's all I have to go on. If all my students wanted me to call them by names they invent for themselves, where would we be, Eh? Where would we all be?'

'I tell you where we could be, Dr Todd-" Toddy" " Tod –Tod". We could be down at that little pub by the river, the one with the old beams and that. I could be drinking a nice long, cool Double vodka and Bacardi or three and you could have a James Bond-shaken not stirred thing . You could be proving to me that you're all man, that you know about real life, not just life in books ,not all this sex in the head rubbish, we could be making it, know what I mean?'

She had risen from her chair, thrown her notepad and books down and was standing, legs apart, in front of his desk, jutting out her remarkable pointed breasts under his wine tinted nose.

'I think that we can say that this tutorial is now at an end; no purpose is to be served by prolonging it. I must ask you to leave, Miss James. I shall try to expunge from my memory all that you said in your anger. Ill advised, ill advised,. I'm not a vindictive person, but you will appreciate that in the interests of all concerned, I shall make application for you to be transferred to another tutor for the modern Literature paper. Mr. Endicott has just joined the Department and he might well be more in tune with your expectations of the behaviour of a subject supervisor, but I have no way of knowing that. Please leave. Now!'

His trial was not to be ended so neatly She bent her head forward ,trained her eyes on him in a half closed, meaningful way and breathed down her nose at the same time making rumbling noise deep in her throat. Charlie, her latest, had found this a fittingly stimulating prelude to their afternoons of sex in his room.

Todd must do something.

'Would it be indiscreet to ask, Miss James". She butted in with an insistent, 'It's Trace, please.' He ignored her.

'To ask you why you have come to this university and what you can possibly hope to achieve here?'

'OK, I'll tell you,' she said, abandoning her sexual semiology exercise for the moment and breathing normally. ' I came here to get as much sex as I could, to get a student grant to keep me in fags and to get a bit of reading done in peace. I like reading, but not all that guff you expect me to wade through. I 'm young, I want a good time. I'm going to be unemployed when I leave here so why can't I enjoy myself. Get off my back.'

'But you must have had some understanding and even appreciation of the books you studied for your A Level to get here, surely?' He asked in amazement.

'No. If you must know, I didn't take the bloody exams. Girl I know took them for me, used my name; there's a lot of people at a poly and they can't check on everyone. So I'm here and I really, really want to talk about some of the books I like-know what I mean?'

One indisputable fact stared Todd in the face; no one except the pupil in front of him had opted for his course on Modern European Literature that year If he lost his one pupil, he could be faced with redundancy. The European Literature course itself, already under subscribed, might very well be threatened; Literature as a serious field of study in this small university could become obsolete. Only one course was open to him.

'Miss James...er Trace.' She acknowledged his concession smugly. 'There is an alternative to studying set texts, you have the choice of submitting your own manuscript, provided it illustrates your familiarity with the current styles in European writing.'

'You mean I could write my own novel and that would do?'

'That's exactly what I mean, Miss...er Trace, I could even help you.'

'I don't need no help, Mr. Toddy, I can get all I want to write out of my head. How's this for starters?;

"Bloody hell, another sodding fuck up", Tina shouted to her mate at the checkout till and she was getting no sympathy from the Saturday morning queue. "Young woman, if you persist in using that sort of language, I shall never come into this shop again." "Great! Sod off," shouted Tina."'

' Howdya like it? Gets to it at once, like, don't yer think?'

Todd blinked, swallowed twice and then said in a strained voice, ' It certainly shows you have a versatile grasp of the current vernacular; it makes a definite statement from the outset. Yes, I definitely found it, er, arresting. With a little tidying up, I think we can say that we've made a start. We could even, when it's finished, of course, submit it as a true example of the contemporary genre.'

'Brill. You're moving into the present century, Toddy. Let's get down to that pub for a bit of "Local colour"- know what I mean?' I've always fancied writing a novel. I'll bring you the first chapters next week '

' I shall await that event with barely bated breath,' Todd remarked acidly. But she was already opening the door to leave.

At the next tutorial Trace turned up with a business-like briefcase which she placed carefully on the floor and from which she quickly withdrew quite a number of typed pages and held them out to Todd. He was amazed. He had expected never to see her again after their last meeting, certainly not to be confronted with an actual piece of work in progress.

'I congratulate you, Trace. You must leave this with me- you have copies, of course?'

'Well I wasn't going to take a chance of you leaving it in a bus, was I ? Any case, I need to know where I'm at; need a copy so I can progress from the last bit. That's usual, I expect.'

'Absolutely normal. I congratulate you on your sensible and practical approach. Leave it with me. I'll see you next week, then.'

The success of "The Reckoning" was phenomenal. As a hardback it topped the sales of the Booker that year. Todd was congratulated on having produced a best selling novelist whilst she was still a student. He had dutifully read each chapter as it was completed but had determinedly refrained from making any uncomplimentary remarks whatsoever. He had kept the completed pages and then made his decision; he would write the novel himself and submit it as the work of his pupil. A friend of his, a past pupil, had obliged him by publishing the completed book As he guessed, Trace never bothered to reread any of her manuscript and therefore had not read the final version.

Now, on the day of the award, he was slumped in the furthest chair from the presenters' table and Trace was making her acceptance speech.

'I just want to say that my success with, "The Reckoning", my first, and so far, my only novel is all thanks to my teacher, Dr Sidney Todd. It was him that got me started on the writing, before that I was just getting bogged down in all the stuff I had to read- heavy! You would not believe how deadly it was, but he said I could have a go at a novel and he even sent it off to this competition. And now I've won!'

Then there were photographs, more champagne was splashed into glasses and everyone was wanting to give her a hug or shaker her hand. Todd, found it all too much. He tried to blot it all out with glasses of wine from the passing trays. His Pygmalion had turned into a Medusa and was blighting his whole life.. What on earth had made him suggest to her that she might write a novel? As a result of her success, his classes were hopelessly oversubscribed and it seemed that every student who opted for the Modern European Literature paper wanted to do the "Free Choice" and then submit it as a novel instead of studying the list of Todd's favourite books which over the years that he had taught them, he knew so well that he could quote from them easily by heart and never needed to prepare or update his tutorial material. He could do it in his sleep, he often boasted and for years he had been doing just that; teaching his ever decreasing number of pupils as though in a dream. His life had been wonderfully leisurely, his work undemanding and he had been able to spend his lunchtimes and his evenings drinking wine and being made a fuss of. He was a *Character* and licensed to do as much or as luittle as he pleased. He had always elected for the latter. Now he was faced with the ghastly prospect of having to advise, listen to and generally spoon -feed God knows how many ghastly students who were all hoping to follow Trace's example. Of course he could not admit to the university powers that be that the novel that had won Trace her prize was his work. She had left her scruffy papers with him and he had reshaped them, metamorphosed them and blown life into the dreadful little story she had produced as her opus. If Trace had simply sent in her own stuff and been given the fail mark that it deserved, all this would never have happened, but he hadn't let her do that, he had told her that she could even try for one of the literary prizes open to new young writers. He would help her, he'd said And she had won! Except, of course, that he had won; his travesty of a novel , written in the pub, mostly, and certainly not soberly, had been judges worthy of a , no *the* prize. 'It's a mad, mad world, my masters' he kept repeating to himself.

. At the end of Trace's first academic year she had come to see Todd. Her appearance made him gasp,

'Trace, you look absolutely stunning. Are you all made up for a television appearance or something?'

' Not exactly, I'm just off for a couple of weeks to L.A. Taking my mate, Charleen- don't want to be alone on my first visit to the States. But I wanted to say ta for all you'd done- I'd never have got on with the bloody book if you hadn't wound me up like you did. I don't think I'll be coming back; think I probably know everything about all that literature stuff now, don't you think?'

'I think you may have a point there, Trace. You've certainly taught me a lot more about it than I knew before certainly if you take Literature as a mirror of a society.'

' Yeah, well, I never did understand what you were on about, but I do know a bit more about human nature than you thought, eh?'

The implications of her long wink at him as she left unsettled him even more for the rest of his now horribly busy days. And her legacy was to darken his life until his retirement. A preternaturally lazy man could now no longer avoid that four letter word- work. It was a reckoning for his devious behaviour that he had not anticipated but which fate had seen fit to visit upon him.

❧ The Best Policy ❧

"The Wheatsheaf" was the epitome of everyone's ideal of what a *Dickens' Days* English country pub should be. Set back from the road, the low, wisteria covered, thatched building gave out welcoming signals to the weary traveller or to the locals who loved its reassuring and warm atmosphere. Here the same friends met each week without fear of changes in the service or in the menu or alterations being made to the familiar 'traditional' decoration which they all loved.

Eleanor and John Freeman had lunched at "The Wheatsheaf" on Sunday ever since they had both retired; John from managing a building society office and Eleanor from teaching in a girl's preparatory school. The same couples occupied the same tables each week. The menu was brief; a choice of three dishes for each course, and unfailingly the first listed of the main courses always included "Prime Rib of Aberdeen Angus Beef, Yorkshire Pudding, seasonal vegetables." John would run his eye down the list; 'Hm, Poached Turbot. Jugged Hare. I wonder.' But, with a grateful sigh, as always, he'd settle for the roast beef.

One Sunday in May, a group of the regulars were sitting in the lounge and helping themselves to the excellent and plentiful coffee served after their substantial lunch.

'What do you make of this chap in the paper: killed his wife when she confessed to him that he wasn't the father of his two grown up sons?' Peter, a retired estate agent asked.

'She should have kept her mouth shut; never pays to go admitting anything that you don't have to,' Peter's wife, Barbara announced, looking around conspiratorially at the other wives.

'Well perhaps she was lying; she just wanted to hurt him. Seems a bit far-fetched that she'd keep a thing like that quiet, for what – twenty eight years, wasn't it?' John Freeman suggested.

'You can never tell; people do very strange things at times, but outsiders will never know the truth,' Eleanor said dismissively. She hated newspaper stories. The pros and cons of telling or not telling things to one's spouse continued. Liqueurs and brandies were ordered, an unprecedented indulgence for the Sunday group.

Eleanor took the wheel instead of John for the drive home after the lunch party broke up at about three thirty. Eleanor had drunk two glasses of wine with lunch, but John had had a glass of brandy, and that was a different matter altogether.

Now that they were both retired, things got done without discussion, as though the wishes of the one must inevitably be the wishes of the other. John did most of the shopping whilst Eleanor gardened. John would come home with two cuts of fresh salmon and Eleanor would say, 'Salmon! Funny, you know, I just fancied a piece of nice poached salmon for supper.'

In winter they had *supper* in the lounge on the long coffee table in front of the fire, *dinner* meant that they ate in the dining room, when guests were invited. John brought in the tray with two bowls of vegetable soup which he had made and which, they considered, being home made, was better for them than the cholesterol laden prawns or deep fried whitebait which they both loved but in which they now rarely indulged. John poured them both a glass of the white wine which they had discovered at a knockdown price on their last trip to France and with which they had filled the boot of the car.

'Ah, this is nice,' Eleanor would sigh as she sipped her wine.

'You sound tired, darling; don't go over doing things in; the garden, will you?' said John, solicitously.

'I'm not likely to do that, in fact, to tell you the truth, I had a couple of hours' sleep this afternoon when you were out. Just dropped off. Getting old, I suppose. My grandfather was always 'snatching forty winks' in the afternoons. I thought it very boring.'

'Don't you always tell me the truth, love?' John asked, not looking up from his soup spoon.

'Of course I do. Why do you ask, silly?' Eleanor countered.

'No reason really, just thinking of that discussion last Sunday in the"Wheatsheaf". Do you remember Peter's wife, Barbara, saying that she thought it better never to tell a husband more than a wife absolutely had to?'

'And quite right too – you wouldn't like it if I told you about the affairs I'd had whilst you were out pottering round the shops or looking into boatyards, just to remind yourself what boats look and smell like', Eleanor had joked.

'If having an affair is really your ambition, then I'll be the complaisant husband. But I warn you, I might have to buy another boat; I do miss all that pottering, and dreaming whilst I got her ready for the season.'

'I think that's really what you liked most about boating; chatting for hours with your mates, down on the hard, comparing notes, boasting about all the "Pretty tough passages" you'd made and all that. And if you really miss it that much, why not get another boat? It doesn't have to be as big as your old "Cleopatra", a nice little pottery boat, wooden so that you could do all the lovely business of rubbing down, varnishing and so on which kept you so busy and happy.'

'Hmm, I never liked the "rubbing down" bit. No, my boating days are over – "To everything there is a season." Now is the season of putting our feet up, taking it easy, spending a bit of the cash we both worked for when it was the season for working. But to go back to what Barbara said about married couples not telling each other everything, do you always, I mean always, tell me "everything", Eli?'

'"Everything"? "Everything" sounds pretty ominous said like that, Johnny. Don't people always say, "everything" when they mean being unfaithful; having an affair and all that?' Eleanor laughed.

'Or else being terminally ill – 'Doctor, have you told me "everything?"' ' John said, and added, 'but you're right, we don't actually tell each other all *the truth*, do we, when you think about it.'

'When haven't I told you the truth, then? Give me some examples,' said Eleanor, narrowing her eyes and putting her soup spoon down.

'Ok, now. You didn't like my soup, did you? Don't bother to deny it, I didn't like it either. Tasted of nothing much in particular and had a sort of musty, old potatoey smell, didn't it?'

'Yes, since you mention it, it did. Not one of your best ,but full of nourishment, I've no doubt,' she replied.

'Yet you say no one can make a soup like I can.'

'Yes, but that doesn't mean it's a good soup, it might just mean that nobody can make a soup, a ghastly soup perhaps, like you can make a ghastly soup'. They both laughed.

John put some more logs on the fire and Eleanor took the soup bowls out to the kitchen and brought in a cauliflower au gratin, her contribution to the evening's structured relaxation.

The whole matter of telling each other "Everything" might have rested there, a mere blip in the tranquillity of their ordered life together, had they not watched a production on television of Ibsen's "The Doll's House". They had both enjoyed the performances of two of their favourite actors in the lead roles. When it was over they had both said simultaneously, 'They don't write them like that anymore'. The play's disturbing attack on complacency in marriage and the subordination of a wife to a domineering, but loving husband had brought back the memory of that lunch time at the "Wheatsheaf" when honesty in marriage had kept them all talking for so long.

'She should have told him. He would have forgiven her. It was her fault for not trusting him', John asserted, turning off the television and poking the fire into a last blaze.

'You're quite wrong Johnny, she knew him all too well, she knew he'd never understand, never forgive her; he valued his wretched honour and reputation more than he valued his wife,' Eleanor argued.

'But he was never given the chance to understand; he was condemned without a trial. But at least it's made us talk about something important; the usual sex and violence rubbish on the box won't do that. It takes the Classics to do that. I've been thinking, not just about what this play was saying but about what you said about not telling each other things.'

'I remember not telling you that I didn't honestly like that veggie soup you made. I didn't want to hurt you, Johnny.'

'I hope I'm up to facing honest criticism; about soups or anything else for that matter.'

'Ok. Let's give total honesty with each other a go for a bit. Don't keep back things from me and I'll do the same for you. Do you agree?' she enquired, with an unusually penetrating look.

John didn't answer at once, he was turning over the possibilities.

'Ok love, it's a deal. Shall I start? It's something you do that annoys me, although I've never told you,' John declared.

'Shoot; I'm braced for the attack' Eleanor said, a note of self-conscious drama in her voice betraying her slight anxiety.

He smiled to reassure her, but she did not smile back immediately.

'You never wait for me after we get out of the car; I stop, you get out, I lock the car and check the locks, but you're already off down the road, as though I were just a paid driver or something. Well, I've got that off my chest; the awful truth is out. It's your turn now, but we don't want to spend the evening listing all the things we find infuriating about each other do we? I think my list would be very short. I can't think of anything else you do that annoys me.'

Eleanor considered this then said, 'Well that's not true, you know there are other things. You're cheating already by keeping things back. I'm right, aren't I?'

John had to concede that she was. 'You're right, but let's not spend the whole evening finding fault with each other. You can take this sort of thing too seriously you know.'

'Coward,' Eleanor shot back. 'But you're not going to do me out of having my go. Right, here goes. Why do you always have to give such total attention to reading the paper and look so infernally serious, as though it were a weighty problem which you, and only you could solve. The damned paper's only what hacks write; they earn their living by making mountains out of mole hills; presenting their prejudiced opinions as facts; stirring up the readers. It's rubbish, tittle-tattle and scandal, yet you sit there, your whole body radiating attention to all that stuff and when I dare to say something, 'Dinner's ready' or 'What's on the box tonight?' you look over your spectacles at me and frown, as though you'd been distracted from averting some world disaster! And another thing'. But John had left his chair and was pouring himself a drink.

After opening Pandora's forbidden box so determinedly that night, John and

Eleanor felt that honour had been served, for the time being at any rate, and let the matter rest, and that accursed box might have remained closed for years, perhaps forever, if something apparently quite trivial had not happened.

Eleanor had seen in the library a notice about Creative Writing classes. She was interested and took down the details. As a teacher she had enjoyed making up stories for her young pupils. She'd told her own children stories, some of them she had written down and kept. Eleanor had joined the writing group and spent two hours each Thursday evening at the local College of Further Education discussing the stories and poems which she and members of the class had produced.

There had been a competition in one of the papers asking for a "Modern Fairy Story". Without saying anything to John, Eleanor had written out one of her stories and sent it off to the paper. John had come across the newspaper with a circle around the competition and mentioned it.

'Bloody nonsense, but a nice little earner, as they say; all you have to do is get stupid mugs, housewives with nothing better to do, to send three pounds to the paper with their "Modern Fairy Story" and the winner, probably the editor's granny, will receive a prize of two hundred pounds. Stands to reason there must be at least three or four thousand mugs ready to send in the story they wrote when at school. My bet is they don't even bother to read any of them, just award it to one of their mates. Or their old granny, of course.' Eleanor fixed him with one of her basilisk gazes.

'You knew that I had sent in a story, didn't you? You saw the circle round the ad. and thought, now I can hurt her, make her feel silly, just like you've done in so many, many ways over the years and I've had enough of it, I don't have to listen to it any more. There are times when I really despise, even hate you, do you know that? Eh? Eh, Mr Clever?'

There was the sort of silence that follows when a tray of plates crashes to the floor – horrified realization, then sudden reaction; shouts, cries of amazement, curses and giggles. Almost John wanted to do just that – giggle. Eli's outburst over something he thought so silly seemed grotesquely out of order; unprecedented. It was another whiff of the pit surging out from Pandora's Box. He was at a loss for words. Not so Eleanor.

'If you think I'm joking, having a fit of tantrums or something, think again. And another thing; why don't you ever put your socks on the chair, or back in the drawer or anywhere instead of just chucking them, as you always do, every night of our lives, onto the floor?'

'Good God, woman! What the hell's my socks got to do with your going in for some daft competition in the paper, for Christ's sake? Are you having some sort of breakdown? No, I know- it's your "Total honesty" thing isn't it? That's what it is, isn't it? Isn't it, eh? You're playing a very dangerous game with our marriage. And while I think about it, why don't you ever finish the cup of tea I bring you in the morning and why is it always me that bothers to get out of bed and go down to make the bloody tea? I like lying in bed for those few minutes too, watching the sky and just quietly thinking about what I'm going to do that day.'

'I don't finish the tea because you're incapable of making a cup of drinkable tea. I don't say anything; I don't want to upset you. Now you know it all.' Neither of them spoke, they looked at each other, then burst out laughing.

Strangely, from then on, they accepted the concept of being totally honest with each other and were brought closer together whenever a forgotten and rather moth-eaten skeleton tumbled from one of the cupboards of their earlier lives. The most secret and ridiculous reservations that they had once had about each other could not survive total exposure in the open air of reason.

The weeks passed; the years passed; they had accommodated themselves to the new system and rejoiced in their freedom and became quite smug when they heard about marriages failing because one partner had found out "the horrid truth" about the other. They considered their marriage as being "bomb-proof".

A testing of that impregnable position happened one Sunday, again in May, when they were celebrating their fortieth wedding anniversary. John had been round to "The Wheatsheaf" earlier in the week and ordered flowers for all the tables of the friends with whom they usually passed their Sundays. There was champagne, and John had arranged to pay for the total bill for all the Sunday regulars; he was fond of them; he was grateful to them for being in part responsible for the new lease that their marriage had taken on as a result of the honesty discussion in the pub all that time ago.

'We raise our glasses to you. You two are quite the happiest and best suited couple we've ever come across,' said Peter when they were in the lounge chatting after the anniversary lunch.

'I always say that a good marriage is made in bed, but I don't expect you to tell us all your secrets in that direction', Barbara said with one of her conspiratorial laughs.

'We've nothing to hide *in that direction*', Eleanor declared, her voice confident and dramatic from the champagne she had drunk. 'John and I are always absolutely honest with each other, so when it comes to sex, well we tell each other exactly what we want the other to do.' The Sunday regulars had not bargained on the embarrassment of hearing the revelations of two old people about their sexual peccadilloes. They looked away from Eleanor; they coughed, they blushed; they hid their faces in their glasses. 'And do you know what we do?' Eleanor continued. 'Do you want to know exactly what we do in bed?'

The discomfort of the whole group was now obvious and John felt that he must intervene.

'I'll tell you what we do, my dear old partner and I, we do absolutely nothing.' The silence lasted a few seconds, then they all burst into laughter, clapped and cheered.

Brandies and more champagne were ordered. One couple after another felt bold enough to make their statement on the forbidden subject and they all had something in common; neither partner had dared to admit that he or she no longer had the slightest wish for all the paraphernalia of making love; the pretences, the concerns to "get it right"; to please the partner by some taxing and uncomfortable contortion, which, if they had both been honest with each other, neither of them wanted.

It was Peter finally who brought the party to order. He used the words that John had once used about his boating days being over.

'To sex in marriage. To everything there is a season, and thank God too, say I.'

Eleanor and Barbara said, 'And so say all of us'.

There were no dissenting voices; total honesty for all seemed to be the order of the day, for once.

〜 Boxed Pair 〜

There was no lock or catch on the door of the confessional box, perhaps this was to emphasize his vulnerability. Why were they called.boxes? These were cubicles, but to the old priest that word suggested, undressing, nakedness, steamy swimming pools, children shouting, noisy fun. He was here for a serious, life and death business. "Box "suited. him well enough; he frequently felt that his entire life was spent in or with boxes. A coffin was a box for the dead and chocolates, for which he had a terrible weakness, also came in a box. The irony amused him.

Each week he must spend several mornings in his confessional box, not to pour out his own shortcomings, but patiently and sympathetically to listen to catalogues of secret misdemeanors- silly little sins, if that is what they were. It was rare that he had to listen to any real crimes or despicable or unnatural actions.Men's vices were so trivial, so domestic and almost always, utterly prosaic.

No one had come all morning; three hours of sitting and waiting. Now it was almost noon. Soon he could go home to his small, cold flat. He rubbed the smooth knots in the wood in front of him. Should he read his book? Detective stories seemed such irreverent reading in his church, but the time hung heavily. Anyway, it was too dark to read. Should he pray; pray to be properly ready for anything that came? Was he truly "holding himself in readiness." He thought of Father Thomas's joke about that and smiled a little smile to himself- onanism was such a tawdry little vice. He waited. Someone was pulling the curtain back on the other side. He heard the scuff of heavy shoe- a man. Then came the laboured breathing of an asthmatic or heavy smoker. He smelt the smoke from the clothes. He waited.

'Father, I want you to hear my confession. '

'When were you last confessed, my son?'

'I have never been to confessional before but I'm interested in asking someone or something for forgiveness. Can you help me?'

'I am not here just for your *interest*, but if you are anguished in your soul, then I and all other priests are here are at your service, to help. Tell me what anguishes you.'

'I am a writer. My every waking minute, it seems, is spent writing about people who don't exist; people who are merely the creations of my imagination. I try to make them attractive to my readers . I'm ingenious in my efforts, I like to think.'

'Like a fisherman preparing the fly for his hook,' the priest suggested.

' A simile that is unfortunately apt, Father. My anguish is that I have no time for the real people in my life because the people I create from my imagination absorb all my attention; what they do, why they do it, what they say, why they say it, and when, and how. These are all important to me. Let me tell you about this morning. My wife asks, ' Do you want a cooked breakfast?' I don't reply. I can't. Why can't I respond to her kindness? What lies behind the question my writer's curiosity makes me ask myself- is she compensating for a feeling that she has neglected me? We don't eat cooked breakfasts unless we are in a hotel and it's part of the deal, included in the price, you see. Is the, cooked breakfast, served in bed, a sign of some sort? Is some guilt gnawing at her so that she is trying to make amends for seeing someone else on the side; having an *affaire* as novelists love to say. Am I to be bought off; my masculine dignity and peace of mind squared by a plate of eggs and bacon? Eggs and bacon, and a sausage, a mushroom or two, perhaps some devilled kidneys? Kidneys! Yes, yes. My imagination, and my appetite call out for the uncustomary dish, my suspicions for the time put aside. But they come back- is she having a secret meetings in some out of town village pub, no doubt, with a married man, a Drama teacher or a double-glazing rep or other such notorious lecher from my novelist's cast list. Am I to be so simply bought off by the prospect of offal, seethed in hot butter, and served on crisp toast.? '

The old priest swallowed his saliva noisily.

' Father, do you have a thing about offal at all?'

'No, my son, not often, but since you mention food, I have had sometimes to fall upon my knees and pray to Almighty God for His forgiveness at my excessive consumption of barbecued chicken flavoured potato crisps . I am not above venial sins and truly I suspect that not even St Peter was, or even the Blessed Mother of God herself. I am exercised in my mind to know why she was so concerned about there not being enough wine at the marriage in Cana. Had the mother of the bride drunk too much of it herself? Had she given a wrong order to the wine merchant? Why had it run out? Had she sampled too much of it in her anxieties about whether all was going well? Maybe she had problems in that direction, women often do.'

The man behind the curtain interrupted,

'But He stepped in ; He saved the day and waved his wand and had every jug, and bowl, mug and teacup filled to the brim with a good vintage Chateau Cheval Blanc, or whatever was the favourite tipple then. Do you think they went in for fine wines in those days? Did they know a drop of the *real* when they drank it? But the wines of the East nowadays certainly can't be called, *fine* wines'. and they probably never were up to much.'

'That's sadly true, my son. Last year I took my flock or at least, those members of my flock who could afford it, to the Holy Land, a spiritual excursion, so to speak. The food ! The food was just terrible, just really terrible. Swill! No milk with meat, and you know what that means- No goulashes, no stroganoff,s - no cream, you see. And the wine! Well Mrs Felstead's lettuce and burdock would have been a Krug champagne to the swill they served me.'

'I shouldn't have thought you'd get a stroganoff in the Holy Land, but if you're into strogs, there's a new place just opened in Frith Street that does a mean strog, and I mean a mean strog.' He drew in his breath in a long whistling intake- 'whewww!' and expelled it luxuriously and nostalgically, 'Ahhhhh!'

The priest felt in his robe for the pocket where he sometimes found a last few crumbs of chicken flavoured delight but there were none to assuage his mid-morning longings.'Is it just the cooked breakfast that you want to confess to me about, because I think a dozen Hail Mary's, maybe two- on account of the kidneys,you understand-should fit the bill.'

'No Father, you're not listening. It's my whole life; being always concerned with just the imagined people in my books not the real people around me that worries me. Am I just a callous cold-hearted shit, if you'll excuse the word? '

'We all have to have our dreams, my son. We can't always be doing the right thing. You have your living to make. You have your wife to support and you must do it in the best way that you know how'.

'The only way,' the writer added after a sad pause.

'Well then, if that's all you want to say, I give you my blessing'

The curtain was pulled back ,the heavy footsteps retreated . Suddenly the priest shouted from behind his grill. He should, by rights, be offering a special last message for the sinner before he left the box, but all he could manage was,' What was the name of the place in Frith Street, the place where you can get the stroganoff?'

He was too late, The man was at the door of the church. A woman staggering under the weight of several filled supermarket bags had just entered and was approaching the confessional box. She had put her bags down for a moment, slipped a packet of crisps out of one of the bags and was munching determinedly. The sound of the munching carried to the depths of the confessional box and stirred something in the heart of the old priest. When she heard the shouted question from the box, she stopped in mid munch and crossed herself. Fortified, the woman picked up her bags again and struggled into the confessional box, blinded for the moment by the musty smelling curtain falling across her face. She seated herself and waited for the crackling from the bags around her to cease.

'Father, I've come to make my confession, if you're ready.'

'Ready? Am I not always ready to hear all the sins and wickedness of my flock? ' The woman sensed definite irritation in his voice.

'Well then, Father, I have sinned again. You remember that I came to make my confession last week, after I'd been to do my bit of shopping. I like to drop in and get a few things off my chest before I catch the number 22 bus, it only runs every two hours and if I just miss the four o'clock, there's such a wait, sometimes in the rain. There's some funny people wait for that bus, so I thought that stopping by for a bit of a sweep out in the conscience department wouldn't be a bad thing; two birds with the one stone, so to speak.' There was a prolonged throat clearing from the priest.

'What do you want to tell me, my child' The last words were not entirely clear being uttered through his gritted teeth.

' I'd been doing my weekly shop. It gets me out of the house; there's nothing now to keep me in, you see. I'm by myself now that Frank's gone. No don't imagine I want him back, again I was glad to see the back of him and his drinking and lying about, and lying about everything; saying he'd been to the job centre when he'd spent the day in the pub, sitting there by the hour with that idle lot of loafing bastards who never did a decent day's work in their lives and couldn't if they tried, well, as I say, I was doing my bit of shopping. ' Another sigh from the priest.

'Did you say something, father?'

' Not yet, I was waiting for the sins you had to tell me about."Ah yes, the sins. Well, now, I like a bit of salmon, tinned, the red sort, not the pink, don't know what part of the fish the pink bit comes from; it's cheaper so it's got to be coming from the bit that no one wants, like the ox tail, although I dearly love a bit of oxtail, you never see it now, but it takes a deal of boiling and you need good onions, not the rubbish they sell now with all that skin inside. You're cutting it up and then there's another layer of skin, that would spoil the taste of the oxtail broth, or, of course, stew. My mother, God rest her soul, she was a marvel with the ox tail, it was on her death bed she told me the secret; '"Bovril," she said, 'add a little Bovril to the stew, it makes it more meaty,' and that's odd because an ox tail is all meat; meat ,and bone, of course. Well, as I say, I like a tin of red salmon, they had them on offer; three for the price of two, so I thought, that's six for the price of four, all I have to do is wait till I see someone buying four tins of salmon, add mine to hers and I'd be getting mine for nothing. No one came by wanting the salmon so I got tired of waiting, I'd be late for the bus, I thought, so I just took the six tins, put two- the free ones- out of sight, in my handbag, and bought my other things; custard powder- you don't always see that on the shelves, women can't be bothered to cook the puddings, you see, so they don't want the custard to go with it- anyway, I got the custard and the thick-cut marmalade, don't you think that should be cheaper, not more expensive, saving all that trouble of slicing it up thin? That used to be my job for my Granny when I was small. 'Slice it up with your Grandpa's razor,' she'd say, but I cut myself, 'Blood oranges! That's a treat,' she said and she'd laugh. 'Blood oranges; your Grandpa will like that', she said, God rest her soul. Well I'd almost finished when I saw the crisps, some don't like them messed about- things added- you know; cheese or cheese and onion-even curry flavoured-Ugh! And...'

'Barbecued chicken flavoured?' suggested the priest.

'That's my favourite,' the woman said, and added, 'they had them on offer. I took nine- three for the price of two. At the checkout I said I'd got five, but I'd got nine. They don't count them, idle , that's what they are, and there was a queue, or maybe it was my honest face; 'you've got an honest face', my mother used to say, 'You'll never get away with seeing another man if you're married'. I didn't want to see another man, Frank was problem enough and the others are just like him; idle, drinking men, always lying, and him turning up his nose at my fine oxtail stew, saying he didn't want anything from so close to the cow's arse- dirty beast that he was.' What about an egg, then eh?' I said. That shut him up. Well I was waiting for the bus and I thought maybe that hadn't been a good thing to do, to take those two extra packets of crisps. I was never any good with the mathematics, so seeing I'd just missed the bus, I thought I'd just drop in here and get a bit of absolution before the next bus was due. Have you the time on you? Five thirty! I'll be off to the bus. Is it the two dozen Hail Mary's, like last time?'

The old priest shifted on his cushion behind the screen. He wondered about the cushion- perhaps he should be doing a penance himself, on the hard bench seat, but the cold was penance enough and the cushion was a very venial sin.

He said, 'You've two packets of crisps you have no right to. Leave them on your seat when you go. That will put things right and God will settle for one dozen Hail Mary's this time. You did say they were barbecued chicken flavoured?'

She was already picking up her bags and leaving the box. It was almost time he went home. No one would come now, not this close to opening time and his lunch time. The crisps would go down nicely with the drop of Jameson's he'd got left; something to look forward to.

Dedication had its small rewards, he thought as he closed the box for the day.

⤚ Flesh ⤙

"There's no way of knowing, There's no way of showing, what you mean to me, sonny boy, " Then the singing stopped. Flora sang through the chorus in her head. The singer started to whistle the rest of the tune, and if she had been able to whistle, Flora would have joined in. She couldn't so she waited for the whistling to stop. It did abruptly and the whistler gave a long sigh. 'That's what it was. I thought as much;the washer on the spin bearing has disintegrated. It's an old machine, it's to be expected. It's lucky I always carry a box of spares, 'he said and went out to his van to get the washers.

Flora felt a sudden longing to cheer or shake Mr. Bennet's large hand, or give him a hug, or somehow show him that she felt more than just gratitude for his reassurance about the broken washing machine. This tall, solid man, over the seven years she had lived in the old house, had repaired the washing machine three times, the dishwasher eight times, the waste disposal unit six times and the vacuum cleaner four times. She felt that she and Mr Bennet had established an affinity. She would become distraught if one of her household appliances let her down. Each time she saw the catastrophe in terms of the beginning of the total collapse of her home; the leak on the washing machine would be caught, like measles, by the dishwasher, and then on through all the other appliances, electric devices, then the central heating burner, then the double glazing, the loft insulation, the automatic door lift on the garage, then the zips,buttons and fastenings of every sort on her clothes, and Reggie's clothes. The curtains would disintegrate. The carpets would follow. There would be no end to the avalanche, the landslide of domestic disaster. She would never be able to sit with her feet up, reading a magazine, sipping her favourite coffee whilst listening to "Woman's Hour", the afternoon play and all the diversions which sometimes helped to keep loneliness and boredom at bay.

Mr Bennet returned with the new washer, fitted it, reassembled the washing machine, put his tools back in their box and wrote out his bill. Flora asked if he wanted a cup of coffee, or tea, or anything but he said thank you very politely but no. He had three more calls to make that afternoon. The house felt so empty and threatening when she was alone again. What would Mr Bennet have said if she had told him that she wished he could mend her, put her back together again, get her life to run again smoothly without all the moments of sheer panic that made her hold on to the furniture, her eyes staring as she gasped for breath with fear. Fear of what? Should she, could she tell him that she dreaded hearing Reggie's key turning in the lock when he came home from work. He always, always said the same thing in the same way, his words making the same song. 'Flora. It's me. I'm home. Come and give me a kiss.'

Perhaps if they'd had children, perhaps if she'd been able to keep a job, had something else in her life the panic would have stayed away. Now there was nothing to be done. She couldn't tell Reggie how she felt, she just went on, just the same; the little wife, the little mouse at home, the listening ear to his stories of the stupidity of his boss, the unreliability of his colleagues at work. The silence of the house threatened her, like the recess of the cave she used to visit as a child. In the furthest, darkest part was something, something watching, waiting. At last she would run out of the cave to the sun, but still she was watched.

She put the dishes in the dishwasher clumsily. She wanted to throw it off balance. She stacked it incorrectly so that it would take its revenge and go wrong. Then she could send for Mr Bennet again, send for him so that he could come, listen as she told her problem, and he would mend her, restore her to good working order. Had she ever been in "good working order" she wondered? Not since her sister had died and her father and mother had separated, the safe home broken up, the house sold. No, she needed repair, someone to put the sprockets back on the centrifuge, fit a replacement cold water pump, replace the overload fuses on her spirit.

Reggie was reading his paper. He'd come in for his coffee in a minute and then he'd tell her about "His day". What about her day? Could she tell him about Mr Bennet coming to repair the washing machine? He'd complained that she was always making things go wrong and complained about the costs of the repair. The cost! The cost of Mr Bennet; of the wondrous way that he gave her hope as he repaired things; of his strong capable hands doing a job that he knew so well, putting things right. You .couldn't put a price on that. She overfilled the percolator and the hot coffee sprayed everywhere. Reggie came in, mopped up, stared at her, shook his head, refilled the percolator to the right level. All things had to be made right. He took his coffee, when it was made, into the lounge and watched the news on the television."Telly", he called it. She hated it; stupid watching, staring eye. She viciously wrenched all the knobs on dishwasher. It was time it went wrong again.

On Wednesdays she went shopping. She would catch the bus at the corner and go to the supermarket in the town. She hated it; decisions to be made; things not to knock down; things to remember to get; the right things; the sensible things. She would fill her trolley with so many things that she couldn't carry the plastic bags and had to leave things behind and take the wrong things home- the "Telly dinners" that Reggie hated, the baking powder yet she never baked, the special offer packet soups that she always threw away when she had made them. What had she got right? Nothing. She never got anything right. And then she discovered that she'd left her purse at the check out. She must go back, but she knew it wouldn't be there. There wasn't any point in even bothering to ring up, go back or even hope.

She wanted to be mended.

Mr Bennet was surprised, as always, when she phoned him because something had gone wrong with the dishwasher. Could he come as soon as possible. Friday, he'd said was the earliest. Not today or tomorrow? Friday.

Reggie was away for three days, on a course, he'd said, but she knew that really he had gone away with that woman from work, the one he'd said had joined the company last month. He'd gone away from her, his wife, because there was something wrong with her. She needed to be mended. This time she'd tell Mr Bennet and he'd put her right, get her back together again.

On Friday morning she was ready. Everything was prepared. Everything necessary had been done. Nothing must be left to chance. The doorbell rang and she opened it at once because she had been standing at the door, waiting for Mr Bennet's van to stop outside. "R.Bennet. General Household and Appliance Repairs" it said on the van. So reassuring-"General Repairs." He was here. He was inside the house. He had his tool box.

In the kitchen Mr Bennet tested the dishwasher. He found nothing wrong. 'Maybe you overloaded it and it stopped', he suggested. In her head Flora knew that he was talking about her problem; the reason why she needed to be repaired. She was overloaded and she'd stopped. She held her hand so tight against her chest. Now she could tell him that it wasn't because of a fault with the dishwasher that she'd called him, but a fault with her. She wanted to be put right.

'I think you've got me here for nothing', he said and turned to go.

'No, no, There's something wrong for you to repair. Can't you help me? I need you to put me back together again,' she managed, at last, to gasp out.

He watched her for a full minute. He looked puzzled and annoyed at the same time.

'I repair machines, not people, not flesh,' he said The word, "Flesh" he'd stumbled over as though it was an intimate word, like breasts, like lovemaking, like orgasm. He wondered why she held her arm to her chest so hard that the effort showed in her face.

'My flesh', she said so softly; an invitation or a confession? 'My flesh', she repeated. He looked puzzled. She let her arm fall away from her chest and the great open cut, like a mouth, pulsed out her life blood through her clothes, through her weariness, through her empty days of waiting.

'Heal my flesh and repair my spirit', he thought she'd said and said so at the inquest.

Beauty and the Beast
A "Hill-Billy" story.

My mother never gave advice. If she wanted to influence things according to her own particular views, she would content herself with quoting an old proverb or folk saying. When my father lost his job the day after most of the tiles fell off the roof in a storm and near about everything we owned was spoiled, my mother just closed her eyes up tight as though she was going to shut it all out, opened them again and said, ' It never rains but it pours'.

My brother, Sam, was against work of all and every sort. When my father said that Sam should maybe do some school work on account of his teacher giving him such bad grades and a report to match, mother pointed her finger in the air and proclaimed,' A watched pot never boils.' These pieces of wisdom were not appreciated at the time but when I look back I can see how what she did get to saying at the big moments in our lives turned out to be prophesies

When I met Alice Scudamore at the church hall dance and later brought her home to meet the folks, mother said nothing at all, but I knew she was thinking something. Alice was a twin, her sister, Bella, was definitely the ugliest girl I had ever seen. At school her ugliness made her a sort of hero. Alice, on the other hand, was truly a beauty, that fact no one would ever have disputed.

At the weekly dances Alice was always on her own, boys were just too damned frightened to go up and ask her to dance, I guess. I only asked her because Tom Joad bet me a quarter that I wouldn't and I was always short of money. Alice said yes at once as though she'd been expecting it all along. She didn't dance too well, but then she didn't get the practice that other and less overwhelming girls got. I couldn't look at her as we danced and I didn't say anything neither. At the end of the dance Alice took my hand and said something like,' Yes, .Billy, I do have a mind to stepping outside to get a breath of air, if you were thinking to ask me that.' We went outside and she stood in front of me. The porch there gave a little shadow, free from the street light. You could still hear the music from the hall. They were playing one of my favourite tunes, " The Red River Valley."

The stars that night were real clear, but it wasn't too hot outside. I was just wondering how I was going to get back into the hall and what I should say to Alice to get us both back inside, when she let out a sigh, put her arms around my neck, clamped her eyes tight close and kissed me straight on the lips. I guess I'd kissed maybe a dozen girls in my life up to then and when I kiss, I reckon to make the first move myself. The girl would act all reluctant, of course, then she would just go along with it and the spirit of the thing.

I always enjoyed kissing girls, but with Alice it was different. It was like she was carrying out a holy ceremony, like when the Reverend ducks the Baptists in the river; very solemn and formal. Well I never had it clear how I came to be bringing Alice home to meet my folks later that week As we went back inside after she'd done the kissing, she said, 'I don't have any reason that I can think of not to meet your Mom and Dad after the church service on Sunday. If you want me at your house by four thirty, that's when I'll be there.'

On Sunday Alice was all dressed up in her fine clothes and she had on a hat with a great wide brim. I hoped as how she'd forgotten about coming to our house and I just walked on when I saw her outside the church. She stood and waved her hand at me, but I wasn't going to let on as I'd seen her do that.

At four thirty Alice pulled our door bell and mother let her in. Father was reading his paper. He took one look at Alice and then went silent which was certainly unusual for Father. When Mother had done scanning Alice's face, she sniffed her special sniff, it was a danger sign, and then she let Alice in, sat her down, poured out tea and handed out some cakes she always made for Sunday afternoons. No one said anything else. I suppose, by rights, since she was there on account of me, I should have been talking to her. I tried hard to think but I didn't have an idea what to say. Alice sat and drank her tea. Turned out that it didn't much matter that I hadn't found anything to talk about at that time as Alice had so much to say. She knew the names of all the flowers that Mother had planted in the yard in front of the house and said how fine they looked and that it wasn't everyone who could get a double begonia to take and that Mother must have green fingers, Alice opinioned.

It seemed that Alice knew about cakes; she held up the slice of angel cake, nodded at it and said that you could always tell a good cook by her angel cake. It had to be real light but with something called "Consistency of texture." If I recollect aright.

Mother just said,'Ugh hum', she knew that we knew that it was the only cake she could bake and she made it from a packet, just adding water and an egg. There wasn't nothing special about that cake, but Alice had to say something, her wanting to please Mother, I guess.

When Alice had finished about the cake and the flowers and all, no one spoke, they just looked at the floor. Then I thought of something, I told my folks what happened at school last Friday, about how Miss Butterly had tripped over as she was in such an all tearing rage to get to the back of the room and hit Gary Attenbury before he could dip Emily Hackenbacker's pigtail into the inkwell again. We had all enjoyed that fall. We acted it out again in the recess and laughed all over again. Sam Hudderson put on Betty Cooper's glasses, the ones with the thick glass, then he'd skid down between the desks and he'd shout in Miss Butterly's high voice,' You stop that , Gary Mathews, this minute, do you hear, or I'll strike you!' Then Sam would fall down, grab a desk and then lie on his back giving out a squeal. Then someone else would take the glasses and do it all over again. It got funnier each time. I was close to throwing up I laughed so much.

Alice didn't look as though she appreciated my story, she looked serious, but Father grunted, I could tell from that grunt that he considered it a good joke too, but Mother wouldn't want him to show that he thought as I did; they were different that way.

At six o'clock Alice said I could take her home so I got up to do just that. Father caught my eye, it was the first time I had ever seen him look at me in a man to man way; he felt sorry for me I knew. Walking back, Alice took my arm, said as how she had a good time at my folks. She walked fast and I was pulled along, or that's how it felt to me. I got to wondering how I could stop what I had started. It would never have happened if Tom Joad hadn't dared me to dance with Alice. She kept on holding onto my arm and talking about something she called," Our future together."' I felt like I wanted to vanish or turn into something else, maybe a lizard; anything but a sixteen year old boy, but I was in a trap and I didn't know how I could get out. I could see what this "Future together" was going to mean, it would mean there was no way that I wouldn't end up married and all to Alice, then I'd have to live on her father's farm and do all those jobs, and there were a heap of them, that Alice's father didn't have relish for doing himself. But all that was stopped thanks to Bella, Alice's ugly sister.

I had been seeing Alice every Saturday since she came to our house. Sometimes I'd have to go with her to visit one or the other of her kin, mostly old maiden aunts who treated us like we was some sort of travelling show. Alice would wear her Sunday best dress and I'd have to put on a clean shirt and shine up my boots. We would drink the tea, eat the cake and then it would begin,

'Just look at that girl. I declare she doesn't look real; she's a work of art, that's what she is. Just stand still, girl- oh, those eyes! Billy, you're a real fortunate young man, you know that? A real fortunate young man. You must look after Alice and never let her do anything that might spoil that beauty. That beauty is a gift from God hisself, yessiree.'

I didn't see any way I could get out from under all their plans for me and Alice. Even were I to maybe drop a hint that I might want to go some place where Alice wouldn't have been on show, she would just look at me. She'd fix me with her eyes the way a mongoose fixes a snake and I couldn't do anything or say anything after that. I was her prey and she wasn't about to let me loose, then or ever. I got to hating those .Saturday trips and I would be shaking when I saw Alice waiting outside our house, all dressed up to go visiting again.

The way Bella saved me must have been as big a surprise to Alice as it was to me. It happened after Alice and I had been dating each Saturday for about a six month. I missed my Saturday fishing trips with the other guys, they never ever thought to wait for me, just taking it for granted I'd be seeing Alice, I guess.

Mother said as I was just fixing to pick up Alice, as usual, one Saturday afternoon in June, 'Constant dripping will wear away a stone'. She said it under her breath, to herself, but I heard it and it hurt.

Well, as I was walking down the long, hot road to pick up Alice and go visiting another old aunt or something, I must have been dragging my feet that day and then I heard someone come up behind me. The steps slowed down to my pace and I saw who it was, it was Bella.

'Bet you wish you was going fishing, Billy, eh?' Bella said, right as if she could read my thoughts. My face must have shown her that she'd guessed right I stopped and looked at Bella; oh she sure was ugly, but in a way that didn't seem real, like Alice's beauty didn't seem real. Bella's ugliness didn't force you to watch, listen and obey, the way that Alice's beauty forced you to do. When I stopped on the sidewalk and looked at Bella, her face was so familiar, so full of friendly understanding. It was like looking at a face you had always known. Sure there were wrinkles and moles and the nose was too wide and squashy and the lips too big, but none of that mattered. You felt when you looked at Bella that it was how you felt when you looked at your own face in the mirror, close up, when you were shaving or slicking your hair down neat. It was a face you could trust; it was the face of someone who knew all your little secrets; things you kept hidden from yourself. Bella knew them as well and just laughed about them so you didn't ever feel bad about them or think you didn't measure up to others because of them.

When Bella looked at me, I felt full of power; ready to do anything, face anyone. I had never felt that way before. It felt good and I just stared at Bella, wanting that good feeling to go on forever. Something in my chest wanted to get out; it swelled up, making me want to sing I felt so happy and so- well- free! Yes Bella made me free to do anything- to go fishing, free not to see Alice, free to laugh at Miss .Butterfly falling over, free to be myself as I'd never felt before.

I took Bella's hand; she had a small, warm hand. I held it, it felt good. She returned my hold. I knew that when I was with Bella, I didn't have to try to be or do anything I didn't have a mind to, not ever.

Next Saturday it just seemed right that I asked Bella to come to meet my folks. Father liked Bella's jokes and laughed and Mother laughed too. I felt bad about not telling Alice that I would not be dating her anymore, but Bella said she had talked with Alice and it was all ok and that Alice understood.

After I had finished up at school, I took a job on the farm of some folks near us. It was a big farm and he was an old man who needed the help of a strong young man, which I was. A neat log house came with the job. The log house was for the farm help, if he was married so I married Bella and Mother cooked a big angel cake.

Everyone said Alice looked so beautiful at the wedding. She had on a new blue dress with flowers on it. Bella looked more ugly, somehow, in her wedding outfit, but that only made me love her more.

Alice's old aunts were there and they kept talking and clapping their hands together and exclaiming stuff like, 'We'll all be coming to Alice's wedding next; a girl looking like she does and all- you'll see.'

But no one did see for next Fall they found Alice drowned in a very shallow pond. Bella knew why her sister had done what she had, but all she said was,' I wish I could have given her some of my looks, as she wanted, poor Alice.'

All my mother said was, 'Beauty is in the eye of the beholder.' She didn't have anything else to say.

Ecstasy

Ecstasy:state of exalted delight, joy, rapture. Overpowering emotion characterized by loss of self-control,often associated with orgasm.)

Dinner parties were always hurdles for Thomas; his mobile index finger would lie impotent on the silverware and could do so little. At Angelina's dinner party he just watched her. On all previous occasions, when they had been invited, he had used one of his many excuses to avoid attending, but this time his wife, Helen, had wanted to go so much; had wanted Thomas to meet her new friend and her husband, the friend she had made at the Art classes she had recently joined, that he gave in; they both went to Angelina's for dinner.

It was late summer. It had been a busy year.
Thomas was tired, too tired, he thought, for anything.
But he was wrong.
First; the introductions: "Nice to meet you, Angelina,
And Peter too, of course."
"He's just been given the Chair of Fine Arts."
"I'm sure Angelina's paintings are fine art,"
Thomas said, and took her cold, thin hand and stared.
"She's a very gifted painter and teacher too,"
His wife had said.
"Then I shan't afford your paintings,"
Conversationally he'd said.
" A surgeon short of money! That I can't believe,"
Said Angelina and they went in with the other four
To take their drinks and chat whilst dinner cooked away.

Time passed.
Helen ate.
The others ate.
Thomas stared and stared at Angelina;
He could not help himself; she was his fate.

Course followed course;fishy things on tenuous salad, intriguingly dressed.
Then a sorbet- something sweet with just a hint of nuts;
Subtle. expensive, thought Thomas, toying with his share.
Then followed seared breasts of duck, vegetables cut very thin,
A port drenched sauce and porcini mushrooms piled on high.
All was so very, very neat and arty on each plate.
Last: mangoes crushed with plums in Armagnac and cream.
They stayed on and talked at table over coffee.
But the only thing Thomas revelled in was Angelina;
Her nubile thigh, her trimmest abdomen.
His X-ray eyes traced the dimple of her navel;
He knew exactly how it would feel;
Warm beneath his exploring, noting hand.

"Don't you ever hesitate or tremble
When you make that first incision?"
Billy's silly wife felt moved to ask.
"The first cut, you see," he said," is as all important:
One can't go back or do a second take.
 It must be done so neatly; at a stroke
And then completely."

Billy's wife grew bulbous eyed and pushed away her sweet.
"Anyone seen the play at the Yvonne Arnaud?"
Someone suddenly asked.
 Then someone else enquired quite quickly
If he looked at the face when he made that first cut.
"It all depends, you see… but really-
That's more the anaesthetist's job."

But Oh how he longed to see Angelina's fair face
When he'd make that first incision beneath the ribs.
He'd go right on then to explore her inner recesses of delight.
No other penetration of her body could be the same;
All his sexual drive was called out
As his probing fingers teased out
Every tiny little vein beneath his hand.
His silly little penis would be just a thrusting monkey
If it squeezed and pulsed inside her pelvic cage,
At its business so restricted midst gasps and careful sighs
As he worked to find his pleasure in her thighs.
But to plunge his whole hand into Angelina's stomach
And touch the secret treasures that he'd find;
The spleen, the kidneys, the liver and its lobes,
The portal vein, heptic artery, the glomerulus
And the plungent cortex- a wonderland,
Engulfed and bathed in deepest red

Tom's eyes moistened, his mouth fell open at the thought. He could not speak. All
the the routine jobs on old and flabby bodies had made him want to retch but
had brought him ample money. Now he just pined and cried
For Angelina's inside
"You're looking pretty seedy," fellow surgeon Henry had remarked in his delightful
Irish way
"Just need a bit of holiday; I've been working bloody hard."
But he spoke a lie; it was for Angelina's fair inside
That he longed for and he pined for.

His hair grew thin; it came away in bundles.
His eyes lost their inner light and he went right off his food.
And then, when all hope seemed lost, he had a sign;
A letter came from heaven, it seemed, to welcome him there.
Angelina was booked in; was on her way to lie out on his table
Needing. It seemed, a blessed hysterectomy.
Thomas broke right down and cried
In all his joy and ecstasy;

He'd have his hands inside her ere night fell.!

❧ All Fools' Day ❧

My late father was very gifted as a raconteur and could bring the most unlikely scenes to life by doing all the voices in one of his anecdotes, usually about low life in the "Australian" pub in Saville Row.. On Saturdays, when civil servants had to work until midday, he would usually stop off with his bachelor friend and bad influence, Gerry, to enjoy the badinage of the actors whose local "The Australian" was. He would then catch the Southern Rail train back home to sleepy Malden, arrive late for mother's roast and have to be as entertaining as he knew ho could be in order to deflect mother's wrath at his late arrival for the weekly roast lunch after "Wasting time and money again with those no goods in that wretched pub". Whether the sort of thing below actually used to take place, a boy of ten had no means of knowing, but in my father's dramatisations it certainly seemed to be drawn from life. This piece of nonsense is dedicated to my father, a man who could make even a water bill sound funny.

Friday, again. How he hated Fridays; the end of the week always found him exhausted and not looking forward, as most of his colleagues did, to a weekend of inactivity or else wild activity with children or in the garden or something. He remembered his wretched schooldays when, on Friday he would bring home his satchel bulging with homework to blight the whole rest period. It was not that he actually got on with it, despite his mother's habitual insistence; 'Get the wretched homework out of the way on Friday night so you're free and we can all go for a walk or a drive down to Brighton; discipline yourself!' but that he had found difficult. All his life; any sort of order or planning was inimical to his nature and made him want at once to rebel or just sit and stare fixedly at a spot in the carpet. And here was Friday, the first of April. All Fools' day, no less, upon him again like a curse. Midwinter, from the Sales Department fell into step with him as he walked away from the office and towards Midwinter's station.

' Anything planned for the weekend, George?'

He had felt like giving one of his flippant replies which usually gave so much enjoyable offence, but instead, because Midwinter was one of the few men in the company that he did not actively loathe, he replied, ' I don't like weekends much, I'm afraid; they seem so unstructured'

'Know what you mean, old chap; there's no sense of urgency, is there? Time to do several of those infernal, "Little jobs" that inevitably turn out to be bloody big jobs which take the whole weekend. "Just see if you can fix the fence, or the mower, or the boy's bicycle or- well you know, but, of course, you don't; not being married. No little woman to keep you up to scratch. Lucky chap, you can do just what you like at the weekend, can't you?' George had had to endure this part envious, part resentful attack, if it was an attack, many times recently and had reacted in a way that had left him few if any friends in the vast and anonymous company for which he had worked since leaving school thirty five years. ago.

'Thought of going down to Sidcup to sort out a graveyard for myself this weekend, as it happens'.

' Thinking of leaving us soon then, George?' Midwinter joked.

'May sound morbid, but it's one thing I enjoy doing at the weekend- looking for a place where I might finally rest. Did you know that it's getting almost impossible to find a place where you can be actually buried nowadays? Everyone wants to be cremated; cheaper, of course, and all you need is a sort of token little plaque, "Sacred to the memory of Joe Bloggs who fell asleep on Friday, Ist April, 1958" or something like that. "Fell asleep!" sounds so careless- fell into the machinery or just got bored out of his mind by life's dreary predictabilities? You can't even put, "Here lies", because ashes don't really "lie", do they? No, I've done a bit of driving about on weekends and so far the only place left with a bit of room for new guests is in the Sidcup Municipal Graveyard. Has a ring to it, don't you think? ' Midwinter gave George a long look and then quickened his step to reach the station. ' Have fun. Sort a place out for your old chum from Sales; be nice to know where I'm going for a change.' The two men parted to go to their separate ways

'Think he really thought I was serious,' George muttered to himself with a laugh as he weaved briskly through the impatient crowds surging to get a seat perhaps on the over crowded Friday trains. But it was his birthday so he deserved a bit of fun, didn't he, he thought to himself.

The public bar of the "Australian" was pretty crowded when he arrived there for his accustomed "Bracer", as he liked to call his habitual large gin and tonic and a packet of peanuts taken religiously on his way home each Friday.

Mention my birthday or just keep it to myself? That was the question. Whether it would be nobler in the mind to avoid any offers to, "Have this on me" or more convivial to announce as he came into the bar, ' Drinks on me-it's my birthday!' In the event he said nothing and was merely nodded to by the two or three regulars seated round the bar at 6 o'clock

' George, did you see that bit in the paper today about Global Warming getting worse? Looks as though we'll be flooded out of this little place if the tides go as high as they predict. Bastards!'

'Shooting's too good for them; they've buggered every bloody thing up that you can think of', his companion added cheerfully, and put his empty pint mug back on the bar hopefully. George could always take such a hint;' Fill us all up, Bertie, before we're all swept away into a watery grave.'

The long suffering young landlord knew his cue; ' Chap was in lunchtime telling me about how he'd just found a place to park his new Merc.- you know what it's like here for parking- anyway, he was just reversing in when a young chap in one of those little "Smart" cars shot in and pinched his place. The Merc. bloke stopped and gave him the eye, " Didn't you see me backing into that place?" He calls out to the young chap. "Yes," says the young bloke, "but this is what you can do if you're young and very fit, know what I mean?' Well, the Merc bloke just reverses into the Smart car, crunches the side in and pushes it out of the way. " And that's what you can do if you're very old and very rich", he says. Nice one, eh?'

'That's what I do like to hear,' said George; 'demonstrations of bad behaviour, man's natural inhumanity to his fellow man, warms my heart and makes me believe there might be a God after all. By the way, what have you got on the old menu tonight, Bertie, for all those who have no "Little woman" at home; slaving away over a hot stove to get something savoury, nourishing, restorative and enjoyable on the table when the breadwinner brings his weary old bones home after slaving his pitiful life away at the office face?'

'Usual, said George; 'steak and ale pie or plaice and chips; just the stuff to put hairs on your chest,' Bertie declared theatrically.

'So long as that's the only place where the hairs get- do you remember that pork pie you sold me last year?'

' I wish you hadn't brought that up,' said the embarrassed Bertie.

'So did I , at the time, ' said George, but kept a straight face. ' If you can see your way clear to earmarking me a basinful of your hairless and incomparable steak and ale pie in about an hour's time, when I've had a chance to "chew over the fat", as they say, with my fellow customers, I shall be forever in your debt., my dear fellow.'

'What's got into you, George? You're not usually so talkative, and on a Friday too, said Bill from his high bar stool.

'Just full of my usual sweetness and light, Bill It's nice of you to actually listen to what anyone's saying- must be a first for you. Eh? But I'm forgetting myself; I haven't congratulated you on your choice of suiting- off to the Camptown races, are we, or did you strike lucky at the dogs' home charity shop? My , my , how I do enjoy a bit of colour in my life; puce, is that what they call it?'

' You're working up for a bunch of fives up the snout if you're not bloody careful and if you don't buy me a large Johnny Walker and water pronto,'

'Badinage, old thing; rise to it; pat it back to me; keep the ball in the air,' laughed George.

' Yours certainly will be in the air all in its solitary state if we have any more.'

'Not bad; a ralantando, I believe; back handed, off the edge of the racket notwithstanding,' George rallied.

' Talking of rackets,' said the other customer who was beginning to feel out of things, 'what about the bloody government's increasing the tax on beer?'

' In your particular case, Terry, it can do nothing but good; give a welcome surge of income to be spent on the indigent poor and save you from an even bigger overdraft and more monumental pot belly.' And here George raised his glass to his plump drinking companion.

'The hours just seem to fly by when you're having fun and enjoying good company,' George at last spluttered out after finishing his bar supper and draining the last of his seventh gin and tonic. He waved his hand, pulled his overcoat round him and stepped out into the cold lonely world outside. The rain was falling relentlessly as he tottered up the road to let himself into his unheated , lonely and uninviting one bedroom flatlet above the dry cleaners. His hour of glory; his Falstaffian exercise was over for another week, but this time he rather thought that it had been better; more acerbic and thrusting albeit so close to the lonely weekend- perhaps something to do with it being All Fools' Day, or just because no one had remembered his fiftieth birthday?

Laurie Lewis was born in 1934 in Cambridge. He spent his early childhood in the West Indies and then Tiffin School, Kingston-on-Thames. He read English at Cambridge and went on to teach in Eastbourne, Cheltenham, Sherborne and Truro and also lecture in Drama and Literature for the Extra Mural Department of Exeter University and the W.E.A. for some years. He has run creative writing classes.

He retired early to follow his love of sailing and writing. He is an occasional feature writer for Yachting magazines. He has a son and a daughter and lives by the sea with his wife, Cicely.